Ruth

MOTHER OF KINGS

Ruth

MOTHER OF KINGS

DIANA WALLIS TAYLOR

WHITAKER
HOUSE

Publisher's Note:
This novel is a work of historical fiction and is based on the biblical record. References to real people, events, organizations, and places are used in a fictional context. Any resemblance to actual living persons is entirely coincidental.

RUTH, MOTHER OF KINGS

Diana Wallis Taylor
www.dianawallistaylor.com

ISBN: 978-1-60374-903-9
eBook ISBN: 978-1-60374-904-6
Printed in the United States of America

Whitaker House
1030 Hunt Valley Circle
New Kensington, PA 15068
www.whitakerhouse.com

Library of Congress Cataloging-in-Publication Data

Taylor, Diana Wallis, 1938–
Ruth, Mother of Kings / Diana Wallis Taylor.
pages cm
Summary: "The book of Ruth has captivated Christian believers for centuries, and now the story of this remarkable woman comes to life in the pages of this dramatic retelling"—Provided by publisher.
ISBN 978-1-60374-903-9 (alk. paper) — ISBN 978-1-60374-904-6 (eBook) 1. Ruth (Biblical figure)—Fiction. 2. Women in the Bible—Fiction. I. Title.
PS3620.A942R87 2013
813'.6—dc23

2013021394

1 2 3 4 5 6 7 8 9 10 WH 20 19 18 17 16 15 14 13

Dedication

To the Sarahs of the world who have waited on the Lord for the promise and seen it fulfilled, in His time.
And to my family, for their consistent encouragement as I write the stories God has put on my heart.

Acknowledgments

My sincere thanks...

To my publisher, Christine Whitaker and Whitaker House, for the opportunity to write a very different story of Ruth;

To Courtney Hartzel, for making the editing of the manuscript such a pleasure;

To my agent, Joyce Hart, of Hartline Literary Agency, for her loyalty and friendship through the years and for giving me the opportunity to write my stories for great editors;

To Dr. Vicki Hesterman, for her contribution of editing ideas and suggestions;

To my critique group—Martha Gorris, Ann Larson, Jean Nader, Mary Kay Moody, and Sandi Esch—for their suggestions and ideas when I bogged down on a chapter;

And to my daughter, Karen, for her insights when I hit a snag.

To all of you, I could not have completed the book without you.

—Diana Wallis Taylor

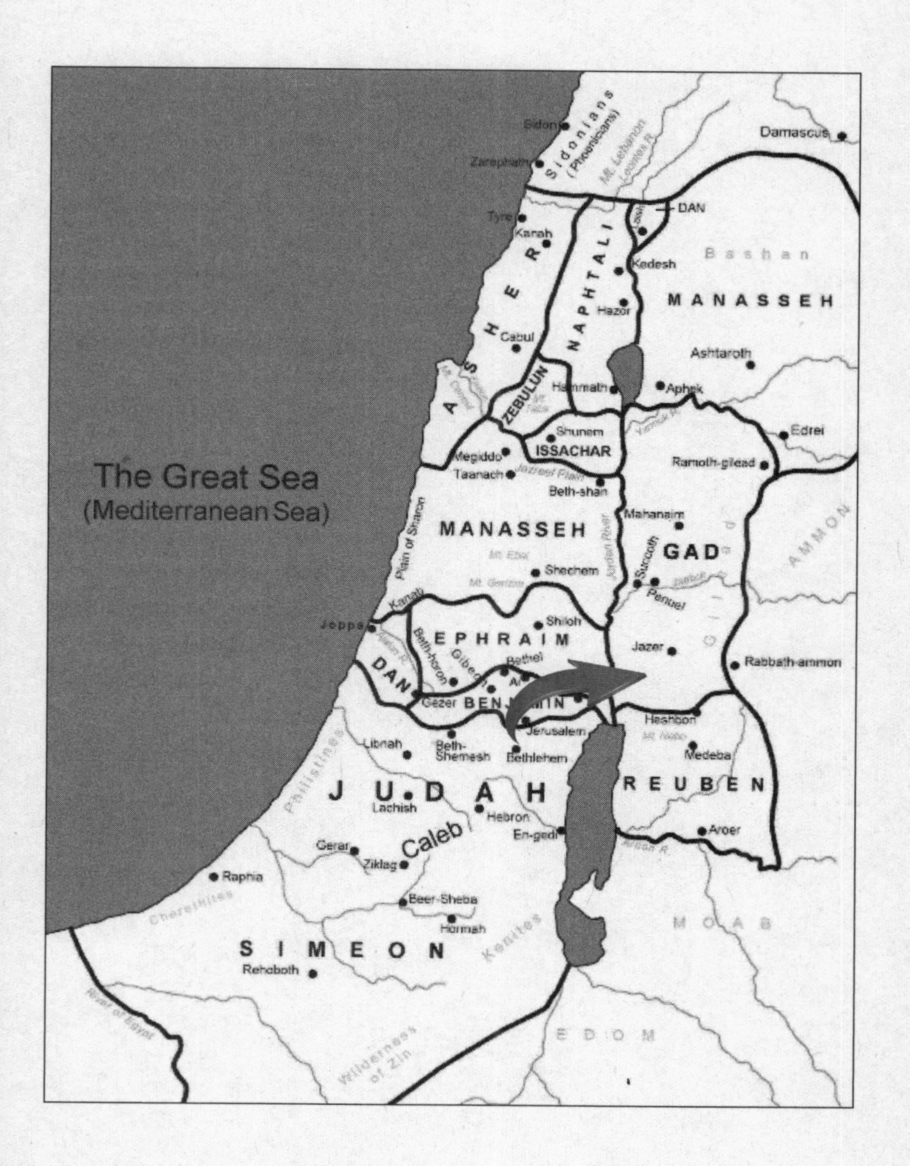

The Great Sea
(Mediterranean Sea)
Sidonians
(Phoenicians)
Sidon
Zarephath
Damascus
DAN
Tyre
Kanah
Kedesh
Bashan
ASHER
NAPHTALI
Hazor
MANASSEH
Cabul
Ashtaroth
ZEBULUN
Hammath
Aphek
Shunem
Edrei
Megiddo
ISSACHAR
Ramoth-gilead
Taanach
Jezreel Plain
Beth-shan
Plain of Sharon
Mahanaim
MANASSEH
AMMON
GAD
Shechem
Succoth
Penuel
Joppa
Shiloh
EPHRAIM
Jazer
Bethel
Rabbath-ammon
DAN
Gibeon
Beth-horon
Gezer
BENJAMIN
Heshbon
Jerusalem
Libnah
Beth-Shemesh
Bethlehem
Medeba
JUDAH
REUBEN
Lachish
Hebron
Caleb
En-gedi
Aroer
Gerar
Ziklag
Raphia
Beer-Sheba
Hormah
MOAB
SIMEON
Rehoboth
Kenites
EDOM
Wilderness of Zin

One

Ruth sat with her brother, Joash, on a small rug in the neighbors' courtyard, listening fearfully as the adults discussed what to do with them. Ruth wanted her mama. Why would they not let her see her? Was she still sick? Her papa had tended her for several days and told them not to disturb her. No one baked any bread for their breakfast.

She scrunched up her small face, her lower lip trembling. Yesterday, her mama would not wake up, and her papa began weeping and acting strangely. He struggled to stand up, and perspiration ran down his face. She remembered his words, spoken like he was out of breath. *"Joash, you must help me. Take Ruth and go to the house of Naaman. Tell him I need his help. Stay there until I call for you."*

Joash grabbed her hand and almost pulled her to the neighbors' house. She had been holding her mother's shawl, and she wrapped it around herself that night as they slept in the neighbors' courtyard. She could hardly breathe for the fear that seemed to rise up from her chest. Why would the neighbors not let them go home? Had Papa not called for them?

Everyone looked at them with sad eyes and whispered to one another. She clutched her mother's shawl and turned to her brother.

"Why will they not let us go home?"

"I don't know. Something is wrong." He looked at a woman standing nearby. "We want to see our mama and papa."

The woman answered quietly, "Children, your mama and papa are dead. You cannot see them...ever again."

Ruth heard the word "dead." A bird fell in their small courtyard one day, and her papa said it was dead. It lay on the dirt, unmoving, its eyes closed. She could not imagine her mama and papa like that bird. She turned to her brother again.

"Mama and Papa are dead?"

Joash nodded, tears rolling down his cheeks. He put an arm around her, and they clung to each other.

Naaman's wife spoke up. "I have fed them for two days, but I cannot continue to care for them."

"Do they have family elsewhere?" said another neighbor woman. "I have children of my own to feed."

Naaman murmured, "Phineas has family near the Plains of Moab, outside Beth-Jeshimoth. He told me before he died."

"What family? His parents? Are they still alive?"

There was silence. Then, "How would the children get there? They can't go alone; the boy is only six, the girl almost four. Who would take them?"

"That is something to consider. It is a two days' journey."

Teary-eyed, Ruth turned to her brother and whispered, "Where do they want to take us?"

He straightened his shoulders and tried to sound very strong. "I don't know, but do not be afraid, Sister. I will care for you."

A couple entered the small courtyard and hurried up to the group that had been talking. The woman spoke. "We just heard about the parents. The mother, Timna, was my friend. Do you know what is to be done with the children?"

Someone said, "Naaman told us they have grandparents, outside Beth-Jeshimoth, but we don't know how to get them there. They cannot travel alone."

The man nodded, then said, "I will take them. My wife, Mary, will go with me."

"But, Gershon, can you leave your shop for that long? It will take at least two days or more, just one way."

"*Ha'Shem* will watch over my shop. It is the right thing to do. If they have family, that is where the children should go. I will prepare my cart and donkey."

The first woman spoke. "May the Almighty bless you for your kindness, Gershon, and your wife also. It is a good thing you do. I will gather food for your journey. The other women in the neighborhood will help."

Ruth listened to the women click their tongues and murmur among themselves.

"Those poor children were alone in the house with their sick parents for days before Phineas sent them to Naaman and his wife."

"My husband wondered why Phineas had not come to work in three days."

"The Lord only knows the last time they had eaten."

"Both of the children are so thin."

One of the other men spoke up. "What if you get there and find that the children's grandparents are dead?"

"We will just have to trust the Almighty to guide us; we will pray that they live and that these orphaned children will be welcomed."

Joash clutched Ruth's hand tighter. "See? We will go to *Abba*'s family. They will take us there."

Ruth, too frightened to speak again, could only nod, dried tears still on her cheeks.

Early the next morning, they were fed some lentil soup and fresh bread, and then Gershon and Mary took their hands and led them home, telling them they would now gather a few things to take with them. Mary clicked her tongue and sighed as she and her husband looked around the small house. "There is little of value here," Gershon said. "The girl seems determined to hold on to her mother's shawl."

Mary glanced at Ruth. "It is a comfort to her. We must not take the bedding, because of their sickness. I will bring bedding from our house. Oh, Gershon, they were so poor. How did they live?"

"Evidently he made just enough to survive."

Ruth, with her mother's shawl still wrapped around her shoulders, clutched a doll made of rags that her mother had sewn for her. She looked around. There was no sign of her mama or papa anywhere. She watched her brother slip a small leather box out of a cupboard when the man and his wife were not looking. He put a finger to his lips and hid the box in his clothes.

When the cart was loaded, Ruth climbed in after Joash and settled in as the journey began. Never having ventured beyond her street, she looked about, wide-eyed, as they passed through the town.

"What is our town called?" Joash asked.

"It is Medeba," the man answered.

His wife turned around in her seat at the front of the cart. "Have you not been in the town before?"

Joash shook his head.

"It is large. Your father made many fine bricks to build houses with."

Ruth looked up at her. "I miss my mama."

Mary sighed. "I know, child. Your mama and papa were so sick from the fever. They just didn't get better, like so many others. But soon you will be with your grandparents."

"Will they let us stay with them?" Joash asked.

There was a pause, and Mary looked at her husband. "Oh, of course. I'm sure they will be glad to see you." She turned around again. "Have you ever met them?"

Ruth looked at her brother, and both children shook their heads.

They spent the night with some other families that were traveling. Gershon said something about it being safer to stay with a group.

Mary made sure Ruth and Joash were settled for the night and then lay down next to her husband. The two adults whispered to themselves, probably thinking that Ruth was asleep. She kept her eyes closed and listened in.

"Oh, Gershon, I pray that the grandparents are still there. What will we do if they are not?"

"We must trust the Almighty, Mary. I feel we are doing the right thing."

"Then we will do our best, and know the outcome soon."

"Timna was never well, from what I understand."

Mary murmured, "If the parents of Phineas had a farm, why did he leave? Would he not work the farm with his father?"

"A disagreement of some kind. I don't think the parents approved of the marriage. Medeba is a larger town. He probably thought he had a better chance of finding work there."

She sighed. "Then the grandparents may not even know about the children?"

"It's likely they don't. Let us get some rest. We have many miles to cover tomorrow."

Ruth yawned. What did it all mean? She was so tired. It was too much for her to understand. Moving closer to Joash, she settled down and, despite missing her parents, allowed sleep to draw her into its embrace.

Two

When they arrived in Beth-Jeshimoth, in the afternoon of the third day, Gershon began making inquiries of the people they came upon. "I'm looking for the farm of the parents of a young man called Phineas."

The first two people he asked shook their heads. The third person squinted at the cart and the children before saying, "I know a man named Misha and his wife, Eunice, whose son Phineas left some years ago. They have a farm on the Plains of Moab, about a mile outside town."

"This couple lives there still?"

The man nodded his head.

By this time, a group of people had gathered around the cart and stood looking at them. Ruth huddled close to Joash.

"Are you relatives?" the man asked.

"No, but the children are. Phineas and his wife, Timna, were taken by the fever, and we are bringing the children to their grandparents."

There were murmurs of sympathy from the women. One woman stepped forward. "May the Lord bless you for your kindness. The girl Timna's parents are dead. Eunice and Misha never knew if they had grandchildren. You will bring joy to both of them."

Ruth's heart was comforted to know that her grandmother would be full of joy to see her.

"I told you it would be all right," Joash whispered. "Our grandparents will let us stay, I know it."

With a word of thanks to those who had offered help and encouragement, Gershon drove the cart in the direction he had been told, and they rode quietly for about a half an hour. Finally, Ruth could see animal pens and trees and then a house. Chickens scratched in the yard, and a herd of goats moved restlessly in their enclosure. Two donkeys tethered to a post were munching on some grain. As the cart approached, they looked up and regarded the visitors with their large brown eyes.

Gershon pulled his own donkey to a stop, and a woman came from the house. She approached them cautiously, a puzzled look on her face.

"Welcome. Can I be of help to you?"

Gershon got out of the cart and helped Mary down. He turned to the woman, and Ruth held her breath as she listened to the exchange.

"My name is Gershon, and this is my wife, Mary. We are from Medeba. We are looking for Misha and Eunice, the parents of a young man named Phineas."

The woman's hand flew to her heart. "We are his parents; do you bring word from him? We have not seen him in almost seven years. Is he well?"

Mary shook her head. "We are grieved to be the bearers of sad news. Both he and his wife died of the fever. We have brought you their children, Joash and Ruth. We understand you are their only relatives."

The woman gasped. "Our son is dead?"

Mary nodded. Gershon helped Ruth from the cart, followed by Joash, who insisted he could manage himself.

The woman's eyes filled with tears. "Phineas is dead." She stood there a moment, lips quivering, and wrung her hands. "I must call my husband. He is in the fields."

Gershon stepped forward. "I will be glad to find him for you. Show me where he is."

The woman nodded and pointed. As he strode off, she turned to Ruth and Joash.

"Oh, may the name of the Most High be blessed. We have grandchildren."

Ruth, clutching her mother's shawl, looked up at the kind face in front of her—the face of her grandmother. Tears rolled slowly down her cheeks as she waited, not knowing what to do. Then, her grandmother opened her arms, and Ruth, with a sob, went into them.

She saw two figures hurrying down the road—an older man, followed by Gershon.

When they reached the group, the older man panted, "What is this I'm told?"

"Oh, my husband, our son is dead," Ruth's grandmother said. "He and his wife died of the fever that afflicted our town some months ago."

Her husband tore his garment and raised his hands to the heavens. "The Lord gives, and the Lord takes away. Blessed be the name of the Lord." He bowed his head, shaking it from side to side, with a grieved expression on his face. "He would not listen. He would marry that girl, in spite of our warnings."

"They had a disagreement," Ruth's grandmother offered, "and he left the farm with his wife, and we have not seen them since."

The man paused and peered at Ruth, still clinging to his wife's clothing. "And who are these children?"

Ruth's grandmother turned her to face him. "Ruth, this is your grandfather, your *Sabba*." She motioned for Joash to come forward. "Joash, come and greet your grandfather, Misha."

Her brother stared at Misha for a moment, then swallowed and said politely, "I am glad to meet you, *Sabba*."

Misha stepped forward and looked down at Joash, his face alight with wonder. "Our son left us a legacy, and we didn't know."

Eunice beckoned everyone to come into the house. She brought out wine and fresh bread. Ruth devoured her half of the date cake offered to her and Joash.

Eunice glanced at Gershon and Mary. "How did the children fare in Medeba?"

Gershon cleared his throat. "They lived on little. Their father worked for the brick maker and did whatever jobs he could find, but there was little in the house. The wife became ill first, and then your son. The children were in the house for a day or so before anyone realized your son and his wife were ill. The neighbors fed the children but didn't know when they had last eaten."

Misha looked at them, his eyes misting. "And you good people brought them here all the way from Medeba?"

Gershon shrugged. "I felt it was what the Almighty wanted us to do. It was better for them to be with family than to be passed around among the neighbors."

Ruth, drinking some fresh goat's milk along with her date cake, watched her grandparents carefully as the adults spoke.

"I grieve for my son," said her grandmother. "But I am thankful to the Almighty for bringing us such a gift in our later years."

Misha nodded. "Please, stay the night with us and partake of our evening meal. We will send fresh provisions with you in the morning."

Gershon thanked them. "We accept your hospitality. It will be necessary to leave early. I must get back to my shop. I am a carpenter and have many projects to finish upon my return."

Eunice suggested that she and Mary take Ruth and her brother outside to let them explore their new home and allow the men to talk. Her grandfather was saying something about making a room.

Outside, Joash wanted to see the donkeys. Ruth was fascinated with the goats, especially the kids, who chased each other in the pen, butting heads.

Her grandmother and Mary stayed close by. Ruth heard Mary ask, "Was the wife of Phineas not to your liking? You said your husband and son had a disagreement of some kind, and my husband heard the same."

"Ah. Misha wanted Phineas to take over the farm, but he wanted to do other things. Then he met Timna and was determined to marry her. She just didn't seem very healthy, certainly not strong enough to bear children. She was so shy, she would hardly talk to us. When we voiced our concerns, Phineas became angry and, to spite us, married the girl and brought her home as his wife. He and my husband did not speak for days, and then, one day, we woke up and they were gone." Eunice hesitated, her voice breaking. "We have not seen our son since, and now we never shall."

"They are good children, Eunice, and young enough to train in the duties of a farm. They shall bring renewed energy to your household."

Eunice sighed, watching Joash climb on the fence of the goat pen. "I wonder if I am up to that, but we will do our best. Things were getting too quiet. Perhaps we needed grandchildren to bring a change."

Mary smiled at her. "I'm sure they will bring a good change."

The women ushered Ruth and Joash inside again, and Mary helped Eunice prepare the evening meal. Ruth and Joash were shown where to wash their hands and faces. After the meal, Eunice made space in the storeroom of the house for Ruth and her brother to sleep. She put down extra rugs so they would be warm.

Ruth and Joash politely said good night to their *Sabba* and to the couple that had kindly brought them so far. Ruth was weary from the long trip and was glad to have a place to sleep.

As she and Joash lay down, Joash hesitated, looking up at his grandmother's face, then said resolutely, "Good night, *Savta*."

"Good night, Joash. May *Ha'Shem* give you a peaceful night's rest."

Ruth clutched her mother's shawl to her and smiled tentatively. "Good night, *Savta*."

Eunice wiped her eyes with one hand, then reached down and brushed several strands of hair from Ruth's face. "Good night, my little Ruth. Sleep well." She quietly left the room.

Ruth watched her go and then turned to Joash. "This is a good place. I will like it here."

"I will like it, too." He reached into his clothing and pulled out the little leather box. Ruth watched carefully as he opened it. Inside was a shekel.

"I heard *Abba* say it was for a special time. We shall save it, also, for a special time."

Ruth nodded and watched him put the small box behind some bags of grain. Then he settled back in his bedding and closed his eyes.

Ruth pulled the shawl over her, thinking of the gentle mother who had worn it and the arms that had rocked her at one time. Missing the voice that had sung her to sleep in times past, she felt a large tear make its way down her cheek.

"Good night, *Imah*," she whispered.

I must do this. I have no choice. My herds are dying, my friend, and my sons are ill. It is my only hope. When the drought and famine have passed, I will surely return."

The elders murmured among themselves, and Micah, his close friend, raised his eyebrows. "You would leave your home, Elimelech? What of your family? How can you know the rumors of good grass and water across the Jordan are true?"

"For the sake of my family, I am trusting that it is so."

Micah shook his head in resignation. "We will pray the Most High, may His name be praised, will watch over you. But may He hear our prayers and send the rain."

Elimelech, having left his home and all that was familiar for a land he'd never seen, now sat in the opening of his tent. The setting sun, like a ponderous orange ball, shimmered in the waves of heat as it began to slip below the horizon. He lifted his chin as a faint breeze stirred the few trees that lined the Jericho Road. An owl hooted in the distance, and a bird called from a bush nearby. As he looked out over the herds of sheep and goats, he listened with a heavy heart to the plaintive sounds of their distress as they milled about.

He, his sons, and two herdsmen had driven them for days in the hot sun and choking dust. While he had moved them at as slow a pace as possible, many of the young had been lost. How much further would the animals be able to travel? They must find grazing land as soon as they crossed the Jordan.

They had purchased water for the animals from the villages they passed, but the people, while hospitable, were reluctant to give too much of the dwindling water supply needed for themselves and their own animals.

Was it wise to leave his home in Bethlehem and insist on bringing his wife and two sons this long way? He had been forced to sell his house and land. Would the new owner properly care for them in his absence? And what would they return to, if indeed they were able to return?

"My husband, will it be much longer?"

He hadn't heard his wife's approach, and he gave her a wistful smile. How he relied on her calm demeanor and gentle nature. She did not rant and rave, as other women might have done if uprooted from their home and taken on a journey to a land far from what they knew. When Elimelech told Naomi of the grazing land untouched by drought or famine, and of the chances of their sons' health improving, sudden hope lit her eyes. The memory was enough to assure him he had made the right decision.

He looked out at the desert again. "We will reach Jericho tomorrow and follow the Jericho Road to the river. The Jordan is low, and we should be able to ford the river with the animals safely. I've sent Abib ahead to scout a good crossing place."

She stood quietly beside him. "The Most High will help us find refuge in the land of our brethren."

"I have heard from reliable sources that there is good grazing on the Plains of Moab, across from Jericho. There are Israelite settlements and villages there. The Reubenites have not suffered from the drought and famine that plague Canaan."

"This journey has been hard on our sons, my lord. I pray, as you do, that they will find better health in this new land."

"As much as I do not wish to weary them more, I must send them out to relieve the herdsmen during the night."

"I know." A small sigh escaped her lips.

His sons had been at the heart of his decision to leave Bethlehem. Both boys were subject to frequent coughing spells. Their older son, Mahlon, meaning "weak," had indeed been weak from his birth. It was thought he would not live. Chilion, whose name meant "pining," was not much stronger. Both boys seemed to do better as they grew into young manhood, until the drought sucked the very life from the land, eventually bringing famine. Now, though eighteen and sixteen, they had become listless in the dry, dust-laden air, and he'd had to hire help to manage their animals. Leaving Canaan had become their only hope.

Elimelech's shoulders sagged. He had been an elder, used to sitting at the town gate with the other elders to determine matters of law. Of the princely tribe of Judah, he held a place of honor. What distress and concern he'd caused when he'd announced his decision to leave.

The whole town of Bethlehem had gathered to see them go, the men's faces stoic, and some of the women weeping with Naomi.

Tomorrow they would pass Jericho on the road that led to the Jordan River. Once across, he would have to find a town that would agree to give him grazing rights. It wearied him to contemplate all that was ahead.

Naomi laid a gentle hand on his arm. "Will you seek your rest, my lord?"

He covered her hand with his own. "I shall join you later."

When she had gone to the corner of their tent to lie down, he looked up at the darkening evening sky. It was clear and still. Not a cloud in sight. A short coughing spell from the adjoining tent broke the silence. One of his sons. Elimelech straightened his shoulders and strengthened his resolve. His sons would get better in the new land, and tomorrow his thirsty flocks would drink from the Jordan.

After saying his evening prayers, Elimelech turned to join his wife. Whatever the future held, though unknown, he could only go forward and trust in the Most High.

Ruth watched the caravan's progress as it made its way from the Jericho Road to the Jordan River crossing. As she strained her eyes to see what she could from her vantage point below the escarpment, her herd of goats wandered unguarded over the still green grasses of the slopes. She'd never seen a caravan so large and with so many animals. Even from a distance, she could hear the sheep and goats complaining loudly at the choking dust of the trail. So many animals were a sign of wealth, and she wondered who the travelers might be who, though prosperous, sought refuge so far from home.

She sipped water from the goatskin bag that hung at her waist and followed the caravan with her eyes until they disappeared into one of the rift valleys. The herd became restless and wandered farther down the slope to where a small stream forced its way from a small crevasse and gushed down into the lower valley. There was enough level land for the goats to drink easily, and as she caught up with them, she bent to fill her water bag.

The narrow trail wound up through the escarpment to the great plateau where her grandparents lived, and her charges moved at a faster pace, sensing home. A covey of wild partridges, startled from their hiding place in the bushes, flung themselves into the sky with a great beating of wings. For a moment, she wished she was as good with a sling as her brother, Joash. It would be nice to bring home a fat partridge for her grandmother to cook for supper.

The afternoon sun was close to the horizon as Ruth guided their herd of goats into the pen. Her grandmother came out of the house, tucking several strands of gray hair behind her ear and clicking her tongue.

"Ruth. You are late again. Shall I die of worry for you and the herd? It's not safe upon the trails this time of day. The sun is nearly down, and *Shabbat* will begin. Do you not fear the wolves of evening that prowl when the shadows touch the mountains?"

Ruth knew her grandmother was never truly cross with her, but she hung her head. "I'm sorry, *Savta*. I was not watching the time."

"Daydreaming again, child?" Eunice shook her finger at her. "And how many times have you had to go back and find a stray because you did not pay attention?"

"I will be more careful, *Savta*." Ruth gave her a beaming smile. "I saw another caravan today. There were many people and a large herd of sheep and goats."

Eunice sighed. "Ah, the famine in Canaan brings more people to our plains. We are glad to share the pastureland, but it can graze only so many. Perhaps this one will go north."

Ruth shrugged. "Perhaps."

Her grandmother put her hands on her hips. "Since you are so late, you have just enough time to make sure the donkeys have water and then wash yourself before *Shabbat* begins." With a lift of her eyebrows, she returned to the house.

Ruth glanced at the lowering sun and then hurried to the cistern to fill jugs of water for the trough. The two donkeys crowded each other and drank noisily. She watched them a moment and then went to help her grandmother, who was tending a small brazier. The smell of lamb stew made Ruth's mouth water, and she hurried to put their wooden platters on the table and take the bread out of the clay oven.

The gate opened, and her grandfather entered, having just come in from the fields. He glanced at her as he performed the ceremonial hand washing before *Shabbat*.

"Ah, my little Ruth, how were your pastures today?"

She blushed. "I am not little anymore, *Sabba*. I am nearly fifteen."

He dried his hands on a clean white cloth and then stroked his beard, as though giving the matter great thought. "So you are. So you are." His eyes twinkled. "We must find a husband for you, you are getting so old."

She knew he was teasing her, but he was right; she was eligible for marriage and should have been betrothed by now, according to their customs. She had considered the young men of their village more than once, but the thought of marrying any of them evoked a large sigh. In their small village, there were not many to choose from.

"I am in no hurry to leave you, *Sabba*. *Ha'Shem* will show me who my husband is to be." She looked out across the fields. "When will Joash return?"

"After *Shabbat*. Betharam is over thirty miles away. He cannot travel until the first day of the week." He glanced at his wife. "I hope he bargained well for the young kids. They are fine stock animals." He shook his head. "Ah, there was once a time when I could make that trip. It is good that our grandson does not let the merchants intimidate him."

Ruth thought of her brother, Joash, who, at nearly eighteen, towered over her. With his broad shoulders and strong arms, he was a man now.

Eunice nodded. "May *Ha'Shem* give him favor. He will need it to bring the long list of supplies I sent with him."

Her grandfather gave a great bellow of laughter, and Ruth smiled.

Eunice huffed. "Joash can bargain well for the price of the young goats. I pray he will do so for the supplies on my list, as well."

As the sun went down, her grandmother blew out the fire in the brazier and lit the *Shabbat* candles. Pulling her shawl over her head, she intoned the familiar opening prayer of *Shabbat*. "Blessed are You, Lord our God, King of the universe, who has sanctified us with His commandments and commanded us to light the *Shabbat* candles."

Ruth listened, wondering when the day would come that she was the woman of her own household, saying those same prayers over Seder table.

After the meal and prayers of *Shabbat* ended, Ruth looked forward to her grandfather's stories.

"Tell me again, *Sabba*, how we came to this land."

Misha's eyes twinkled as he settled down to his favorite occupation of storytelling. "Once, my child, there were great nations dwelling here in the tablelands and valleys, the people of Bashan, the Amorites, the Ammonites, Moabites, and Edomites. When our ancestors were brought out of Egypt with the great lawgiver, Moses, they went around Edom and the land of Moab, crossing the great Arnon River into the territory of the Amorites. Now, the Amorites had displaced the Moabites in a great battle years before and drove them out of these lands, except for the territory below the Arnon River. The Amorites took over this land and remained a long time."

"And what happened to the Amorites, *Sabba*?" She knew the story, but she also knew her grandfather loved her rapt attention.

"Well, child, Moses asked the Amorites for permission to go along the King's Highway, not touching their fields or vineyards, or even their wells, until they were past the borders of the Amorites." He paused, stroking his beard.

"But King Sihon..." she prompted him.

"Ah, Sihon was a foolish king. He refused the request, went to the other kings, including the king of Moab, and gathered an army to fight against our people."

"And the armies of Israel were victorious," she blurted out.

Her grandfather gave her a baleful look. "Now, who is telling this story?"

She sat back on her heels, meekly.

"As I was saying, the Israelites, in the strength of *Ha'Shem,* under their new leader, Joshua, were victorious and smote the forces of Sihon, destroying the people and taking all his land from the Yarmuk River to the mighty Arnon. Then *Ha'Shem* delivered the people of Bashan into our hands, and every inhabitant of their land was destroyed, giving us the land east of the Jordan even unto Mount Hermon. The Moabites that survived were driven to the land across the Arnon River, where they are today.

"When the battle was over, the leaders of the tribe of Gad, half of the tribe of Manasseh, and our tribe of Reuben went to Joshua and requested the land of the Amorites for their cattle, seeing that the land was good for grazing."

"Why do they still call our land the 'Plains of Moab' if there are no Moabites living here?"

He shrugged. "The Amorites didn't change the name when they occupied the Moabite land, and it remains the Plains of Moab to this day. Many lands are called after the people who first lived there."

In her mind, Ruth could see the fierce battles as the armies clashed with one another. "What are those people like, *Sabba,* the Moabites?"

He scowled. "They are idolaters who worship the god Chemosh. They do terrible things, even sacrificing their own children in the fires of their god. That is why *Ha'Shem* ordered them all to be destroyed from this land and their altars of sacrifice broken down."

Ruth shivered at the thought of small children being burned to death to appease a pagan god. She remembered a pile of stones on the way into their village that her grandfather had pointed out to her one day. It had once been a pagan altar. She couldn't pass it even today without thinking of the terrible god it represented.

Her grandmother interrupted, flinging one hand in the air. "How shall she sleep when you fill her head with stories of death and war, Misha?"

"Dear wife," he responded patiently, "is it not important that she know the history of our people?"

She folded her arms. "And how many times has she heard the history of our people?"

Her grandfather merely shrugged. "She likes the stories."

"Yes, yes, but enough for now. It is time to seek our rest. Tomorrow is *Shabbat*."

He rolled his eyes but rose slowly.

Suppressing a smile, Ruth said good night to her grandparents, then headed to her pallet.

Now, as she lay still, listening to the night sounds, the hooting of an owl interrupted her reverie. She pictured the bird, sailing on strong wings in the night sky over the fields as he sought his dinner. Going back over her day, she remembered the scolding she incurred from her grandmother for returning late with the herd, all because her attention had been distracted by the intriguing caravan. She was not a child anymore. She needed to show her grandmother that she was responsible. With a sigh, she settled herself down and closed her eyes. Her brother would return soon, and she looked forward to his arrival. She missed his teasing, but, more than that, she knew he would bring her a small gift. He always did.

Remembering her words to her grandfather, that *Ha'Shem* would choose her husband, she smiled to herself. Perhaps her prince would arrive on one of the caravans, a handsome stranger who would sweep her off her feet.

Four

Ruth woke as the sun streamed into the open door of the house. She said her prayers and rose quickly, rolling up her sleeping rug and putting on her sandals and mantle. Her grandmother was already up. There was yesterday's bread and some fruit on the table in the courtyard. It was the Sabbath, so no fresh bread was baked this morning.

Ruth settled down to eat her simple breakfast. When the Sabbath was over, as long as the weather was warm, they could cook and eat outside. She wrinkled her nose, knowing that soon they would have to bring the small brazier inside. She didn't like the smoke that lingered in the house at the end of the day.

Her grandfather covered his shoulders with his prayer shawl and spoke the morning prayers for his family, then left for the home of one of the other villagers to gather in a minyan of ten men for the special prayers of *Shabbat*. Though many in the tribes had fallen away, her village followed the laws of Moses and assembled when they could to study the Talmud together.

When her grandmother went for a walk, Ruth sat under a mulberry tree, looking out over the fields. The wild hollyhocks, yellow daisies, and tall stalks of white asphodel were gone. Likewise, the little bell flowers that had colored the landscape had bowed their heads and withered under the summer sun.

She looked in the direction of the town, far in the distance, and wondered if the caravan she'd seen the day before had gone there or had turned north, as her grandmother hoped. Her curiosity about the caravan would have to wait until after *Shabbat* to be satisfied. Reaching their small town required more than the short journey allowed under the law on this holy day.

A hawk caught her eye. Bold creature that it was, it dived down on an unsuspecting sparrow on the ground. As she watched the hawk fly away with its prey, she felt sorry for the small bird. Yet it was the way of life—the larger preyed on the smaller. She looked again toward the town.

At the sound of her grandmother's call, she reluctantly turned back to the house to help her grandparents prepare for the *Havdalah* prayers, marking the end of *Shabbat*. After *Shabbat*, she would find out where the caravan had gone. Her friend Orpah and her family lived nearer to the village. Orpah's father, Abiram, was a potter, and her mother, Rhoda, always knew what was going on. No doubt Rhoda would have news to share.

Out in the fields the next day, the coolness of the fresh morning was rapidly giving way to shimmering heat, and Ruth took another sip of water from the goatskin bag. Today she was impatient. If she took the herd as far as the spring, it would take too long getting the goats back to their pen, and her grandmother had promised that she could go to Orpah's when she returned.

So far, the animals were content to feed at a high point on the grassy slopes. She laughed as she watched two of the young kids playing. One would stand on the rock until the other butted it off, and they would exchange places. It took her mind off of the caravan, but only briefly. She looked up at the sky. The sun was beginning its descent from its midday pinnacle, and she knew she must drive the herd back home. As if to spite her, the goats wandered in different directions. She picked up a small stone and heaved it at the flank of one of her reluctant charges, and it quickly rejoined the herd.

"Go!" she hollered at them. The sharp tone of her voice startled the goats, which were used to a calmer demeanor from their shepherdess. They quickly headed up the path, and she almost had to run to keep up with them.

With the small herd safely penned, Ruth fairly flew down the trail to Orpah's. She knew her friend was as curious as she was.

She nodded to Orpah's father, Abiram, who was working on his potter's wheel in the courtyard. She stopped to watch him press his hands into the soft clay on the upper horizontal wheel while kicking the bottom wheel with one foot. It always amazed her to watch him guide the clay into the shape he wanted. So caught up was she with the process that she almost forgot the reason she had come. She turned and crossed to the other side of the courtyard, where her friend was chopping vegetables. Ruth began to gather them and put them in a nearby bowl. Orpah's mother, Rhoda, came out of the house and nodded at her. "You are a helpful girl, Ruth."

"Grandmother said I could come by after I took the goats out today. I was wondering if you had seen any new caravans lately."

Rhoda stopped and gave her a knowing look. "So, it is news you have come for." She smiled broadly. "Yes, there are two camped outside the town gates. One is moving north tomorrow, but the other is staying."

"We saw them pass by," Orpah whispered.

"I saw one moving through the valley when I was in the hills the other day. It was a large caravan with many animals. They must be very prosperous."

Rhoda nodded. "It is the caravan of Elimelech. They are Ephrathites of Bethlehem. It is said he is of the tribe of Judah. A wealthy man. He comes with his wife, Naomi, and his two sons, Mahlon and Chilion. Another family escaping from the terrible famine in Canaan."

Before she thought, Ruth burst out, "How old are his sons?"

Orpah and her mother exchanged glances. "The older is of marriageable age. The other is younger," Rhoda answered.

Ruth's mind was turning again. "I wonder if they will settle near us."

"The elders will surely grant grazing land to a man of his stature, child." Rhoda eyed her, then Orpah. "Oh, go, but do not get too close, and do not bother anyone in the caravan."

The two young women needed no further urging. They hurried from the courtyard toward the town. It was not difficult to find the encampment of Elimelech, for the bleating of many sheep and the sound of the goats could be heard in the distance.

Thinking to keep out of sight, Ruth and Orpah crept up behind a pile of rocks to look over the vast number of animals.

"Look, Orpah, at the splendor of their tents, and so many sheep." Out of the main tent came an older woman. She was dressed in a beautiful tunic of deep blue, with a waistband of gold threads that caught the afternoon sun. A younger woman hurried along behind her, dressed in the garb of a common woman. Ruth decided she must be a servant.

"They will need a lot of land to feed all of them," Orpah whispered fiercely.

So intent were the girls on the scene before them that when a man's voice addressed them, they nearly fell backward. Ruth's mantle slipped off her head and fell about her shoulders.

"Are you spies come to see the camp of Elimelech?" A tall, slender young man stood on a flat slab of rock, watching them.

Ruth recovered herself and responded quickly, "We were only curious. You are strangers to our land."

His dark eyes twinkled, and she could see he was not really angry. She faced him with what dignity she could muster. "Who are you?"

"I am Mahlon, elder son of Elimelech."

His smile caused little crinkles to form in the corners of his eyes. Though he was slight of build, and his skin paler than that of most men who worked the flocks, Ruth thought him the handsomest young man she had ever seen.

"And may I ask the names of my two curious ones?"

Ruth, aware her auburn hair was blowing in the afternoon breeze, adjusted her head covering and drew herself up. "I am Ruth, granddaughter of Misha, of the tribe of Reuben. This is my friend Orpah."

He acknowledged them with a slight nod of his head. "Well, since you are curious, would you like to come to the camp and meet my mother and father?"

Startled, Ruth looked at her friend. Should they go? What would *Sabba* say? It was too tempting. "We can come for only a short time."

He led the way down the rocky escarpment, and they passed through the herd, which parted for them with much bleating. Near the tents, several large camels were tied, some standing and watching them with large, limpid eyes, and others resting and chewing their cud. Ruth had never seen so many camels up close, and she stared at them with fascination.

The woman Ruth had seen earlier stood at the entrance to her tent. She watched them approach and raised her eyebrows in question.

"*Imah,* I have brought two of our new neighbors, Ruth and Orpah." Mahlon gestured toward the woman watching them. "This is my mother, Naomi."

Ruth and Orpah bowed their heads politely.

Naomi gave them a gentle smile. "It is good to meet you, Ruth and Orpah. What brings you to our camp?"

Mahlon broke in, "I invited them, *Imah.*" His mouth twitched with a smile. "They were, uh, watching from afar."

Ruth blushed furiously. "You had such a large caravan. I saw you from the hills before *Shabbat.*"

Naomi raised her eyebrows. "Ah." She turned to the servant standing nearby. "Kezia, prepare refreshments for our guests."

The girl hurried into the tent, and Naomi beckoned Ruth and Orpah to enter.

Once inside, Ruth was overcome with the richness of the tapestries and handwoven rugs that adorned the tent. Elimelech was indeed wealthy.

Kezia served them sweet tea in brass cups and freshly made baklava. It was a rare treat for them, and both Ruth and Orpah savored the sweet dessert.

Pleasantries were exchanged, and Ruth and Orpah told about their families. One never got to the purpose of a visit before the formalities had been attended to. Finally Ruth could stand the suspense no longer. She had to know more about them. "We have heard the famine is great in Judea, and many have come to our fields. Have you come far?"

Naomi glanced up at her son, who replied, "We traveled from Bethlehem."

Orpah raised her eyebrows. "How did you cross the Jordan, and with so many animals?"

"It took quite a while to get them all across. It is fortunate that the Jordan is at its lowest this time of year. We ferried the women and our household goods across, but the animals had to swim for it."

Before Ruth could comment, there was a commotion outside, and then an older man entered the tent with a younger man behind him.

"What have we here? Guests already?"

"Father, this is Ruth and her friend Orpah. They are neighbors. This is my father, Elimelech, and my younger brother, Chilion."

Both Ruth and Orpah stood and bowed before this great patriarch.

Elimelech studied the two young women from beneath his bushy brows. "Perhaps a day of providence." He turned to Naomi. "Good wife, we have been given grazing land for our herds. We may settle here."

Naomi had also risen to greet her husband. "That is welcome news, my lord. They will prosper now."

Ruth took a moment to glance at the younger brother, Chilion, and found him looking at Orpah with a curious expression. They seemed to be around the same age.

Feeling suddenly awkward, Ruth sensed that it was time for them to leave.

"It is getting late, my lord, and we must return to our homes, lest our families worry." Ruth turned to Naomi. "Thank you, my lady, for the hospitality of your tent. Should you wish to visit our farm, my grandfather will most kindly receive you."

Elimelech nodded sagely. "You are most kind in your offer. We hope to meet more of our neighbors soon."

With another respectful bow to Elimelech and Naomi, and then a quick glance back at Mahlon, Ruth followed Orpah from the tent. The sunlight was waning, and they walked quickly to Orpah's house.

"Where have you girls been?" Rhoda scolded. "I was sure you had met with wild beasts in the field."

"*Imah*, we met the family of Elimelech, from the caravan that arrived yesterday."

Rhoda put her hands on her hips. "I thought I told you both not to bother them. What will they think of us?"

Ruth came to her friend's rescue. "We didn't bother them; we were only watching from a pile of rocks above the herds. One of the sons surprised us. His name is Mahlon. He offered to have us meet his parents, and we didn't wish to be impolite."

Orpah closed her eyes and smiled. "We had sweet tea and wonderful baklava." She loved sweets.

Rhoda shook her head. "It would be better if their first guests were elders of the village, not a pair of young girls."

"Mahlon is most handsome, Mother, as is his brother, Chilion, though somewhat younger," she added, heedless of the reprimand.

This caused Rhoda to raise an eyebrow. "Handsome, are they?" Then she glanced at the lowering sun. "You had best hurry home, Ruth. Your grandparents will no doubt be worried also."

Ruth scampered along the pathway. She had so much to tell her grandparents.

When she reached the farm, she recognized the donkey Joash had taken with him. Her brother was home. She entered the house and found him talking earnestly with their grandparents.

Her grandmother pressed her hand to her chest. "*Ha'Shem* be praised. She has returned. Ruth, we were worried about you. It is late. Where have you been?"

Joash grinned. "Here, I return from my journey, and there is no sister to greet me."

She gave him a warm embrace. "I am glad to see your safe return also, my brother." She glanced at the pile of goods he had unloaded from the donkey and gave him a saucy look. "What have you brought me?"

"Vain girl! Should you deserve to have me bring you something?"

She waited. Finally he went to one bundle and pulled out a beautiful woven scarf of green and blue, with gold along the edges. Her eyes grew wide. "This is for me? It must have cost dearly."

He shook his head. "The merchant was closing his tent for the day and was in a good mood to let me bargain for an outrageous price. It will be for your wedding, my sister."

She frowned. "But I am not getting married."

"You will be soon, I am sure of it. I have seen the way the young men of the village look after you." Her brother grinned. "No doubt their fathers will be pounding on the door any day, competing for your hand."

She swatted him on the arm. "There is not one I wish to marry."

"Enough," her grandmother interrupted. "Tell us where you have been."

Trying not to look too pleased with herself, she answered, "I have been with Orpah to meet the patriarch Elimelech and his family. They have just arrived with their caravan and have been given grazing rights by the elders of the village. They are going to settle here."

Misha gave her a stern look. "And what were you doing at the camp of Elimelech?"

She explained how they were invited by Mahlon, given refreshments by the lady, Naomi, and met her husband, Elimelech, and other son, Chilion.

Eunice rolled her eyes at her husband. "And what must they think of us, allowing our granddaughter to roam the fields alone? They will think we are disrespectful of the ways of our people."

"I was not alone," Ruth said in a small voice. "I was with Orpah. We were polite, and they were very warm and friendly to us."

"The good manners of an elder of our people." Eunice sniffed. "They would entertain their worst enemy for three days."

Joash listened to all this with an amused expression. "I do not think any harm has been done, *Savta*. Ruth would not disgrace our family."

He always took her side, and she was glad he did so again.

Eunice merely pursed her lips in disapproval. "Since you have decided to return to us from the great tents of our visitors, you may put the bread and platters on the table for the evening meal."

Her scolding over, Ruth hurried to obey, but not without catching a wink from Joash.

Five

Boaz stood in the blazing sun with his son, Jacob, and his father, Salmon, who leaned on his walking stick, his face drawn and tired. Jacob shook his head. "The fields are so dry, *Abba*."

Boaz turned to his son, marveling again that, at fourteen, Jacob was only slightly shorter than he. "We need to keep praying for rain. It may be that the Almighty will have mercy on us."

Salmon walked several steps into the devastated field, the wilted plants crunching under his feet. The spring rains had not come to bring their life-giving moisture to the barley, and it did not look hopeful for the wheat. Now they faced a season with no crops.

Boaz shook his head. "At least we heeded the warning last year when the rainfall was so low. *Imah* and Miriam have harvested and carefully stored all they could."

Salmon looked heavenward. "The Most High, blessed be His name, has afflicted us, my son. You must carefully parcel out what we have stored. We do not know how long this will last."

"*Abba*, I have heard that famine has already begun in parts of Judea," Jacob said.

"I have heard that also, my son."

Salmon, still staring out at the fields, murmured, "We will help those we can, as we have always done, but we must be prudent, Boaz, and take care of our own family."

Family. Boaz considered himself blessed. He'd had his pick of the young women in Bethlehem and had chosen Miriam, the daughter of Micah, one of the elders. She had given birth to their son in the first year of their marriage, but there had been only miscarriages in the intervening years. Then, at the end of their ninth year of marriage, when they had long since given up hope of any more children, Miriam miraculously found herself with child again. The child was breach, and Miriam had given birth in great pain. Boaz cringed whenever he remembered her screams of agony. To their everlasting gratitude, the child had lived—a daughter they'd named Jael. She had been so small, he'd been almost afraid to touch her, but when she grasped his finger with her tiny hand, his heart leaped with wonder and love. Now, at four, Jael was a miniature of her mother, and his heart rejoiced at the sight of her.

He surveyed the fields again as he stood with his son and father and thought of the famine that was creeping into the land. A tendril of fear clutched at his heart. His family would not go hungry. Whatever it took, he vowed, he would make sure his wife and children had food, even if he had to deprive himself.

The three turned and slowly walked down the road to their home. They passed their flock of sheep and heard the animals bleating forlornly at the dry grass. The shepherds appeared, carrying water to a trough for the thirsty animals. Boaz sighed. How long would the wells last? The streams?

Salmon, leaning heavily upon Boaz's right arm, watched the flocks also. In his other hand he held his walking stick. Boaz glanced at the old man. His father's strength was waning. Would he survive a famine if it lasted several years?

Salmon paused. "You knew that Elimelech decided to move his family across the Jordan. It is said the Plains of Moab are still plentiful with grass, and the famine has not touched our brethren there."

Jacob looked up at Boaz. "I miss my friend Chilion. Do you think we will ever see them again, *Abba*?"

Boaz put an arm around his shoulders. "I don't know, Jacob. Perhaps if the drought and famine end." He frowned. "How could

Elimelech not trust our God for his needs? Surely the famine will not last."

Salmon waved a hand. "Ah, but have we forgotten the story of our ancestor Joseph? The famine in Egypt lasted seven years. Shall the Most High not do as He wishes? I said as much to Elimelech, as did his good friend Micah. But he would not listen. His sons are sickly and can't help much with the work. He will have to move the herds slowly if he doesn't want to lose any of his animals. He was adamant that it was the only thing he could do."

"Where will he settle, provided they give him grazing rights?" Jacob asked.

Boaz thought a moment. "When he crossed the Jordan, he would enter the territory of our brethren, the Reubenites, in the Plains of Moab. Those grasslands are rumored to still be fertile and abundant." He stroked his beard. "I wonder if he considered how many others have gone there and requested grazing rights."

Salmon sighed. "I don't know, my son. I could not dissuade him. Others tried also, but he would go where he had decided to go."

Boaz only nodded, but a thought nagged at the back of his mind. Would the drought ever reach a point where he had to move his own family? Surely it would not come to that.

Jacob, full of the energy of youth, hurried ahead of them, but Boaz walked slowly to keep pace with his father. His spirits lifted, as they always did when he approached their home. Situated on the edge of the town, it was larger than most, and it had seen three generations. His father, now chief of the tribe of Judah, had been the first to break with tradition and give his son a name other than Salmon, against his own father's wishes. Boaz already sat with the elders at the gate, and one day he would take his father's place, wearing the red cape designating him chief of their tribe.

They reached the house and entered the gate leading to the courtyard. Salmon sank down on a bench under one of the shade trees.

Boaz's mother, Rachab, hurried from the house. "You are weary, my husband? Let me refresh you." She presented Salmon with a loaf of fresh bread and a cup of wine.

Jacob was already eating a small date cake. Boaz observed him for a moment. "Enjoy that, my son, for there may not be more when those are gone. We must be more discerning in how much we eat from now on."

Jacob's hand paused in midair, and he put the remaining half of the date cake back on the platter. "I'm sorry, *Abba*. I did not think."

Boaz put a hand on his shoulder. "But it shall not affect today."

Jacob raised his eyebrows, and when Boaz nodded, he snatched up the remaining half of the date cake and ate it with relish.

As Boaz turned back toward his parents, he saw his father smile at his mother, and he observed a moment pass between them that warmed his heart. His parents had married for love, not by an arrangement—a rare occurrence in their culture.

Rachab looked up at him. "And the fields?"

"There is little left, even for the gleaners, *Imah*."

"The Most High cares for the sparrows. He will care for us."

Boaz broke off a small piece of bread. "You know Elimelech has gone?"

"Yes, and I will miss Naomi. She was a good friend—always there to help when someone was sick. It was hard for her to leave." Rachab looked off in the distance. "I pray they find the good grazing land Elimelech hoped for."

Boaz thought of the day four years ago when the fields were fertile and all was well in his world. The day his daughter was born.

He hurried to the house. "Miriam and the baby?"

Rachab smiled at him. "They are doing well, my son. The baby is strong, and Miriam seems to have enough milk for her. We will not have to get a wet nurse, after all."

Relief eased the tension from his body as he entered the room where Miriam lay. He knelt down and gently took her hand. "You are better, Beloved?"

Her eyes glistened with love, but her smile was weak, and her skin seemed paler. She looked down at the swaddled baby in her arms. "I have been a disappointment to you. I have finally given you another child, but it is a girl."

"Jael is beautiful, Beloved. You will need her in the years to come. My mother may not be with us forever. It will be good to have another woman in the house."

She smiled at that. "You always think of the good side of everything, Boaz. I shall indeed enjoy having a daughter."

"Just regain your strength, Beloved. Do not trouble yourself. Our daughter will grow up to turn men's hearts, just as her mother did for me."

It seemed as yesterday to him—the joy, and then the anguish, as her face had suddenly contorted with pain.

"Call Zillah, my husband...quickly. I...need...her."

He sent their servant, Hodesh, for the healer, as fear for his wife wrenched his insides.

Hodesh gathered her shawl about her head and rushed out the gate into the street.

Boaz returned to Miriam, hoping his calm words would cover the panic that threatened to engulf him. "Zillah will be here soon, Beloved. Just rest."

Her eyes were closed, her breath quick and shallow. Boaz bowed his head and silently beseeched the Most High to heal her. Jael began to cry, and Boaz lifted his small daughter into his arms. He spoke soothingly to her but was grateful when his mother gently took the baby from him. He turned again to his wife. To his horror, large red stains began to soak through the linens of her bedding.

Rachab handed the baby back to him and grabbed his arm with one hand. "Take your child and go wait in the courtyard. This is a woman's matter. Go!"

He heard a small sob and turned to see Jacob standing in the doorway.

Rachab made a sweeping motion with her hand. "Jacob, go with your father."

"Is my mother ill, Savta*?"*

"Jacob, this is a time for women, not men and boys. Go with your father."

His heart pounding, Boaz carried his daughter in the crook of his arm and, with the other hand, grasped Jacob by the shoulder, propelling him out into the courtyard. They passed Zillah, as she hurried into the house with her bag of herbs and potions.

Boaz sat on the stone bench, bewildered and wondering what to do. In his arms, Jael screamed, her small face contorted. Beside him, Jacob sat forlornly, staring at the door to the house. Hodesh came quickly and took the baby, crooning and rocking her until her cries subsided. Salmon lowered himself to the bench beside Boaz, and the two men sat silently, watching the house. Boaz had never felt more helpless in his life. He put an arm around Jacob, who leaned against him, and they waited, listening to the sounds from the house. What did those red stains mean?

Scenes ran through his mind—Miriam walking through the fields, her raven hair blowing in the wind; her smile, and the way her eyes glistened when she looked at him. He remembered the stolen moments when they were betrothed and not supposed to see each other, the secret meetings under the sycamore tree at night. How he'd longed for her and could scarcely wait for their wedding day—for the words under the canopy that would make her his forever.

"Miriam." The word slipped out, almost a groan. He must not lose her. She was his life and breath. He bowed his head and besieged the Almighty, the God Who Sees, for her life. "Do not take her, Ha'Shem*. Grant me this plea."*

Suddenly he heard moans, and twice Miriam cried out—sharp cries of pain that nearly undid him. He wanted to go to her but knew the women would not allow him in. "Let her live, Ha'Shem, *I beg You." There was one long scream, and then silence, a silence that struck at his heart like a knife. He looked toward the house, and his mother came and stood in the doorway.*

He raised his eyebrows in question, fear filling up his chest until he almost couldn't breathe.

Rachab nodded. "Miriam lives."

Boaz bowed his head in silent thanks as Jacob hugged him. "Oh, Abba,*" he murmured over and over.*

Rachab came and held her arms out to Jacob, who with a cry ran into them and was gathered to his grandmother's heart. In a daze, Boaz stumbled into the house and once again knelt by the side of Miriam's bed. Leaning down, he kissed her warm lips. She was sleeping in exhaustion. The fear lifted, and Boaz put his head down on his arms, weeping in relief and gratitude.

Now, sitting on that same bench, he sighed at the memories that flooded back, shaking his head as if to dispel the anxiety they brought. He didn't have many children, but the two *Ha'Shem* had given him blessed his soul.

Six

Ruth went with Orpah to the village to deliver two of her father's pots that a family had ordered. She hoped to see Mahlon again, for he came into town with his father from time to time. Perhaps he would come again today.

"You are well, Ruth?"

The deep voice startled her, and she turned around. It was Amon, the son of the local blacksmith. He was stocky, like his father, but not as heavy. His mouth seemed to remain in a perpetual frown, and Ruth had heard stories of his temper, which flared when anyone at the local school displeased him. More than once, the rabbi had used his rod, but Amon did not repent or change his disposition. He'd told his father he would no longer go to school. The whole town knew him to be a rebellious son. Why did his father not discipline him? Sometimes Ruth wondered if the blacksmith, a widower, was afraid of his son. Most of the young men in the village were.

"I am well, Amon," Ruth replied.

He ignored Orpah, his eyes glittering as he considered Ruth. She felt uncomfortable under his insolent gaze. He looked at her like a prize ewe. "I saw you in the fields yesterday."

If he had meant to frighten her with his words, he had succeeded. She did not want to be caught alone in the fields with Amon. She fought down her fear and said nothing.

"The lamb is silent?" He snickered. "We should become better acquainted. Perhaps we will have the chance to do that...soon."

Still she did not answer. With a smirk and a slight nod of his head, he went on down the road.

Ruth shuddered. "I do not like him, Orpah. He frightens me."

Orpah looked after him a moment. "There is talk in the village, Ruth. He wants his father to ask for you in marriage."

Ruth gasped. "I pray my grandfather will not hear of such a thing. Amon's reputation is known. Surely my grandfather would not accept."

"All I'm saying is what my mother has heard. You'd better be prepared."

"I would defy my grandfather to keep from marrying Amon," Ruth answered vehemently. The very idea terrified her.

Just then, Elimelech and Mahlon entered the town with Chilion. Mahlon was carrying some tools. Ruth hoped to speak with him, but, to her dismay, they headed inside the blacksmith's shop. Her curiosity overcame her shyness, and she tugged on Orpah's arm. "Let's go closer."

Orpah hesitated, but then she clutched Ruth's arm and came willingly. There was a leather merchant's stall across from the blacksmith's shop, and they pretended to be interested in the display of sandals as they listened to the men's conversation.

"What brings you here today, my lord?" the blacksmith said in his booming voice.

"A repair of these scythes," Elimelech replied. "The edges are dull, and my men will be helping with the harvest."

"So, you are the sons." Amon had spoken, and Ruth did not mistake the sarcasm in his tone.

"I am Mahlon. This is my brother, Chilion."

"I have seen you talking to Ruth, one of our women." The emphasis was on "our."

There was a pause, and the girls leaned in closer to hear Mahlon's reply.

"I have spoken to her."

"She is taken. You need not trouble yourself."

"She does not wear the veil of a betrothed woman. Why do you feel the need to warn me?"

"I'm just letting you know. We don't appreciate strangers bothering our women."

"Amon, enough!" the blacksmith intervened. "You will not speak to these men in that manner."

Ruth peeked through the slats in the sandal maker's booth. Amon appeared menacing, but Mahlon merely regarded him thoughtfully. Though he was of slighter build, he did not seem afraid of the bully. Amon glanced at his father, then stalked from the shop. Fortunately, he headed in the opposite direction from the tent where Ruth and Orpah hid. Fearing they would be caught listening, Ruth smiled at the merchant and shook her head as she put down the pair of sandals in her hand, then hurried Orpah away. Once they had gone a far enough distance, the girls turned and waited for Elimelech and his sons to appear. When they did, Ruth and Orpah pretended to be deep in conversation with each other and unaware of their approach.

"Ah! How are my spies today? Your grandparents are well?" Mahlon stood smiling at Ruth, and under his intense gaze, she felt a fluttering in her heart. Why did she feel like this when he looked at her?

"They are well," she replied. "They have expressed their thanks for your kindness to us."

Chilion joined them and greeted Orpah with a formal nod. "It is good to see you again. How is your family?"

"They are well. We are delivering some of my father's pottery today."

Orpah carefully unwrapped one of the pots for Chilion to examine. "This is fine work. I will speak to my mother and see if she has need of any herself."

Orpah lowered her eyes. "That is most kind of you."

Chilion glanced back at the blacksmith shop. "It appears that not all of the townspeople are glad for our presence here."

Orpah frowned. "If you mean Amon, he is a bully and thinks more of himself than we do. He does not speak for Ruth."

Ruth could have kicked her.

Mahlon smiled, his eyes twinkling. "Ah, you know of that one."

Ruth's heart melted at his smile. Then she had an appalling thought. What if he believed what Amon had said about her being spoken for? How could she correct him without letting him know she'd been listening to their conversation?

Cocking his head to one side, Mahlon studied her. "Should you be speaking with me? You are not wearing a veil."

She tossed her head. "I am not betrothed. I can speak to whomever I wish."

"Ah, I see. Perhaps I've been misinformed."

Her heart began to beat faster. When Mahlon looked at her in that way, she was lost. It was hopeless. Someone of his father's stature would not ask for a poor farmer's granddaughter for his son, yet Mahlon did not look at her with disdain. He looked at her with interest.

Mahlon glanced back at his father, who waited by their mules. "We must go. Good day, Ruth."

As he and his brother walked swiftly away, Ruth looked after them. "Mahlon is very nice, is he not, Orpah?"

Orpah's eyes followed Chilion.

Ruth poked her. "I believe you are lovesick over him. You have a silly look on your face."

Orpah sniffed. "Speak for yourself. I saw your face when Mahlon approached."

"I can daydream, can't I? And I am of marriageable age. You have two years to wait." She shrugged. "What if Mahlon's father approached my family for my hand in marriage?"

Orpah snorted. "Don't be foolish. Why would a wealthy man like Elimelech seek a wife for his son from the family of a farmer? Right now, you had better worry about Amon."

Ruth shrugged off Orpah's unkind comments. They would not stop her daydreams.

Seven

Boaz was taking inventory of their barns. The grain was dwindling, and while they had carefully preserved everything that was able to be saved in crocks and barrels the previous year, it would soon run out. More and more people had left Bethlehem, and the exodus concerned him. It meant fewer people to feed, yes, but if it continued, soon the town would be silent. When he went in to speak with the merchants, even their shops were low on goods. Caravans brought foodstuffs from other lands, but preserving them was next to impossible. They fed those who had money to pay, but the poor of the town depended on the elders like Boaz, Salmon, and Micah to help them. Soon, Boaz realized, even he would need help.

He thought of his young daughter, Jael, who at six was as bossy as her grandmother. When she was two, she had toddled all over the house, getting into everything within reach. He smiled to himself as he remembered his mother scolding Jael one day when she upset a pot on the table, causing it to fall to the floor with a loud crash. Miriam sighed and looked at Jacob, who took his young sister by the hand and led her outside, away from his grandmother's wrath. Then Miriam bent to help Rachab, muttering to herself, to clean up the broken pieces of pottery.

Boaz shook his head. His daughter was a handful—willful and spoiled by them all. Jacob had been an easygoing child and an obedient one. Jael adored him, and Boaz marveled at Jacob's way with her. She would respond sweetly and do whatever he asked when the rest of the family threw up their hands in despair.

Boaz left his musings and considered again the situation with their food storage. He had arranged for grain from their brethren across the Jordan, but it was slow in coming. The caravan was due any day, and even as he thought of the food it was bringing, he heard the bells of camels in the distance. His heart rose. Miriam had been listless lately, and he suspected her of giving her food to Jacob and Jael and depriving herself. To save her husband worry, she ate a little when he was present, but, in spite of his insistence that she eat to keep up her strength, he knew she saved as much as she could for the children.

As the camels approached, Boaz noticed one of the drivers staggering as he held on to his animal.

He put up a hand as they came to a halt. "Greetings and blessings in the name of the Lord."

The caravan master nodded. "And to you," he said, but his eyes darted from Boaz to the ailing camel driver. "We camped along the Jordan, and it is the lowest I've seen. Flies and insects are everywhere. Several of my men are sick from a fever. We will not come into the town but will camp outside. Can you give us water?"

Boaz turned to the servant who had accompanied him to the road. "Bring water for the men and the camels. And tell the healer we need her."

The watering trough was located outside the town, accessible to the animals of the caravans that passed through. It was dry, and the camels snorted and moved restlessly as they put their muzzles down in the trough, smelling water but tasting none.

In a short time, the servant arrived with helpers and carts to unload the goods brought by the caravan. The healer Zillah arrived, moving slowly. She had tended the town for many years but was aging visibly. Boaz wondered how much longer they would be able to call on her.

With her was Basmath, a local widow, who stayed by Boaz, her soft brown eyes regarding him with undisguised longing. Boaz acknowledged her gaze with a nod. He knew her feelings for him. She had been one of the young women he'd considered marrying before he saw Miriam. Word had come back to him through a friend of how Basmath had wept when he'd chosen someone else. She had eventually married, but her husband and son were killed when the mule pulling their wagon was spooked and, in its flight, had overturned the vehicle. Zillah had taken the distraught woman under her wing to teach her the healing arts. It would help her support herself when Zillah was too old to tend the sick.

Boaz turned to the older woman. "Zillah, some of the men have the fever. They will not enter the town, but perhaps you can help them."

The healer approached the two camel drivers, who sat listlessly on the ground. She bent down and examined them with her eyes and put a hand on their foreheads. Then she turned to Boaz, her eyes wide in alarm. "Do not let them go into town and use the well. This is the black fever. It will spread to all in Bethlehem." She gave the caravan master some of her herbs to boil in the water to ease the men's fevers. After whispering harshly to Basmath, she turned back to Boaz. "Do not let them drink from the buckets at the well." With that, she hurried back toward the town. Basmath followed her with apparent reluctance.

Fear struck Boaz like a hammer in his chest. The black fever! It had swept the town of Bethlehem years earlier, and over fifty people had died—mostly women and children. His eyes went to the bags of grain the servants were unloading. Was it the grain that brought the contamination? And how did the fever spread?

The men eagerly drank from the pots of water drawn from the dwindling supply in the town well. More water was poured into the trough, but it barely slaked the camels' thirst.

When Boaz had seen to the unloading of his goods and paid the caravan master, the two men faced each other silently. The caravan master's dark eyes were brooding under heavy brows. "You wish us to move on."

Boaz sighed. "I'm sorry your men are sick. You must keep them away from Bethlehem and camp outside the town until they are ready to travel. We will give you what water we can spare, but the well is low, and our own animals are dying."

"I understand. I've decided to return to my home in Syria. They are not experiencing this problem." He glanced back at his men. "That is, if my men can make the journey." He shrugged. "I will lose some, I fear, but I must trust in my gods to take us safely."

Gods. The man was a pagan and a worshipper of ancient deities. Boaz could only pray that the Almighty would have mercy on His own people and spare them from the fever.

Boaz came back each day to check on the caravan master and his men. By the fifth day, they had buried three men. The caravan master gathered those who were left and hastily departed. He feared that the fever was a plague from the gods, and he wanted to leave Judea as quickly as he could.

The town was not sorry to see them go, even though they'd brought life-giving grain to the people.

Boaz discouraged Miriam and Rachab from going into the town. "There are many who are ill in the village," he told them. "Send Nadab to the well."

Miriam shook her head. "Men do not gather water for households, my husband. That is women's work."

At the stern look Boaz gave her, she bowed her head. "I will remain here."

Eight

On a beautiful day the following week, Boaz and his steward, Nadab, returned from the fields to a strangely empty courtyard. Boaz had expected to find Jacob tending the animals, Rachab and Jael working in the garden, and Miriam resting in the shade of a tree. Alarmed, he rushed inside. His heart sank when he found Miriam lying in bed, with Rachab pressing cold cloths to her forehead.

"*Imah*? What has happened?"

Rachab turned to him, her brow creased with worry. "Oh, my son, I fear your wife has the fever."

"What? How...?"

Jacob stepped into the room. "We went to the marketplace for water today. I'm sorry, *Abba*. It was such a beautiful day, and *Imah* thought that surely it was safe by now to go into town." He sniffed. "We should have known; there were few people about, and many shops were closed. Then a woman at the well told us to be careful, and urged us to hurry home. *Imah* felt weaker and weaker as we journeyed back."

Boaz prayed for restraint. "You meant well, my son, but the fever is rampant in the town. She should not have gone into town at this time, even for water. Our cistern still has enough."

Soon, Miriam developed the familiar rash, and her dry cough brought fear to his heart as he took turns with Rachab tending his wife.

In two weeks, Jacob, who had confessed to having sipped from one of the water pots, also came down with the fever. Then Salmon took to his bed. Boaz and Rachab tended them day and night. By the third week, to his great relief, Miriam showed signs of recovery and was able to leave her bed to tend her son and her father-in-law.

In spite of all they could do, Salmon became delirious, and the cough racked his body. Boaz and Miriam barely had time to sleep, for Jacob began to complain of abdominal pain and also developed a dry, hacking cough.

With fear rising in his heart, Boaz ordered their maidservant, Hodesh, to keep Jael away in separate quarters. As the days went by, to his relief, his daughter showed no symptoms of the fever.

His relief was short-lived. One evening, as he dozed in his chair, weary from the long hours of tending the sick, Nadab touched him on the shoulder. "Master, your father…."

Boaz opened his eyes, bleary with sleep, and looked over at his father. The moonlight was on his face, and his eyes were open, staring lifelessly at the ceiling.

Boaz went out into the courtyard, tears streaming down his cheeks, and tore his garment over his heart. All night, the women worked to prepare his father's body for burial. Later in the morning, some of the men from the neighborhood came and helped him carry Salmon to the burial cave.

When they returned, Boaz went to see his son. Jacob was breathing heavily, his eyes glazed. Boaz and Miriam barely had time to mourn Salmon as they desperately tried to save their son. The boy fought bravely, and at one point he even seemed to rally his strength. The next day, he was worse, and the cough brought blood.

That evening, Boaz sat with his wife at Jacob's bedside, praying desperately for the Almighty to have mercy on his only son. Perspiration poured down Jacob's face. His eyes were sunken and dark with fever. Rachab and Miriam took turns putting cold cloths on his forehead and urging him to drink the potions Zillah had left for him. Jacob closed his eyes and would not take any nourishment or the potions. He looked first at his mother, then his father, but each time he tried to talk, the cough racked his body.

Rachab stood at the foot of his bed, wringing her hands and weeping softly. It was too late. Two days after burying his father, Boaz was forced to bury his only son. He was beside himself and would not be comforted. He did what was expected of him in the deaths of his father and son, sitting *shiva*, but after seven agonizing days, he spent many hours walking the hills and fields. His mother tried coaxing him to eat, but he took little and soon left to walk by himself again. Sorrow ate at his heart like a cankerworm. Miriam was beside herself with grief also and wept bitterly.

In Bethlehem, there was hardly a house where the keening of grief was not heard. The terrible fever spread, and household after household suffered the loss of loved ones.

Boaz fell to his knees in the dust and cried out to his God, "Why? Why has my son been taken from me?"

The heavens seemed silent as he wrestled in agony of soul.

He finally found relief in work. Any of the servants' tasks that required hard labor, he would take over. He pushed his body by the hour, falling asleep at night out of sheer exhaustion. When he was not working, he downed cup after cup of wine to dull the pain.

One afternoon, Jael sat in the corner of the courtyard, playing with some leather blocks and watching her father with sad eyes. When Boaz finally sank down on the stone bench, staring at the ground, Jael approached him slowly and put her hand on his knee.

"*Sabba* is gone, *Abba*. Where did he go?" She had not been allowed to go to the burial place but had been left with Hodesh.

Boaz forced himself to speak as he took her on his lap. "He has gone to join our ancestors, Jael. He was very old and tired. Now he is at peace."

"I miss his stories, *Abba*." A tear rolled down her cheek.

"I will miss his stories, too."

"But where did Jacob go? Is he with our *Sabba*?"

The anguish rose again, almost stifling him. Jael's beloved Jacob was gone, and he forced himself to answer her.

"Jacob has gone the way of your grandfather."

She frowned, her face puzzled. "Then, if Jacob has gone with *Sabba,* will they not return soon?"

Miriam approached them and lifted Jael from his lap. She, too, had tears in her eyes, and she shook her head as she held her daughter tightly. "The Almighty has taken them, Jael. They will not return."

Jael began to cry in earnest. "I want my *Sabba* and Jacob to come back."

Miriam lifted pain-filled eyes to Boaz. "They are dead, child. We cannot have them back. Come, it is time for sleep."

Boaz watched them go, the weight on his chest almost suffocating him. He waited in the silence and finally forced himself to rise and enter the house. When he came into their room, Miriam turned an agonized face to him. The longing in her eyes was plain as she reached out for the comfort of her husband. Boaz, consumed with his grief, had no comfort to give. She lay down with her back to him, her body shaking as she wept silently, but his heart felt as cold as stone.

Day after day, he was aware of Miriam watching him; he saw the fear in her eyes. He lost weight, and his eyes felt like dark holes in his face. Only wine seemed to dull the raggedness of his grief.

After several weeks went by, his mother came to him and said sharply, "Boaz, look at me."

Boaz glanced up from his cup of wine.

"Would you bring shame to yourself and our God?"

Boaz stared at her, not comprehending, his mind a haze.

Rachab continued, "You are the chief now, yet you behave like a willful child. Are you the first man to lose a son? I lost two children before you were born. Each loss caused us heartbreak and agony, but we pressed on, trusting in the wisdom of the Most

High, blessed be His name, and you were born, strong, lusty, and healthy. Put aside this wine and straighten your shoulders. What has happened is the will of the Almighty, and you only fight against Him. You have a daughter who has lost her grandfather and brother. Shall she lose her father, also?"

"He was my only son." His voice was a whisper.

"Your father and I loved each other, but one day the Almighty called Salmon, and I must remain behind. It is the way of all men. Do you think your wife does not grieve for her son? Listen to the keening in the town. There are others who have lost loved ones. Think of your responsibility. As chief in your father's place, will you have those of our tribe look up to you and follow you, or will they shake their heads and speak of your weakness behind your back?"

Boaz was tempted to respond in anger, but he realized his mother's harsh words were meant to bring him to his senses. He had a destiny to fulfill. Would he shame the memory of his father? He slowly nodded his head and put the cup of wine down, staring at the stones of the courtyard.

"Make your peace with the Almighty, my son." Rachab put her hand on his shoulder for a moment and then turned and slowly walked away.

Boaz got up, stood a moment to clear his head, then went to a stone bowl in the corner of the courtyard to wash his face, splashing himself again and again with the cool water until he felt cleansed. The ache in his heart was still there, but he would not dishonor his father, a man he had admired from his childhood.

That evening, he watched Miriam as she ate, her face drawn, with dark shadows around her eyes. He had neglected the one he loved most dearly in giving vent to his own grief. Filled with shame, he vowed to make amends.

When they were alone that night, Miriam stood with her back to him. Boaz reached out and put his hands on her shoulders. He had not touched her in weeks, and as she turned, she looked up at him with such longing, he was broken. He buried his face in her hair and drew her to himself.

"Oh, my husband, I have missed you sorely. Do I not also grieve for the son I bore from my own body? Have you seen Jael? She is like a lost soul, staying out of our way. Does she not miss the brother she adored, and her grandfather? She needs us now."

"Forgive me, Miriam, my beloved; I thought only of myself." He held her tightly and then bent down and kissed her slowly. He led her to their bed, and with their love, comfort came at last.

Later, as Boaz gazed down at his sleeping wife, he saw her face at peace. He went out into the courtyard and observed the stars. An owl hooted in the distance.

He bowed his head. "Forgive me, Lord. I have thought only of myself. Give me strength to be what my wife and daughter need, and help me to get through the days ahead. What shall I do now that I have no heir?"

A small breeze brushed through the courtyard, and it was as if gentle fingers touched his cheek. Then, a voice softly spoke to his heart. *You are forgiven, My son. You are part of My plan, and from your loins will come one who will lead your people.*

Nine

It had been a year since the caravan of Elimelech had arrived. Amon had indeed sent his father to call on Ruth's grandfather, but Misha, while gracious, told him Ruth was not ready for marriage and turned him away. When Amon learned he had been refused, he walked about the village with a perpetual scowl on his face, his eyes narrowing in anger whenever he saw Ruth. She was careful to come to town only with her brother, for protection, and made it a point to avoid him whenever possible.

Mahlon had spoken to Ruth only a handful of times, always when she was in the village with Orpah or Joash. He asked politely about her family, and he and Joash appeared friendly toward each other. The good weather and change of climate seemed to agree with Mahlon. He'd begun to fill out, and his skin was darker now that he was helping his father with the herds. Ruth found her heart fluttering whenever she saw him, but she had given up on her daydreams. Orpah was right. She was only the granddaughter of a poor farmer.

Ruth drove the goats to their pastureland again and sat on a rock, playing her small flute. The music soothed the ever-restless animals. On strict orders from her grandfather, she and Orpah did not go near the encampment of Elimelech again. Orpah's mother told them the elders had called on the newcomers and welcomed the family to their village.

She gazed out at the waving grasslands and watched a hawk sail lazily across the sky, undoubtedly looking for a field mouse for his dinner. In her mind, she envisioned the face of Mahlon and wondered if she would see him again. She sighed. There didn't seem to be an opportunity, unless perhaps at the next festival. She kept an eye on the herd and played another song on her flute, lost in the music.

She was startled at the sight of a tall figure striding across the meadow. It was a man. She thought of Amon's comment that he had seen her in the fields, and, with her heart pounding, she picked up her staff, for she was alone with the herd, far from the village and from the home of her grandparents. As the man drew closer, her heart began to beat erratically, but not from fear.

It was Mahlon.

Seeing the staff held firmly in her hand, he smiled. "I pray you shall not need that."

Heat rose to her face. She quickly laid the staff against a rock.

"I was returning from town and saw your herd, and hoped I might find you," he said. "I hope you don't mind, but I wanted to speak with you. Forgive me if I startled you. If you are uncomfortable, I will leave."

Ruth adjusted her mantle and looked up at him. She didn't want him to leave, but she had never been alone with a young man who was not her brother. Her mind raced. What should she say or do?

"You are well?" he asked.

She swallowed. "I am well."

He smiled down at her. "Am I welcome?"

She blushed. "You are welcome. You are a neighbor and a guest of our village. I am just surprised to see you. I thought you and your brother would be busy with your herds."

"Ah, there is always work to do, but it was a good day for a walk." He rubbed the back of his neck and glanced over at the goats. "I heard you playing your flute. You take good care of your charges."

She looked down, embarrassed that he had heard her. At least the goats could not complain.

He sat down on the rock by her staff. "Would you play for me?"

She opened her mouth to protest. She did not feel she played well at all, but he looked so interested and kind, how could she refuse? Closing her eyes, she raised the small flute to her lips and played again the simple melody she was most comfortable with. When finished, she looked down at the ground, her heart still beating faster than usual.

"Thank you, Ruth. You play well." When she looked at him again, he studied her face and seemed to be contemplating his next words.

"When I surprised you and your friend Orpah looking over our encampment, you were startled, but you answered me calmly. Some girls I've met would have acted foolishly. You were also courteous to my mother and showed respect." He chuckled. "She was very impressed with you."

"That is kind of you to say, Mahlon." She waited for him to say more. Surely he had come all this way for a reason.

"I am of an age to take a wife," he continued, "and my father wishes to arrange a marriage for me. Since we are strangers here, I know little of the young women of your village. My father has the right to select a bride for me, yet he has given me the freedom to choose for myself. I wish to marry someone I can be happy with."

She took a step backward. "Why are you telling me this?"

He turned the full power of his gaze upon her. "When I met you that day by the rocks, I thought you the most beautiful girl I have ever seen. And not only beautiful, but full of spirit. I sensed from that moment there was something between us. I have watched you in the town and have admired you." He paused, his eyes still on her face. "I wish to know if you felt something that day at the rocks, also."

How should she answer? She had always told the truth, but this was a situation she'd never encountered before. Her feelings were jumbled, and she sought the right words. "I felt as if I had known you a long time," she finally replied.

"Then, you did feel something?"

She nodded shyly. "Yes."

His face lit up. "If I have to make a choice, I would like it to be you, Ruth."

Ruth was startled. "This is not the way marriages are arranged in our village."

He shrugged and gave her a rueful smile. "Yes, I know. My father must call on your grandfather with a proposal for the match. I know it is not up to you to choose a husband, but I desire more than just an arranged marriage, Ruth."

Her breath caught. She couldn't speak. The knowledge of what he was asking was overwhelming. She and her family were not wealthy. What did she have to bring to such a marriage?

She considered how to answer him, searching his face as she silently asked for wisdom. How she knew, she could not have said later, but at that moment, it was as if a voice had spoken to her heart, saying, *This is the one I have chosen for you.*

She lifted her head. "I would agree, Mahlon."

He rose from the rock slowly, as if he couldn't believe her words. "You are sure?" Then he smiled broadly and his eyes sparkled. "You have made me very happy, Ruth. I will indeed have my father call on your grandfather to make the arrangements. In the meantime, perhaps it is best to say nothing to your grandparents. I think they would be shocked to hear of our conversation."

She nodded, too overcome by the prospect before her to speak. Then, as he took a step toward her, for a moment she thought he might do something inappropriate. He should not touch her unless they were formally betrothed.

As if reading her thoughts, he stepped back and gave her a tender smile. "I must go. I will speak to my father."

She watched him stride quickly across the meadow and tried to understand what had just happened. The son of the wealthy family of Elimelech had said he wanted to marry her. Her heart beat rapidly as she realized she could not speak about it to anyone until it was arranged. His father must approve the match. She must not even tell Orpah, for Orpah, like her mother, had difficulty keeping secrets.

It was all she could do not to hurry the herd back to the farm. She wanted to shout and sing. Instead, she pulled out her small flute, began to play a favorite melody, and, twirling slowly in the grass, began to dance.

Ten

Ruth kept her promise, but her secret knowledge was like a ripe plum ready to burst. Did she only imagine Mahlon's words? Her mind was full of questions. Was he teasing her? What if Mahlon's father did not agree? He was a prince of Judah, of the direct line of the Messiah. Why would he consider her, a poor young woman living with her grandparents? What could they offer such a worthy family?

A few days later, Mahlon and Chilion were in the village with their father. Ruth, who had come to town with Orpah, lingered in the marketplace to purchase some supplies for their grandmother.

Orpah walked close to where the men were talking. When Ruth had made her purchases, she came out in the open, where Mahlon could see her, but Elimelech, Chilion, and he had concluded their business with a merchant and left without a backward glance. Her heart sank. It was only a dream. Mahlon's father must have turned down his request. Had Amon succeeded in intimidating him? At least she had spoken to no one of their discussion, so there would be no embarrassment or shame. She pretended she had not seen Mahlon, but Orpah hurried over to her, beaming.

"Is Chilion not handsome? He came to speak to me." Orpah frowned. "Why did Mahlon not speak to you?"

"They are busy. Why should he go out of his way to speak to me?"

"I thought you liked him."

Ruth tossed her head and shrugged. "He was nice to us and introduced us to his family. What else could he have done when he caught us spying on their camp?"

The girls walked toward home, and Ruth listened with growing frustration to Orpah's prattling. At Orpah's house, they parted, and Ruth hurried on alone. As she walked, she went over the conversation in the field again. Did Mahlon mean what he said? A week had gone by with no word from the camp of Elimelech. Now she had seen Mahlon in the village, and he hadn't even acknowledged her. She flushed with the shame of being taken in, and she glanced around, glad no one was there to see her face. If she saw Mahlon in the village again, she would not acknowledge him or even look at him.

That evening after the meal, Ruth and her grandmother were putting the kitchen area in order when there was a knock on the door. Anxiety tore her insides like a knife. Was it Elimelech?

When Eunice opened the door, her eyes grew wide and her mouth dropped open. She recovered quickly and bowed her head. Elimelech stood before her. "Misha, come quickly. We have an honored guest."

Joash was carving a small animal by the fire, and Ruth's grandfather was dozing in his chair. At Eunice's words, they both sprang up and bowed their heads. Ruth's grandfather, with a sweep of his arm, invited Elimelech to enter.

"My lord, we are honored by your presence in our humble home. Be seated and let us bring you refreshments."

Eunice hurried to prepare a comfortable seat for Elimelech. "Ruth, bring wine and date cakes for our guest."

Ruth's heart pounded as she gathered the food. She alone knew why Mahlon's father had come.

"Your herd is well, my friend?" It was the opening greeting, and Misha responded, leading to a discussion of their herds and grazing and other subjects. Ruth stood in the shadows with her grandmother, waiting for them to dispense with the social amenities and get to the reason for the visit.

Finally, Elimelech glanced at Ruth, and she lowered her gaze respectfully. "I thank you for welcoming me into your home," he said. "I have come on a serious matter. It is on the behalf of my son Mahlon. He wishes to make an offer of marriage to your granddaughter, Ruth."

Eunice took a quick breath and looked at Ruth. "Perhaps you should check the water for the animals, Ruth. Go now. This is the business of men."

Ruth obeyed, giving Joash a look that said he was to tell her later all that had transpired.

She drew extra water from the rock storage basin and stood looking up at the stars. She remembered from one of Misha's stories that God had told Abraham his seed would be as numerous as the stars. She was filled with awe at the vast display of God's handiwork.

She stood, listening, but couldn't hear any voices. Surely her grandfather would approve such an offer. Finally, her grandmother came to the door of the house and beckoned her anxiously, her eyes glistening. "Present yourself to our guest, Ruth, for he has done you a great honor."

Ruth came and stood before Elimelech. He smiled at her. "Are you willing to be joined in marriage to my son Mahlon, Ruth?"

He was asking her if she was willing? "Yes, my lord. I am willing." Surely he could see the joy spilling out of her eyes.

"Then it is done." Elimelech opened the pouch that hung at his waist and brought out an ornately carved gold bracelet and set of earrings. They gleamed in the light of the oil lamp. "Please accept these as a gift from my son. I have invited your family to partake of our hospitality in three days' time. I will arrange for witnesses and a betrothal ceremony. The *ketubah* will be drawn up according to our agreement."

Ruth took the gifts and bowed low before her future father-in-law. "I am honored, my lord, and I thank you and your son for these gifts."

Elimelech turned to her grandparents and Joash. "I thank you for your generous hospitality and that we were able to conclude our business in an agreeable manner."

When their guest had gone, Ruth's grandmother clasped and unclasped her hands repeatedly, and finally raised them in the air. "Of all people, our humble family has been honored. Our granddaughter, chosen by Elimelech—was there ever such a marriage in our village?"

Her grandfather pulled thoughtfully at his beard. "Have you considered, good wife, that she will now be joined to the house and tribe of Judah? The Word of Jehovah has designated the tribe of Judah as the lineage of the Messiah." He paused, noting the effect of his words on the family.

Her grandmother's eyes widened, and her mouth opened to speak, but she closed it again. She knew, as did Ruth, that every woman in the tribe of Judah, when she birthed a son, prayed that he would be the One—the Messiah promised through the centuries since Abraham. Eunice shook her head slowly.

Joash put his arm around Ruth's shoulder. "My beautiful sister, you must have made quite an impression when you visited their camp. The bride price is astonishing—more than we could imagine. He must desire you greatly. Now you will have an occasion to wear the shawl I brought for you."

Ruth's grandfather eyed her intently. "Do you care for this man?"

"Yes, *Sabba*."

He nodded. "Then it is a good thing. I pray you will be happy in the home of your husband."

That night, as Ruth unrolled her pallet for sleep in the small room her grandfather had built for her, she knelt and thanked *Ha'Shem* for the future she was only beginning to comprehend.

Eleven

The next morning, Ruth longed to hurry to Orpah's home to share her good news. She knew her friend would be happy for her. She looked up at the sky and sighed. Hours to go. The goats must be led to pasture, and she knew the sun would have reached its zenith before she could get away.

She wanted to hurry the animals but knew goats could be stubborn and willful if she spoke to them in a cross voice. She also could not rush the young goats, who tagged after their mothers, bleating hungrily.

Her spindle was hanging from her waist, and she twirled it absentmindedly, her nimble fingers pulling the soft wool from their three sheep into a fine thread. It gave her something to do when the goats stopped to graze. The day seemed as a week until finally she drove the reluctant herd home. They knew she was bringing them back early.

When at last the goats were safely returned to their enclosure and had feed and water, she fairly flew down the path to her friend's house.

Orpah was sweeping the courtyard and watching the road, almost as if she were waiting for Ruth to appear. She grabbed Ruth's arm and pulled her through the gate. "Oh, Ruth, I have such news. There are rumors in the village that Elimelech has chosen a bride for his son Mahlon. We are all wondering which family he called on. I'm so sorry, Ruth. I know you liked him." She looked anxiously toward the village. "When my mother returns, she will know who it is."

Ruth took a deep breath. "Orpah, I am the one *Ha'Shem* has blessed beyond my dreams."

Orpah took a step back and looked her over, eyeing the earrings and the bracelet. "You are Mahlon's chosen bride?"

Ruth nodded her head and couldn't stop smiling. "His father called on my grandfather last night and negotiated the *ketubah*. Joash said the bride price was generous indeed."

Orpah hugged her exuberantly. "Oh, Ruth, I am happy for you. Such a wedding there will be."

Taking her friend's hands, Ruth began to laugh. "I am still trying to believe it."

"Did Elimelech say when the betrothal ceremony would be?"

"In three days' time. Oh, Orpah, Jehovah has blessed me above all the young women of our village and has given me a great honor."

As the two friends embraced once more, Ruth thought of Bethlehem, where Elimelech came from. She looked toward the forests that bordered the Plains of Moab. If the famine ended, would Elimelech return? She would try not to dwell on the possibility as she prepared for her wedding.

Three days later, Orpah's parents stood as witnesses with Ruth's grandparents, along with the elders of their village, as Ruth and Mahlon faced Ahiram, the chief elder. He carefully examined the Document of Conditions. When he nodded to indicate that the *shtar tna'im* was in order, Naomi and Eunice together broke the symbolic plate.

Mahlon took the cup of wine from the chief elder and faced Ruth, handing her the cup. She took it in her right hand and sipped from it, symbolizing her acceptance of his proposal of marriage. There was a murmur of approval from their guests as Mahlon took a gold ring and put it on Ruth's finger. Speaking so all could hear, he said, "With this ring, you are consecrated to me, according to the law of Moses and Israel."

Ahiram gave the couple a stern look as he intoned, "Praise be Thou, O Lord our God, King of the universe, who has sanctified us with His commandments and has commanded us concerning illicit relations; and has prohibited to us those who are merely betrothed; but has permitted to us those lawfully married to us by *chuppah* the canopy and *kiddushin,* this betrothal. Blessed are Thou, God, who has sanctified His people by *chuppah* and *kiddushin.*"

The ceremonial rites of betrothal were observed, making Ruth the wife of Mahlon by the written document. They would not come together to consummate their marriage until the formal wedding under the *chuppah,* the wedding canopy.

Naomi embraced her new daughter, and Elimelech beamed at them. "Come, my friends and guests, and partake of the feast we have prepared for this joyous occasion."

Ahiram stepped forward and raised his hand for silence. "We have welcomed you, Elimelech, to our land, that your herds may be fed from our great plains. You have honored us with your presence, and now you have honored us even more by taking a woman of our own village as a wife for your son. May the family of Elimelech prosper and be blessed by the Most High, blessed be His name, all of your days."

The guests moved into the main tent, where a wondrous repast was spread before them. A sesame-almond-nigella mix was placed by a bowl of olive oil and a basket of leavened griddle bread for dipping. Sliced lamb and a lentil and coriander stew added their fragrance. Squash with capers and leeks with olive oil and vinegar waited on a low table. Decorated pottery bowls held fresh fruit, and baklava was spread on wooden platters next to a bowl of pomegranate seeds and poached apricots in honey syrup. Another platter held moist date and raisin cakes. Cups carved from olive wood waited for the casks of wine that were being opened by a servant.

Ruth watched her grandmother's face and smiled as the older woman surveyed the spread of food Naomi had prepared for her guests. Eunice shook her head and then, catching Ruth's gaze, raised her eyebrows. Never had such food been prepared in her household.

Mahlon's face was tender as he gazed down at Ruth. "My father has set the wedding for one year from today—the time of the date harvest, in the month of Elul. It will be in the heat of the summer season, as it is now, but it is before the goats and ewes drop their young, and Chilion and I will be needed for the lambing."

Ruth did not respond, and he raised his eyebrows. "Will you need more time?"

She shook her head and lowered her eyes. "I have little to prepare, my lord."

He laughed, then reached out with one finger and lifted her chin. "The only thing you must bring to our marriage is yourself, my beautiful Ruth."

Joash appeared at her side and clapped Mahlon on the shoulder. "Beware of my sister," he said with a smile. "She has a mind of her own."

Mahlon pretended to consider this. "Ah, I must deal with a rebel on my hands?"

"I think you are up to the task, brother."

Ruth smiled at the camaraderie between her brother and her betrothed. It boded well for the relationship between her family and the family of Elimelech.

Throughout the evening, Ruth observed her mother-in-law, Naomi, as she moved among her guests and served them. She had a quietness of spirit that was evident to all present. Elimelech would catch Naomi's eye from time to time, and Ruth was touched to realize there was a deep love and respect between them. She looked forward to getting to know Naomi better. She was unlike the mothers-in-law some of the young women in the village dealt with, and Ruth had a feeling she would enter a peaceful household; and, more than that, there were things she would learn from Naomi.

In their village, when a girl married, she moved into the home of her husband, where she lived in a common room—unless the family was more prosperous, in which case a room was added for the newly married couple. Yet Mahlon had no house; he lived in a tent. A tent could be dismantled and moved on a day's notice. It seemed so temporary, like the Bedouins of the desert *Sabba* had told her about in his stories. She pondered the idea of living in a tent with curiosity and not a little apprehension.

After the feast, as the guests parted to return to their homes, Ruth shyly bid Mahlon good-bye. Orpah and Chilion spoke briefly to each other, but Orpah's father had pots to deliver, and Ruth's grandfather was concerned about one of their female donkeys that was due to drop a foal any day. As was the custom, Ruth and Mahlon would not see each other for the entire year of betrothal, which they both would spend preparing for the wedding.

Twelve

The Plains of Moab had been without water for some weeks. The spring rains of Adar through *Nisan* and *Iyar* were over, and the dry season had begun. Ruth's grandfather and Joash checked the cistern to be sure it held all the water possible. In some years, to water the herd, it had been necessary to bind great wooden casks to their donkeys and lead them to the springs that ran underground and spilled from crevasses in the escarpment. But water for household use and for the other animals depended on what was collected in their stone cistern.

Ruth looked toward the forest bordering the grasslands, to the trees that sent roots down deep into the earth, and felt a kindred spirit. She had her roots in this land, where she had been raised. How long would the famine last in Judah? And how long would Elimelech stay here with his family, far from the home he had known in Bethlehem? She didn't want to leave this land she loved, but she was betrothed now, sealed to Mahlon as his wife by the *ketubah*. Even if, for some reason, the wedding did not take place, she could be separated from him only by a *get*, a bill of divorcement. She sighed. She didn't want to be separated from Mahlon and looked forward to being his wife in more than name only. But the future still troubled her.

After the wedding, she would not be herding her grandfather's goats, and she wondered who would take over the task. Joash, perhaps? That brought a smile. There was a rumor in the village that he had an eye for Deborah, the daughter of one of the elders. Ruth liked Deborah. Pursing her lips, she decided that she was a good choice for Joash. Ruth could, in good conscience, turn over her tasks to her.

Her brother's future settled in her mind, Ruth stood gazing out across the Jordan River. Would she enter that land one day? She shook her head. The rains would have to fall on Judea again, and the famine still held the land in its tight grip.

Farmers in the grasslands were harvesting their wheat, and the first figs had appeared on the trees. Ruth and her grandmother dried them on cloths in the sun and then packed them away in pottery jars in the storage room, the brick walls of which her grandfather had built extra thick, so that it stayed cool in the heat of the day. Covered baskets of almonds sat on one shelf, and below them were more stone crocks, filled with the olives that had been gathered in the fall during the month of *Marcheshvan*. The goats had been milked frequently, and the soft, fragrant cheese was carefully stored in stone crocks for the family meals. They often ate a simple breakfast of goat cheese and fresh bread dipped in olive oil.

Though Ruth busied herself helping her grandmother, the months since her betrothal seemed to move more slowly than she wished. She looked forward to the next few weeks, when the grape harvest would begin. Joash and her grandfather would make the wine that would serve them during the year, and Ruth would help tread the grapes. Every year since she had been old enough, she had thoroughly washed her feet and walked around in the grape press, watching the juice run down into the stone holding vat, where it was dipped and gathered to be sealed in wineskins to ferment. Ruth thought her *Sabba* made the very best wine.

She considered what her tasks would be when she and Mahlon were married. His father had no vineyards and had to purchase wine. Naomi had a servant, but did she bake the bread daily? Did she make the cheese? Ruth almost felt guilty, she had so many questions. Yet it would be months before she had answers.

Her grandmother helped her prepare clothing to take to her new home with Mahlon. Wool had been gathered and spun into yarn, and then the different skeins of yarn were dyed with pigment extracted from roots and berries. Leather had been purchased in the village, and the sandal maker had fashioned new sandals. Ruth placed them in the wooden chest in the corner of the house. Her white wedding garment, with flowers embroidered along the hem, also waited in the chest, along with the band of coins for her dowry, which she would wear on her wedding day.

Ruth wanted Mahlon to come out to the fields and sit on a rock, as he had done before. They could talk about their future together—how many children they would have. At the end of their first year, would she be holding a son in her arms? She sighed and looked over the herd to see if any of the goats had strayed. They seemed content, munching the grass that was beginning to lose its moisture. Mahlon couldn't come. She knew that. It was not proper. But then, he had ignored propriety when he had come the first time to speak to her about marriage.

So, she found herself looking in vain toward the town for a figure that did not materialize. Then, at that moment, she felt she was daydreaming. A figure was indeed coming toward her, calling her name.

It was not Mahlon; it was a woman, calling to her and waving her arms. Orpah. A sense of foreboding gripped Ruth. Orpah never came out to the fields by herself.

When her friend reached her, Ruth could see tears running down her cheeks. Orpah caught her breath and took some water from Ruth's goatskin bag.

"Orpah, what has happened?"

"Oh, Ruth, it is Elimelech. He was in the village talking with one of the elders, and suddenly he clutched his chest and fell to the ground. He has been taken to their camp."

"Does he still live?"

"He lives, but I fear he is dying. You must come."

Ruth swiftly gathered the herd and, with Orpah's help, drove them back toward the farm as quickly as they could go. When the animals reached their pen, exhausted, they gulped water from the trough while reproaching Ruth with doleful eyes for their harsh treatment.

Her grandparents were waiting. Misha nodded toward the village. "Joash was in town. I'm sure he has gone ahead of us."

Eunice turned to Ruth. "Wear your veil. You will see Mahlon, but custom must be set aside for your father-in-law. We must hurry."

When they reached the encampment, Elimelech lay on his bed with his sons kneeling on one side, weeping in anguish. Naomi knelt on his other side, putting cold cloths on his forehead. He lay as if dead, but his chest moved with shallow breathing. Elisheba, the woman who tended the sick in the village, stood at the foot of the bed, shaking her head slowly.

What would happen to them all if Elimelech died?

Suddenly Elimelech opened eyes glazed with pain and began to speak, with great effort. "I must...go...to join my ancestors." He turned his head slowly to Naomi. "My good wife, you are the joy of my heart. You have served me well." His gaze shifted to his sons. "Care for your mother, and when the famine is over, take her home to her people."

Mahlon nodded. "We will do as you ask, Father," he choked out.

"You have been good sons. I leave our flocks and herds in good hands." He stopped as a wave of agony contorted his face. Then, "Raise strong sons from the wife you have chosen."

Naomi clutched his hand. "Do not tire yourself, my lord. You must rest."

He turned his head slowly to look at her again. "Yes, my dear one, I will rest." He closed his eyes and, with a shudder, breathed his last.

Mahlon and Chilion tore their garments over their hearts, and Mahlon haltingly recited the blessing, acknowledging *Ha'Shem* as the one true Judge and accepting the taking of his father by his God. Naomi began the death wail, followed by the voices of the other women, so that those standing outside the tent would know that Elimelech, prince of Judah and the head of his family, was gone.

The procession to the burial cave in the forest beyond the plains was a long one, as most of the villagers came to pay their respects. The body of Elimelech, wrapped in a burial shroud and covered with the *tallit,* his prayer shawl, was laid on a plank carried by Mahlon, Joash, Chilion, Misha, and two other men from the village. They carefully placed it in the cave, and then the entrance was sealed.

Ruth spent most of the day grieving outside the cave with Naomi, Eunice, Orpah, and other women of the village, throwing dust in the air and crying out to the Lord over their loss. Ruth had never really experienced death before. She could barely remember the death of her parents, since she was nearly four, her brother six, when they died of a fever that swept the village. *Sabba* told her that she and Joash had been brought to him and *Savta* by some kind neighbors. And *Savta* told her how grateful they had been, in spite of their grief, to discover that they had grandchildren. Ruth and Joash had grown up knowing only love.

As she wept with her mother-in-law, Ruth wondered what would happen now. Would Mahlon change the wedding date? Question after question rolled around in her mind, yet there was no one to give her any answers.

Mahlon, Chilion, and Naomi sat *shiva,* the mourning period, for the first seven days. Joash and Misha joined some of the elders to make up the *minyan* of ten for the daily prayers of mourning. Ruth was responsible for their goat herd, but she came each day to sit, veiled and silent, in the corner of the room for a short time, to let Mahlon know she shared his grief.

Ruth listened carefully as Mahlon stood up before the *minyan* and spoke the Mourner's *Kaddish,* never having heard it before.

"Glorified and sanctified be God's great name throughout the world which He has created according to His will. May He establish His kingdom in your lifetime and during your days, and within the entire House of Israel, speedily and soon, and say, Amen.

"May His great name be blessed forever and to all eternity.

"Blessed and praised, glorified and exalted, extolled and honored, adored and lauded be the name of the Holy One; blessed be He, beyond all the blessings and hymns, praises, and consolations that are ever spoken in the world; and say, Amen.

"May there be abundant peace from heaven, and life, for us and for all Israel; and say, Amen.

"He who creates peace in His celestial heights, may He create peace for us and for all Israel; and say, Amen."

He prayed for the kingdom of God to be established in his lifetime, but she knew that the prayer spoke of the Messiah to come. The Deliverer had been promised to their ancestor Abraham generations before, and each generation hoped they would be the ones to see Him come.

For seven days, Mahlon would stand before the ten of the *minyan* and repeat *Kaddish.* Food was brought by neighbors and left quietly nearby. Some visitors slipped away quickly, so as not to disturb the mourners. Others entered to sit with the family, stopping first to wash their hands in the basin outside the door and to dry them with a towel as an expression of respect for the dead.

During *shiva,* they could not speak, but Ruth felt Mahlon's eyes on her from time to time, and she knew he was glad she was there. When *shiva* ended and *shloshim,* the thirty days of mourning, began, Ruth would no longer sit with the family.

At the end of the last day of *shiva,* Ruth's heart was heavy as she and Joash walked along the road home. How would the depth of his grief for his father affect her betrothed?

"Joash, will Mahlon postpone the wedding?"

He thought a moment. "You have ten months still to the time set by Elimelech. I believe a wedding can take place any time after *shloshim*. Because it is his father, he may decide to wait out the year of mourning, or he may wish to marry sooner. You would be a comfort to Mahlon after the death of Elimelech."

She nodded, and another thought crossed her mind. She turned to him. "And how are things with Deborah?"

He did not brush off her question as he had done before. "You are leaving to marry Mahlon, and *Savta* will need help."

"You would marry for that reason?"

He laughed. "No, foolish girl. *Sabba* and I were making plans to call on Deborah's father before the death of Elimelech. She will make a good wife."

"It does not hurt that she is also pretty."

He stroked his beard, and his eyes twinkled. "Yes, I've noticed that."

She batted him on the arm.

As they approached the farm, Ruth blurted out another question that had been on her heart. "Joash, if the famine in Judea comes to an end, do you think Mahlon will return to Bethlehem?"

"He promised his father he would do so, and take his mother home. The famine has lasted three years so far. Only the Most High, blessed be His name, knows when it will end." He paused and turned to her. "Do you remember the story of Rebekah and Isaac?"

"Yes. She was obedient to the Lord and went with the servant of Abraham to marry Isaac, far from her home."

"The Most High, blessed be His name, will give you the strength you need when it is time, Ruth."

Ruth glanced around the farm where she had been raised, and tears came to her eyes. It was her home. She wanted to be with Mahlon, but if they left the rich pasturelands of the Plains of Moab and returned to Bethlehem, she knew she would never see her grandparents again. Perhaps the famine would last a long time. Immediately she brushed away the selfish thought.

To Ruth's dismay, Mahlon sent word through Ruth's grandfather that he would observe the full year of mourning for his father, and they would marry then, two months later than the date his father had set at their betrothal. Her grandfather tried to comfort her, explaining that for a young man to take over the headship of his family and fill the shoes of a patriarch like Elimelech was a great task. Ruth swallowed her disappointment. She knew she must be patient and could only pray fervently for him as she longed for the day when he would come for her. She prepared her garments and, with money from her grandfather, went to the village with Orpah to purchase perfumes and salves to make her body soft and smooth. She wore her veil so that everyone who saw her would know she was betrothed. On the occasions when Mahlon came to the village on business, she slipped into the shadows, longing to speak to him but forcing herself to watch and wait.

She passed Amon on the street one day when she was walking with Joash and Orpah. The man's face was like a thundercloud, and he brushed against people rudely as he passed. He looked at Ruth, and the anger in his eyes was frightening to behold. For a moment, she feared for her beloved. Would Amon do him harm? She'd heard he had gotten drunk when he learned of her betrothal to Mahlon. He was still smarting over the refusal of Ruth's grandfather, and half the village had heard him rail against his father for his loss.

Joash stepped in front of his sister in a protective stance, but Amon only spit on the ground and continued on his way. Ruth sent a silent prayer for *Ha'Shem* to protect them all from Amon's wrath.

She made her purchases quickly, and then, after seeing Orpah to her house, she and Joash hurried home.

"Perhaps it is best you do not venture into the village for a while, my sister," he cautioned her. "I do not trust that one."

"Oh, Joash, I am frightened of him. What if he comes when I am out in the fields with the herd?"

He put a hand on her shoulder. "The elders will speak to him, Ruth. If he continues to be rude to all and disobedient to his father, he will answer to them, with serious consequences."

Thirteen

Lying in bed, Ruth opened her eyes and listened to the sound of the bulbul bird. Today marked a year since the death of Elimelech, and Mahlon could come for her at any time. She knew she must be ready, for he would arrive at night to steal her away. Her heart began to beat faster. Would Mahlon come for her tonight? She would have no warning but for the shout of the bridegroom, so she rose to make sure her wedding chest was ready and the small lamp she wore hanging from her waist was filled with oil.

Warmth crept through her body, and she shivered slightly, wondering what the day would bring. She rolled up her pallet, put on a cloak, and slipped outside. Her grandmother was already taking the loaves of fresh bread out of the clay oven. She looked up at Ruth and smiled.

"So, you are awake, at last. Joash has already taken the goats to the pasture. You are feeling better this morning?"

Ruth nodded. She had not been able to partake of the evening meal, for she had suffered a slight headache. Her grandmother had excused her, muttering something about her being too anxious for the wedding. It was a good excuse to retire early and think her private thoughts.

"Go and relieve your brother. He has work to do to help your grandfather."

Ruth scooped water from a small pottery bowl and washed her face. Then, taking her goatskin bag, she filled it with water from the cistern, wound her shawl over her head, and secured her veil.

Before she left, her grandmother handed her a portion of fresh bread wrapped in a cloth.

It was a beautiful fall day. Ruth's heart sang as the morning breeze caressed her face. She was too old to skip on the path to the meadow where Joash waited with the goats, but she hummed to herself as she hurried along.

When she reached the meadow, the goats were grazing happily in the rich grasses, and Joash smiled as she approached. "You are feeling better? I thought I would have to stay here all day."

"It would not hurt you. Besides, soon it will be Deborah's task."

"Is that so? Well, perhaps Mahlon will not come for you, and you shall have to herd the goats until you are an old woman."

She waved a hand at him. "Take your teasing and go help *Sabba*."

Still smiling, he strode toward the farm.

Ruth unwrapped the bread and ate slowly as she watched the herd. When the bread was gone, she stood, looking toward the escarpment and Canaan. Would she go there someday? She wondered what it was like. If the famine lingered, she could imagine the dry fields. Were people suffering? Her tender heart contemplated what they would do here if the rains did not come to water the crops. She was thankful for the underground waters that flowed beneath the fields to spill out in small waterfalls from the escarpment.

Her reverie was broken by the sudden restlessness of the herd. Fear gripped her body, and she looked up. Standing a short distance away, watching her, was Amon.

"Hello, Ruth."

She eyed him warily and gripped her staff as firmly as she could. "Why are you here, Amon?"

"I wanted to talk to you." He took a step closer.

The tone of his voice sent chills through her body. She tried to sound unafraid. "I am a betrothed woman. You must not come near me."

He sneered. "Betrothed to that thin figure of a man? A strong wind would blow him away. Your grandfather should have chosen more wisely, a man who could give you strong sons." He took another step.

"My grandfather chose for me."

"Of course, his father's wealth would buy any woman his sickly son wanted. Elimelech thought he was a great man, but he has taken our grass and water for his flocks and herds. The family doesn't even live in a house."

"Amon, please go. You will shame me if someone sees us."

"Is that so? Well, I am leaving for Bethlehem. I can take what I want and be gone before anyone else comes."

Her heart began to pound harder. "What is it you want?"

His eyes narrowed, and he smirked. "You."

"I won't go with you, Amon. I love Mahlon, and we are going to be married." She raised the staff to warn him away.

He lunged forward and grabbed the staff from her hand. It fell to the ground as he caught her around the waist and pulled her to him. His breath reeked of wine. "I will have my revenge. No woman spurns me. When I am done with you, no man will have you."

She pounded on his chest and cried out. "O God Who Sees Me, help me!"

He only laughed as he pressed her back toward the rock, tearing her robe. "You're wasting your breath. There is no one near to hear you."

"Let her go!"

Relief rushed through Ruth at the sound of her brother's strong voice. He stood facing them with a sling in his hand. He began to twirl it slowly in the air.

Amon pushed Ruth away, and she fell to the ground, sobbing. He whirled to face Joash. "You think you can hurt me with that? I am not one of your she-goats." He rushed at Joash, who twirled the sling faster, then suddenly released a stone. It struck Amon in the forehead, and he dropped to the ground.

"Have you killed him?" Ruth could not keep the hysteria out of her voice.

Joash helped her up. "He is not dead. The stone only stunned him. He's still breathing. Did he hurt you?"

"No, you came just in time." She started to weep again. "Oh, my brother, how did you happen to be here? He was going to…."

"I know, my sister. When I was in town with *Sabba,* I saw him leave the blacksmith shop with a traveling pack on his back. He was looking around, as if he didn't want anyone to see him. At first, I thought he was leaving the town, but as I watched him, I realized he was not going toward the road to the river crossing but in the direction of the fields. It was then that I remembered what a friend told me—that Amon was drunk one night and muttered something about spoiling Mahlon's bride. It was as though a voice in my head told me to follow him. *Ha'Shem* must have led me." He put a hand on her shoulder. "Can you return to the farm?"

She nodded, her lower lip quivering.

"Quickly, then, take the goats and return. Tell *Savta* what happened and stay in the house with her until I return."

She looked at Amon, still lying unconscious on the ground. "What are you going to do?"

"I am going for the elders. It is written in the law that if a man accosts a maiden in the fields, far from help, he shall be judged by the elders. If he had carried out his plan, he would be stoned. The elders will decide what to do with him."

Ruth nodded and then hurried toward home, driving the goats as fast as she could. She couldn't believe she had been saved from Amon, and she marveled at what miracle had brought Joash to her rescue. She pressed her hand to her heart and gave thanks to the God Who Sees for sending her brother when she needed him. She feared what would happen when Amon woke up and prayed earnestly that he would indeed leave their town and not come to the farm and try to find her.

She wiped her tear-streaked face with her mantle and looked down at her torn clothing, a vivid reminder of her ordeal. The goats complained the entire way home; they knew they were being driven back from the good grass early. Suddenly they broke away and charged toward their pen. She hurried to catch up with them. When she reached the farm, she was half running.

Her grandmother met her and helped herd the complaining animals into their pen. She closed the gate, then turned and gripped Ruth by the shoulders. "Your clothes are torn. What has happened?"

Tearfully Ruth related the incident in the fields. "Joash has gone for the elders. Oh, *Savta,* what will Amon do when he wakes up?"

Her grandmother's face was clouded with anger. "Your brother is right to go back to the town. Your grandfather will know what to do." She put an arm around Ruth. "You are fortunate your brother got there in time." She frowned. "But why was he there? He was supposed to be in town with your grandfather."

Ruth explained what Joash had told her about his suspicions upon seeing Amon in town.

Her grandmother gave her another hug. "Come, let us get inside, so you can refresh yourself." She led Ruth to the house, then sighed as she closed the wooden door behind them. "The blacksmith has never been able to control his son, and now that young man must face his judgment. The Almighty will see justice done."

After Ruth had washed herself in the stone basin, she changed her garments, then came and sat on a small stool near her grandmother, who handed her some thread to mend her torn clothes.

"Work will occupy your mind. Do not think of what happened. You are safe now."

Ruth tried to sew, but in her mind, she could still see Amon coming toward her with that terrible look on his face. She still didn't know if she was safe. If Amon woke up before Joash returned to the fields, he might come and find her. She shivered involuntarily, and her hands sank listlessly to her lap. Joash and the elders had to get to Amon in time. She trembled again.

Finally, she sat still, her eyes on the door. She and her grandmother could only wait.

Fourteen

When she saw her grandfather and brother coming to the house, Ruth hurried out to meet them, followed by her grandmother.

Ruth searched their faces. "What happened to Amon?"

Misha shook his head. "He is dead. Drowned in the river. He saw us coming toward him and thought he could get away."

"We thought we had him," Joash added, "for he couldn't find the path down to the river, but then, just when we got close, he found it. The river is high, and I don't think he knew how to swim. He must have been desperate to try to get across. The pack on his back weighed him down. He grabbed a log in the river, but it rolled away from him. He was flailing his arms before he disappeared under the water. We watched for him to come up again, but he didn't."

Ruth felt her heart strangely stirred with compassion. "I am sorry for him. His life was so sad. And to drown in the river like that. Are you sure he did not just get swept with the current?"

"I am sure," Joash told her. "He would have had to come up for air. His body will be recovered. There are men looking for it even now."

Her grandfather stroked his beard thoughtfully. "His father will need to give him a burial."

Ruth turned to Joash. "Why was he so angry? Why would he want to hurt me?"

"He wanted you for his wife. He was angry that Mahlon was to be your bridegroom."

Her grandmother put her hands on her hips. "We will never know all that went on in that young man's mind. But now, let us put this sad incident behind us."

Misha turned to Ruth. "Word will reach your betrothed. We can only hope he believes that Joash got there in time and you were not compromised."

Ruth caught her breath. "Would he divorce me? Mahlon must believe the truth."

Joash spoke up. "I'm sure he will, my sister. The elders will make the truth known."

The meal was subdued as the small family contemplated what had happened that day and how the family of Elimelech would react.

Ruth waited to hear from Mahlon. It was with surprise and anguish that she learned that the elders of the town wished her to come and speak to them.

She lifted her chin. "I have nothing to hide or confess. Amon was not able to do what he had in mind, thanks to Joash."

Her grandfather nodded. "We will accompany you."

The council was convened, and Ruth stood before them, puzzled as to why they would need to speak to her.

She looked past them and saw Mahlon, his face grave as he contemplated her. Next to him were Chilion and Naomi, their faces filled with concern.

Simon spoke up. "We wish to hear what happened to you in the field."

She looked from one to the other and summoned her courage. "Amon tried to…." Her voice trembled. She could not finish.

"Did he succeed?" This from another elder.

She shook her head. "No, my brother came just in time."

"You did not encourage him?" asked another.

"Why are you putting her through this?" Joash broke in angrily. "I said I followed Amon because I suspected he would make trouble for her. I heard about the threats he made."

Misha turned to his grandson, his voice stern. "This is not the way to speak to the elders. You will show them respect."

Joash pressed his lips together and bowed his head.

Ruth, gathering courage from Joash's boldness, raised her eyes and looked Ahiram in the face.

"Before all of you, as the Almighty is my witness, I am still a virgin daughter of Israel."

"You did not provoke Amon in any way?" spoke a voice from behind her. "You did not agree to meet him in the field?"

She turned around. It was the blacksmith, and his face was like a thundercloud.

"I did not speak with Amon, nor did I ask him to come to the fields." She faced the elders again. "I have been brought up to tell the truth. I have done so."

Then she addressed Mahlon. "You have my word, and the word of my brother, who was watching out for me. I can tell you no more than I have said. I am sorry Amon lost his life in the river. No man deserves to die that way. But he was a bully and frightened me."

Misha put a hand on Ruth's shoulder. "Ruth has been an obedient granddaughter to my wife and me. She has always been truthful. My grandson has told us he followed Amon, and thus there was no time for the young man to carry out his deed. Let us release this matter and put it in the hands of the Almighty."

"You knew he wished to seek you for his wife," Simon pressed on.

"I did not wish to marry Amon."

Mahlon stepped closer. "Ruth is my betrothed, and I, for one, believe her account of the matter. I will not call her brother a liar. He was watching out for Ruth, and I am grateful she was unharmed."

Ruth's heart soared with hope and gratitude.

The elders conferred among themselves a few moments, and then Ahiram turned to Ruth. "We have agreed to accept your account, daughter of Israel. You may return home."

With a serious expression, Mahlon came and looked into her eyes a moment, and then his face softened. "We will agree with the elders."

She gave him a grateful smile. The warmth of his look encouraged her.

Ruth's grandmother came and put her arms around her. "It is best forgotten, child."

In a moment, Naomi was at her side, also. "Forgive them for their unbelief, Ruth. We look forward to welcoming you into our family."

When Naomi looked her in the eye, Ruth almost believed her mother-in-law could hear the thoughts going through her head. Yet the innate kindness of the woman strengthened her.

Bowing, Ruth nodded, then let her grandmother lead her away. Soon, anguish and anger rose within her. How could they accuse her of such a thing? These people had known her all her life. She was sure the tongues of the women in town were already busy adding to the story.

On the long walk home, Joash let them all know his mind. "How could they do that? Is my word nothing? How could they make a spectacle of her in front of the town?" He turned to Ruth. "Well, at least your bridegroom had the courage to stand for you. That is in his favor. If he had not, I would no longer respect him. Obviously he loves you."

Ruth's grandmother waved a hand at him. "Let us be done with your words, Joash. We have had quite enough for one day."

Her grandfather touched her arm. "I am sorry too, child, but it is the way a matter like this must be handled. We have elders to act as judges, to see that justice is done for all concerned. They were only doing what they had to do."

The tears that Ruth had been holding back began to trickle down her cheeks. "Ending the matter will not stop the tongues in the town. How can I bear to go into town again or look anyone in the face? I will see condemnation in their eyes, even though I am not guilty."

Savta drew herself up. "You will face them the way the women of our family have always faced the enemy—with your head high. You were not compromised. You are not guilty of wrong. Do not give them the opportunity to believe their foolish thoughts."

She knew her grandmother was right. She had to face them squarely, with the knowledge that she was innocent. She nodded. "Thank you, *Savta*. You are right. I have done nothing to be ashamed of."

As they walked along in silence, all of them entertaining their own thoughts, Ruth thought about her next trip into town. She took a deep breath as she wiped her eyes with her mantle. Her grandmother was wise, but Ruth would have to face the women alone. Could she do that?

She caught her brother's eye, and he smiled at her, seeming to sense her thoughts. He did this from time to time, yet it always surprised her. "And I will be at your side," he said.

That evening, Joash took Ruth aside. In his hand he held a small leather box. When he opened it, she stared in astonishment. "I'd forgotten about Papa's sheckle. Has it been hidden away all this time?"

"Our father said it was for a special occasion. Your marriage to Mahlon certainly qualifies." He held it out to her. A small hole had been drilled near the edge so that it could be added to the ring of gold coins she would wear on her forehead on her wedding day.

She felt tears sting her eyes as she took the coin out of his hand. "Oh, Joash, thank you. I shall treasure it always."

"Be happy, my sister, with the husband *Ha'Shem* has given you." He smiled and touched her cheek, then turned away toward his own quarters.

Fifteen

Ruth had been asleep and for a moment thought she was only dreaming. Her grandmother was shaking her shoulder. She awoke to a commotion outside the house as a cry arose from a crowd gathered there.

"The bridegroom is coming!"

As she had been doing each night, Ruth had bathed carefully in preparation, and now she rose joyfully as her grandmother brought her wedding garments.

"At last, you will be married, Ruth. You must dress quickly."

After she'd donned her wedding tunic, her grandmother placed the ring of gold coins around her forehead. The wedding scarf Joash had given her was arranged and topped with a wreath Ruth had woven. She slipped on her new sandals, and her grandmother wound the embroidered sash around her waist. With Ruth thus prepared, they hurried near the front door to wait for the knock from the bridegroom.

When it came, Ruth almost could not breathe for excitement. Her grandmother opened the door to admit Mahlon, accompanied by Chilion and Orpah. Mahlon lifted the veil and exclaimed over the treasure he had found, and then they left the house, with Ruth's grandparents and Joash following. Some of the villagers had followed the groom's procession. The young men carried torches, and the maidens carried small clay lamps to help light the way. It was a long walk to the encampment of Mahlon, where Naomi waited for the wedding party to arrive, and Mahlon tucked Ruth's arm in his so that she would not stumble and spoil her finery on the way.

Naomi greeted them graciously, and the bridal couple was led to the *chuppah*, where the rabbi waited. The words and prayers that had united young couples since the beginning of their race were spoken. Then, with ribald comments from the men of the village, Mahlon took Ruth into his tent and closed the opening. Chilion, as the brother of the groom, stationed himself outside the tent to keep watch until it was time for the bride and groom to reappear. They would have seven days to themselves to consummate the marriage before presenting themselves to the returning guests and presiding over the wedding feast.

Mahlon faced Ruth for a moment. Then he took her in his arms and began to kiss her, gently, then passionately. He removed the veil, and as her wedding garment dropped to the carpet, he led her to their marriage bed and kissed her again. With a sigh of happiness, Ruth yielded herself to her husband.

After their first night together, the stained cloth from the marriage bed was handed outside the tent to Naomi to present as proof of Ruth's virginity. Her grandmother would later tell her that the people gathered there had all nodded in approval, and that it had put to rest the rumors believed by some that Amon had indeed had his way with her in the field, despite the adamant protests of her brother.

In the days that followed, Ruth and Mahlon began to learn about each other and talk of the future.

"I hope we will have many sons, Mahlon, as many as *Ha'Shem* allows."

He chuckled. "That will be a good thing, Beloved. The sooner the better. And I will build you a house. You will not have to live in a tent."

"Oh, Mahlon, I thought that mattered, but I would live anywhere you were."

He kissed her again, and his eyes sparkled. "Perhaps we should make sure there is a son by this time next year."

The week went by quickly, and they were so caught up with each other that they had no sense of time. Their meals were passed through the entrance of the tent each day.

On the seventh day, Mahlon lifted the opening of the tent, raising joyous exclamations from the crowd of villagers who had gathered to welcome the newly married couple and partake of the wedding feast.

When Ruth and Mahlon emerged, Naomi welcomed their guests to the wedding feast she had worked all week to prepare. It was more sumptuous than the feast at the betrothal. Slices of succulent roasted lamb filled three platters, along with bowls of goat meat stew and platters of squash seasoned with capers and mint and goat cheese interspersed with slices of melon. There were bowls of leeks in olive oil, vinegar, and mustard seeds; fried fava beans; and lentil salad with watercress and goat cheese. Other platters held date cakes and baklava. Baskets were piled high with fresh leavened griddle bread and sauces to dip it in. On one table were small casks of spiced pomegranate wine, as well as red wine from grapes, aged in goatskins.

While a wedding celebration could go on for a week, this event was subdued out of respect for the loss of Elimelech. After a full day of feasting, the guests returned to their homes and resumed their daily tasks. Chilion had helped Naomi to oversee the herds and the servants during the wedding week, but he was inexperienced, and the servants had taken advantage of him. Elimelech had ruled his household and flocks with wisdom and a firm hand, but Chilion did not have his father's skill and was too young. He was more than happy to turn these tasks over to his older brother after the wedding.

Mahlon made some inquiries and found that two of the workers had been lazy—not only did they leave the herd unattended but they also fought with the other herdsmen. He gave them enough wages to return to Judea; but, even so, one of the men, Abib, grumbled as he snatched his money pouch from Mahlon's outstretched hand.

"The cubs seek to follow the full-grown bear, but they are only cubs. I shall not forget this," he grumbled.

The other worker scowled also but did not speak.

Mahlon looked after the retreating servants a long moment.

"What did he mean by that, my son?" Naomi stood with Ruth behind Mahlon, both of them having observed the actions of the two hired men.

"Do not be concerned about them, *Imah*. Their threats mean little. They were just angry they were found out. If they return to Judea, I'm sure we shall not see them again. I will hire more dependable workers from the village to take their place."

Naomi returned to her tent, but Ruth remained by her husband. A shadow of apprehension clutched at her heart. Mahlon's words sounded comforting, but his face was troubled.

Sixteen

Ruth sat in the shade of the sycamore tree, unable to stop the tears that rolled down her cheeks. For a month, she had mourned the death of her beloved *Savta*. Her grandmother had been baking bread one morning when suddenly she clutched her chest and fell to the ground. How she would miss the woman who had been the only true mother she had known. Her grandfather grieved so much, the family feared for him.

In five years of marriage, there had been joy and sorrow. Joy because Chilion and Orpah finally married, and Ruth had the comfort of her friend nearby. Yet her joy of being married to Mahlon became anguish as months and years went by, and there was no child to hold in her arms. Out of her sorrow, she fervently prayed to *Ha'Shem* to break the curse that seemed to hang over the household of Elimelech. Orpah suffered the same anguish.

The village healer, Elisheba, had prescribed many herbs and potions, and each time Ruth tried one, her hopes went up, only to be dashed when, month after month, the time of women came without fail.

She considered her husband and sighed. Mahlon seemed tired all the time. Trying to take his father's place sapped every ounce of energy he had. He oversaw the herds and the servants, but at night he was exhausted. He was losing weight from a body that had little mass to spare.

"My daughter, I have searched for you. Why do you sit here weeping?"

Ruth turned her head and saw Naomi standing nearby. "Forgive me, Mother. Sometimes there are things that overwhelm me."

Naomi lowered herself to sit beside Ruth. "I know, but we must accept that it is the will of God, my daughter. How can we question His ways?"

"Have I sinned in some manner that He afflicts me so? You have no grandchildren to hold on your knees. I have failed my husband."

Naomi put a gentle hand on her shoulder. "I do not understand our God, but we are not meant to. He is higher than the heavens, and we must trust that His ways are good."

"Two daughters-in-law and both barren? What more can we do?"

"Give it into His hands, my daughter. I feel your sorrow and have prayed fervently, as you have, to no avail." She put her arms around Ruth. "You have been a good daughter in every way. If we try to understand the ways of God, we are wasting our time. I have wondered why our God led my husband so far from our home. I could only trust my husband. Now I wonder if he was following the Almighty or doing what he himself thought best. He is gone these past years, and the afflictions from the Lord seem to continue."

"You are not angry with Orpah and me that we bear you no grandchildren?"

Naomi smiled sadly but replied, "After my sons, you have been the joy of my heart." Her expression turned somber, and her eyes searched Ruth's face. "I have not been unaware of the health of my sons. They have never been strong. When we first came here, they seemed to gain strength, but now...." She hesitated. "Is my son performing the duties of a husband to you, my daughter?"

Ruth was startled by the blunt question. She had never lied to Naomi, but she did not wish to shame her husband. How could she answer this woman who had been like a mother to her? She loved Mahlon and prayed for him to regain his health. Her mind raced as she pondered how to respond.

"As you say, he is not well, Mother. The burden of taking care of all of us wearies him at times."

Naomi bent her head. "I have known this and prayed for strength for him. I wanted strong, robust sons for my husband, but both of their births were difficult. I lost a son and a daughter before Mahlon's birth and another child before Chilion."

Ruth's tender heart went out to her mother-in-law. Naomi had never spoken of these things before. How she must grieve all the more because both of her son's wives appeared barren. There were murmurs in the village, rumors that the family of Elimelech was cursed by the Most High. She had seen the knowing looks of the other women.

"Oh, Naomi, I am so sorry to grieve you more. Surely the Almighty will answer our prayers."

Naomi sighed and rose. "Yes, child, surely He will, in His time. Come now, it is time to prepare the evening meal."

As Ruth approached their dwelling, she thought how good it was to have a house again. Shortly after Chilion's marriage to Orpah, the elders had called on them with an offer to help build a house. They had decided it was not right for their neighbors to dwell in tents when the rest of the villagers had houses. It had taken many days. Ruth, Orpah, and Naomi, along with Eunice and Rhoda, had cooked and kept the men fed while the work went on. It had been a time of camaraderie for the men and a chance for the women to catch up on the latest gossip.

The men of the village had made time amid their own tasks to work on the house. Brick after brick was formed in the wooden boxes, dried, and laid for the foundation and walls. A main room was constructed, with two smaller side rooms, one for Mahlon and Ruth, the other for Chilion and Orpah. Mahlon added a storage room with the help of Ruth's grandfather.

Heavy poles formed the foundation for the roof, with branches laid across them. The branches were filled in with clay and more branches, until the roof received a final coat of clay, becoming smooth and solid enough to stand on. Stairs were formed up the side of the house to allow the family to go to the roof in hot weather to sleep. Finally the courtyard was formed, with thick walls.

Ruth delighted in the house. It gave her hope that Mahlon would decide to stay. Yet his promise made to his father on his deathbed still hung over them. Was the famine in Judea abated?

Orpah was sweeping the courtyard as Ruth and Naomi approached. She barely looked up from her task. Orpah had been sullen lately, and Ruth suspected there was trouble of some kind with Chilion. Ruth had heard them quarreling in fierce whispers on several occasions.

For dinner, they prepared a lamb and lentil stew seasoned with coriander, then left it to simmer in a pot on the clay stove. Ruth broke up the bread left over from the morning meal and placed it in a basket on the low table. Orpah put a jug of wine and some wooden goblets on the table, along with some goat cheese. Next to the cheese, Naomi placed a basket of fresh figs.

The men ate in silence, except for a few comments on the condition of the herds. When it was the women's time to eat, they also ate quietly. The camaraderie and joy of the early days of marriage had disappeared like the mists of the morning. What was there to be joyful about?

Boaz stood in the courtyard, watching the shadows make strange images on the walls. A bird sang its last melancholy song of the evening and flew off into the night. Sleep eluded him, as it had many nights in the years since the death of his father and son. During the day, Boaz kept his emotions to himself, but it was the darkness that brought restless dreams.

His father had been weak and feeling his age when the fever struck, and he grieved for him, but he could be more philosophical about his passing. It was not so with the death of his son. Jacob had been the light of his life, and Boaz had been proud of the way the boy took to his studies of the Torah and how he loved their home and fields. Boaz had even begun to consider some of the young maidens in Bethlehem as possible wives for Jacob, even when it would be three to four years before he was ready for marriage. Now Jacob was gone and would never know the joys of marriage or the wonder of the births of his children.

Boaz also pondered the miraculous survival of Miriam and Jael, as well as his mother. He marveled that Jael was already ten. Each time he returned home, she hurried to meet him and ask about his day. Already she was adept at helping her mother bake the bread and tend to the house. God had taken his son, but Boaz was finally realizing what a gift He had left him in Jael. He sighed. His wife and daughter filled his life.

Taking a small clay lamp from the stand in the yard, he went to the storeroom. The clay jars of grain were half full and held enough to last them for some months. His mother had packed away everything she could save in stone crocks—date cakes, dried grapes, and figs. Last year's grape harvest was meager, leaving them a limited store of wine. If they diluted it, the drink went farther. The town well was deep, and, surprisingly, the women were still able to draw water from underground springs. It seemed a miracle. Still, each day, there was the shadow of finding the water pot empty. The wells in the fields were barely providing water for the flocks. How long until they ran completely dry? There had been some rainfall this year but not enough. Still, it was an indication that the drought might be passing and better harvests were ahead.

He left the storeroom and looked toward the house. All was quiet. His mother slept heavily. She had done well after the death of her husband; though she grieved, she put her heart into the lives of her family.

Boaz, now in his late thirties, was respected in the council. The men of the village recognized the wisdom of his decisions and had begun deferring to him. While it took a great deal of time to hear cases and settle disputes, it kept his mind busy, at least in the daytime. It was the nights, again, when he found no respite.

Setting the lamp down, he considered Elimelech and the others who had left Bethlehem years before in search of greener pastures. Had they found what they were looking for? Elimelech's sons were not strong, but if he had found grazing land to settle in, perhaps they were better now. A seventh year of Jubilee had passed three years before, a year that would have allowed Elimelech to buy back his property, but Elimelech never appeared, nor was there any word from him. Now it would be another four years until the next Jubilee. Boaz looked in the direction of the Jordan. If the famine did not lessen soon, and the life-giving rains were still withheld by the Almighty, he might consider seeking the fertile Plains of Moab himself.

Suddenly tired with all the thoughts that tumbled in his head, Boaz slowly returned to his bed, weary in body and spirit. He closed his eyes as sleep claimed him at last.

Seventeen

Boaz came back to the house for the evening meal. He employed an overseer, but it still pleased him to walk in the fields and examine the crops. The workers were used to seeing their master stride through the fields, encouraging them and inspecting the quality of the stalks. He knew their families and often inquired about the health of a wife or child who had been ill. Many times he sent the healer to them and paid her fee.

Miriam greeted her husband warmly. "And the fields?"

"The barley is still not producing good heads. The Most High has given us some rain at last, but it's not sufficient. I fear a small crop." He sighed heavily. "If we do not get more rain soon, there will be no crops at all."

She sank down on a bench. "How much longer can this famine go on? Our stores are low, Boaz. We have fed others, but soon we may not be able to feed ourselves."

He lowered himself down beside her and then looked at his mother, who sat nearby, rolling yarn onto a wooden stick. His eyes fell on her hands, and he saw the raised veins and age spots. How much longer would she be with them? And how long could Miriam manage as their food dwindled?

A gentle hand touched his arm, and he sensed Jael had crept up on him. He looked around, pretending not to see her. "Is someone there? Hmm. A bird must have landed on my arm, the touch was so light."

She giggled. "It is me, *Abba*, it is your Jael."

"Ah." He looked down at her, feigning surprise. "It is not a bird."

She put her hands on her hips. "It is me, *Abba*."

He reached down and swung her into his lap, tickling her face with his beard. Her laughter was like small bells in the evening air. He looked into her face, with her raven hair and dark eyes, and saw how like his Miriam she had grown. Setting Jael down again, he rose and took her hand, and they walked to the low table for their evening meal. With his father and son gone, he had no other men to eat with and had finally insisted that his mother, wife, and daughter join him instead of waiting until he had finished. Rachab had protested his bypassing custom but, in time, came to enjoy it as much as Miriam.

After the meal, Boaz led Jael into the house to get her ready for bed while Miriam put away the food and cleaned the platters from their meal. He shivered in the gathering darkness. Another night of sleeplessness lay ahead. The dreams had lessened over the years, but he still prowled the courtyard in the wee hours of the night.

"Good night, my little flower." He tucked the small rug around her.

"Good night, *Abba*."

He sat by her bed until her eyes began to droop. Once they closed in sleep, he watched her for another moment, then rose slowly and returned to the courtyard.

His mother had retired to her bed, and Miriam joined him. "She sleeps. I wonder at the ease of her slumber." She studied his face. "You sleep little, my lord. How is it you can put in a full day's work in the fields with so little rest?"

"There is much on my mind, Beloved—the price of being the chief of our tribe."

She arched an eyebrow at him and moved closer. "Come with me, Boaz."

He was struck again by her beauty. She was no longer a girl, but the face that impudently smiled up at him never ceased to stir his heart. He ran a finger over her cheek and leaned down to kiss her.

"Hmm. I think I like being enticed."

She laughed, and her mouth curved into a provocative smile as she took his hand.

~

Mahlon stood with Chilion at the edge of the field and watched the flock of sheep grazing contentedly. He frowned. "Are you sure of this, brother? There are lambs and young goats missing?"

"The herdsmen say there are only a few missing. But I have counted, and each time, there are fewer than before. We have lost over thirty in the last two weeks."

"How can this be? Are the herdsmen we hired not keeping watch?"

Chilion spread his hands. "If it were wolves, the flock would be restless and noisy. The herdsmen would be aware of their coming."

"True. What of the Moabite raiders plaguing the farms close to the Arnon River? I heard they are coming across where the river is low this time of year, killing or frightening off the herdsmen and driving the herds back across the river."

"I do not believe they would come this far. Moreover, our herdsmen are unharmed."

Mahlon waved a hand in exasperation. "What other explanation do you have, then?"

"I don't know, but I have an idea." Chilion stroked his beard. "I am thinking we could conceal ourselves at night. Perhaps, since there is little shelter in the tall grass, we could hide in the trees at the edge of the fields."

Mahlon laughed then. "Perhaps hidden by the trees rather than in them. I am too old for climbing trees."

"We do not both need to go. I can go one night, and you can go another. We will have to be very careful no one knows what we are doing."

"Are you saying someone in our camp is involved?"

Chilion shrugged. "Until we know who the thieves are, is it not wise to be cautious?"

"Agreed."

"I shall go out tonight when everyone is sleeping. Orpah can say I went to lie down early because I wasn't feeling well."

Mahlon nodded sagely. "It is a good plan, brother."

Ruth watched Mahlon as he sat on the soft rug and absent-mindedly reached for a chunk of bread. He seemed to eat little these days. It was obvious his focus was on something other than the meal. Ruth hesitated to speak, fearing it concerned her situation. Naomi appeared to contemplate her son as she placed a cup of wine in front of him.

"Are the herds well, my son?"

He looked up, startled. "Can you now read my thoughts, *Imah*?" His shoulders drooped. "Someone is stealing the lambs and young goats."

Orpah glanced at Chilion, and he nodded. "It is true. I have sought to quietly find the culprit, but to no avail. Whoever it is comes at night, right under the noses of our herdsmen. They say they have seen nothing."

Naomi frowned. "Could it be wolves?"

Mahlon shook his head. "There are no wolf tracks and no blood. They cannot carry the whole carcass and many times leave it to return to later. We have searched the area and have found nothing."

Ruth hesitated to voice her own thoughts but decided to do so. "Could it be someone from the village?"

Again Mahlon shook his head. "That would be hard to hide. There are few secrets here." He sighed. "If one sneezes in his house, someone across the village says the blessing."

Ruth almost smiled to herself. It was true. Gossip flew like a grass fire. One could conceal little from his neighbor.

"My husband, all who do not have animals buy their meat from the butcher. He would know if a stranger brought in a lamb or goat to sell."

Mahlon shrugged. "That is true. I would like to think it is not someone we know. We have a plan." He glanced at Chilion, who rose, excusing himself for the evening. Orpah followed him from the tent.

Naomi's servant, Kezia, began to remove food from the table, seemingly oblivious to their conversation.

When Kezia and Naomi had retired for the night, Ruth thought of the men's discussion, and something brushed her mind. A memory. Something to do with the herdsmen. She sought to understand what it was that troubled her. Unsuccessful, she sighed. Surely *Ha'Shem* would reveal it to her in time.

Eighteen

A few clouds moved across the moon, creating shadows interspersed with bright moonlight. Chilion settled himself as comfortably as he could in the tree and prepared to watch the flocks. As the hours went by, his head nodded, and he dozed briefly. He was awakened by a stirring of the herd. They had been quiet but now were restless, milling about.

Next, Chilion heard several male voices murmuring. He was puzzled. They had only three herdsmen. Who were the other men? As he watched closely, two men began to move slowly though the herd, and then a ewe bleated forlornly. Someone was taking her lamb.

Anger filled Chilion at the realization that their own herdsmen were involved and had lied to them. What should he do? Alone and unarmed, he could only watch in frustration as the lambs were put in crude wooden cages on each side of three or four donkeys. They cried out for their mothers as the men moved off in the night.

Making sure he wasn't seen, Chilion quietly climbed down from the tree and stealthily made his way back to camp.

Orpah stirred. "What did you find out?"

"Enough. I will speak with Mahlon in the morning. Go back to sleep."

"Will you not lie by me?" Her voice carried a wistful note, but he shook his head.

"It is late. I have other matters on my mind."

She lay back down and was quiet. He sensed her silent weeping, as he had many times before, and hated himself for his hardness of heart. He closed his mind resolutely and gave himself to sleep.

The sounds of the awakening compound stirred Chilion, and he sat up, surprised that he'd slept. Orpah was gone. She would be helping *Imah* and Ruth with the morning meal. He considered his wife. Married three years, and not a sign of a child. Were they cursed? Had they offended the Most High in some way? Ruth was also cursed. No child in five years. He had thought at one time to divorce Orpah, but his mother had asked him to wait. No one would have blamed him. A barren wife was cause for divorce. What was it that held him back? He shook his head. In spite of everything, he still loved her. And he knew it was not entirely her fault. He sighed. If only he were not so tired by the end of the day. Perhaps this next year would bring the longed-for child.

He rose and hurried toward the courtyard and breakfast. There were things to discuss with his brother. They must consider what to do about the lambs. How many men were there, and where did they come from? Were Mahlon and he prepared to confront their herdsmen? What should be the consequences?

Mahlon looked up as his brother approached, and Ruth could see by the determined look on Chilion's face that he had bad news. She and Orpah served the morning meal, listening silently without appearing to hear. It was as if neither woman were present.

"What have you learned?" Mahlon asked.

"Our own herdsmen are helping them," Chilion spat out.

"Our own herdsmen?"

"They were there when the other men came to get the lambs. No shouting, just words murmured. I was too far away to hear what they were saying."

Mahlon stroked his beard. "We must get help. We cannot count on our own men, and there are only two of us. I will go speak with the elders. The men of the village will help us. We must prepare carefully and surprise them in the act."

Chilion nodded. "True, brother. We cannot do it alone."

Ruth glanced fearfully at Orpah and saw the same concern in the eyes of her sister-in-law.

When their husbands had left to speak with the elders of the village, Naomi gathered Ruth and Orpah to her. "We must seek the wisdom of the Almighty. The men will have to arm themselves, and where there are weapons, someone will be hurt. Pray our God is victorious."

Hands clasped, the women prayed fervently for a resolution to the problem and asked that justice would be done.

When they had prayed, Ruth looked up and saw Naomi's servant, Kezia, her head covered and a bundle under her arm, slipping quietly out the gate. Was Naomi sending her on an errand?

Early the next morning, Naomi came to Ruth in distress. "Kezia is gone. She did not return yesterday. She has taken her things and also some of my jewelry."

"I wondered if something was wrong. I saw her leave right after the morning meal. I thought you must have sent her to town, but she was carrying a bundle."

Orpah joined them and spoke up. "I have seen Kezia talking many times to Bela, one of the herdsmen."

Ruth looked toward the gate. "If Kezia knows one of the herdsmen, and he is involved in the theft of the lambs and kids, do you suppose she went to warn him?"

"I think she ran away with him, knowing what our husbands plan to do." Orpah folded her arms.

Naomi clasped her hands together against her heart. "Kezia has been with me a long time. She was not a slave. Her mother served me, and when she died, Kezia asked to take her place. Why would she do this thing?"

Ruth put an arm around her mother-in-law. "If Orpah is right, Mother, perhaps she cared for this man and wanted to save him."

Naomi shook her head. "We will know soon. My sons will try to surprise the thieves to catch them in the act, but their efforts will be in vain if Kezia has indeed warned them."

When Ruth told Mahlon and Chilion about Kezia, Mahlon pounded his fist into his palm. "We will never catch them now. All we can do is deal with the herdsmen. When I found them in the market square, looking for work, they seemed like honest men. After I fired Abib and Hazar, we needed the help. Perhaps I should have asked around the village for men who were known."

Later that day, he and Chilion headed into the fields with a few of the elders and some other men from the village, the women following at a distance. Mahlon led them to the edge of the herd and sent for the three herdsmen he'd hired. Only two herdsmen were found. The youngest, Ashnah, came forward slowly, glancing apprehensively at the crowd of men.

"Where is Bela?" Mahlon asked.

"He is gone, my lord." Ashnah glanced briefly at his fellow herdsman Moladah, who glowered at him but remained silent.

"Gone where?"

"He and the woman, Kezia, have returned to Canaan."

Mahlon fixed him with a stern look. "And why did he leave with her?"

"I don't know, my lord. He just gathered his few things, and they left together."

"I think you do know. You have been helping thieves to steal from my flocks. My brother observed you. Do not deny it. You did not give me warning, and you are as guilty as the thieves."

Ashnah and Moladah, their eyes wide, glanced fearfully at the elders, who conferred among themselves. Then Ruth's grandfather, Misha, spoke up.

"It is said in the law that if one steals a sheep, he must return fourfold what he has taken. You have not stolen the sheep, but you know who the thieves are."

Ashnah glanced around nervously. "Sir, they threatened us. We were told that if we refused to help them or informed anyone, they would come in the night, and we would be dead men."

The elders murmured among themselves, and Misha turned back to face Ashnah. "Who is the leader of this band?"

The other herdsman finally spoke up. "It is Abib. He and Hazar wanted to get even for being sent away by the son of Elimelech." He looked at Mahlon and lifted his chin defiantly.

"Are you able to make restitution for the animals that were stolen?" Chilion asked, his voice harsh. "Can you provide four animals for every one that was stolen?"

The two men hung their heads. "No," they murmured.

Mahlon said, "Then, will you help us catch the thieves? If you do so, you will avoid a more severe penalty. You must also work without pay until the amount of your debt is paid."

The men nodded their heads vigorously, and Moladah spoke up quickly. "They will come tonight, my lord, when the moon is waning. If you hide yourselves, you will be able to catch them."

Mahlon stroked his beard and turned to the elders. "I will need armed men to help us. If they stole from me, they may steal from others. They must pay the penalty for their crimes."

There was assent from the other men. One called out, "You will have help. We will return at sundown, and we will be armed."

Chilion addressed the two herdsmen sternly. "If you warn them or aid them in any way, it will go badly for you. Do you understand?"

The men nodded, relief visible on their faces. They returned to the flock, but Ruth watched them go with a sense of apprehension and prayed silently that *Ha'Shem* would guide their actions this night.

The evening shadows slid slowly over the walls and stretched out across the courtyard as Ruth, Orpah, and Naomi gathered to beseech the Almighty for the safety of their men and the victory of their mission. After they had prayed, they lit a small brazier and gathered near for warmth as they sat quietly, watching the gate and listening for the sound of anyone approaching.

They were dozing when voices awakened them. The gate was flung open, and Mahlon and Chilion entered the courtyard. They were exultant.

Chilion nearly crowed. "We caught them, *Imah*. The herdsmen gave them no warning, and we caught the thieves in the very act of taking our sheep."

"Two of the thieves were killed," Mahlon added, "one by an arrow, the other from a blow to the head. Hazar was fighting us and struck Aaron in the shoulder. He was going to strike him again as he fell, when another man swung his club and struck Hazar in the head. He died instantly."

Ruth put her hand to her heart. "Was Abib captured?"

Mahlon frowned. "Unfortunately, Abib got away."

"Was anyone else injured, my husband?"

"No, Beloved. We at least had the advantage of surprise."

She nodded with relief.

The men rubbed their hands together over the brazier, and Mahlon continued. "The herdsmen, Ashnah and Moladah, have agreed to work off payment for the animals that were stolen. Now that the thieves have been dealt with, they are greatly relieved."

Ruth handed him a cup of wine. "Do you think Abib will return? He seems bound to cause trouble for you."

"All his friends are dead. He would be foolish to return again after tonight."

"I pray that is so, my husband."

"I do not think they will return, *Imah*." Mahlon touched his mother's anxious face.

She nodded, then stood, taking a deep breath. "Good night, then," she said as she turned toward the house.

With the matter settled, Chilion and Orpah left them, and Ruth went with Mahlon to their room.

As they were preparing for sleep, Ruth was startled when Mahlon suddenly reached out and took her in his arms. As he kissed her, she put her arms around him and was alarmed to note how much thinner he was. She looked up at him, her brows furrowed. "Are you well, my husband?"

He stilled and then suddenly put her back from him. "I seem to weary easily these days, but I am fine." To her dismay, he turned away, lay down on their bed, and closed his eyes.

Ruth stood there a long moment, puzzled and overwhelmed by sadness. Why did he embrace her with the promise of love, only to turn suddenly and ignore her, preferring sleep to comforting his wife? Slowly she lay down beside him and, turning her back to his motionless form, let the tears fall on her pillow.

As the cock crowed at dawn, Ruth rose and said her morning prayers. She looked at the sky, a soft pink turning to gold, and thought of Mahlon's morning prayer, which he prayed every day: *"I offer thanks to You, living and eternal King, for You have mercifully restored my soul within me. Your faithfulness is great."*

If God was faithful, why had He not heard her desperate prayers? Mahlon also was required to thank the Most High for not making him a woman. What was it about being a woman that earned such disrespect from her race? It was surely a man's world, and she had little to say about it. She could only ask *Ha'Shem* for strength to endure this strange marriage of hers—the actions of her husband and the closing of her womb by the Most High.

Orpah had spoken many times of returning to the village and the home of her parents but felt they were shamed by her barrenness. Chilion would not divorce her. She and Ruth seldom went into the village, not wishing to endure the looks of pity from the women who almost proudly carried babes in their arms and led other children past them. Had Elimelech's family been cursed for leaving Bethlehem? He was a prince of Judah and a leader in his town. Did the Most High punish him for leaving? Why else was their home void of the happy sounds of children?

Nineteen

The following evening, as they prepared for bed, Mahlon turned to Ruth and studied her face, his gaze gentle. He reached out and gently caressed her cheek. She covered his hand with her own and was gathered in his arms.

"What have I brought you to, Ruth? You have no children. Always our people have blamed the woman, but I feel it is because of me. I have not been a strong husband for you."

She waited, savoring his compassionate words. "You have been more than children to me. I have known your love."

Very slowly, he leaned down and kissed her. That night, for the first time in a long time, he was her husband in every sense of the word.

The next morning, still feeling the warmth of his love, she wrapped a shawl around her head against the morning cold and, taking a last, tender look at her sleeping husband, went to help with breakfast.

Because of its location on the edge of the town of Beth-Jeshimoth, the house of Elimelech was a regular stop for travelers weary after the long trek from Jericho. It was no surprise when someone knocked on their gate, yet, this morning, the knocking seemed urgent, almost a pounding.

When Ruth opened the gate, a man stumbled into the courtyard. His mule stood with its head down, its flanks sweaty. The animal breathed heavily.

"I am from Kirjathaim. I have come to warn you. The Moabites are raiding our towns again and taking livestock."

Mahlon and Chilion came outside and stood with the women to listen.

"My village is near the Arnon River," the man continued, "which separates the land of our people from the land of the Moabites...."

As he talked on, Ruth heard the words "our bitter enemies" and recalled the stories her grandfather had told her of the Moabites, a people who protested bitterly that the tribes of Gad dwelled in what they believed to be their land. One day, she heard her grandfather say to a neighbor, "They boldly cross the river at its low point to increasingly raid the nearby farms and villages. I have heard rumors of whole herds being rounded up and driven across the Arnon."

Now Naomi, her eyebrows drawn in concern, spoke up. "Those towns near the river must be wary, my son. Surely they are watchful."

Mahlon nodded. "We have no army to call on to rally to our defense."

"None of us does, my friend," the man murmured. "Sometimes the raiders are too numerous for the herdsmen. They are killed or driven from their herds."

Ruth felt fear grow in her heart. Would the raiders come as far as their village? She brought a cup of water to the stranger as Orpah took his mule into the courtyard and gave it water and feed. The man drank the water thirstily and wiped his brow with a cloth. "I barely got away with my life. Now I must warn others."

Mahlon called for the elders of the town to hear the man's story. When they arrived and questioned him, he told them, "They are moving farther north. Nebo and Medeba have also been attacked."

Their own village was only twenty miles away. The men murmured among themselves.

"What can we do?" asked Chilion.

"They are fearless," the man continued. "They know we are peaceful farmers and shepherds."

Mahlon stroked his beard. "We could put to flight two or three, as we did four years ago when Abib betrayed us, but a large group of armed men is more than we are able to fight. We are not soldiers." He paced back and forth.

Naomi whispered to Ruth, "We must pray. We might also be in danger."

Mahlon spoke again. "We can hope they do not come this far. It would be a long way to drive the sheep and goats to get back to the river."

The elders nodded and, after more discussion, reluctantly left to return to their homes. For now, there was nothing anyone could do except be vigilant.

Fortified with food and water, the man left them to go back to his village. He promised to send an alarm to the towns again if there was another incident or the raiders returned.

During the evening meal, Mahlon turned to his mother. "*Imah,* I have thought about this a great deal. It is time to take you home to Bethlehem. I'm sure the famine is waning, and you will be among friends again. The lambs and kids are still small, so we must wait for the time the river is at its lowest point, in order that the smaller animals may cross. I have saved the money from the sale of our tents. We will be able to manage until the famine is totally past."

Naomi's eyes had lit up at the mention of Bethlehem. "That is a good plan, my son. I will look forward to going home."

Ruth listened in silence. They would be leaving the Plains of Moab. How would she feel among strangers in a foreign land? The flocks had grown since the incident with the thieves, and there were many young. Ruth understood the need to look out for them crossing the river. The river would drop to its lowest level when the dry season began, in *Sivan,* just a few months away. She had only a short time left here, and she vowed fervently to spend more time with her grandfather and brother before their departure.

Twenty

In the weeks that followed, Ruth felt Mahlon and Chilion relax outwardly. The danger seemed to have passed, yet Ruth watched carefully as she went through the fields to visit her grandfather.

"So, you are going to Bethlehem." It was a statement rather than a question. Her grandfather knew she would go with her husband. He looked down at her, seated on a low stool at his feet. "It grieves me that you must leave us. When will we see you again?"

"I don't know, *Sabba*. I want to be with my husband, but I don't want to leave you."

"You must go where you must go. The Most High, blessed be His name, will watch over you. You can send word to us from time to time."

"How will I do that, *Sabba*?"

"The caravans. Send your message with the caravan master, and he will see that someone gets it to us."

She wiped her eyes with her mantle. "I wish they would stay here, but Naomi is so excited about returning home, I do not wish to spoil her pleasure."

He put a hand on her shoulder. "I will pray that in a new land, the Most High will have mercy on you and grant you children, and also that your husband will become stronger in the land of his birth."

She shook her head sadly. "I, too, have prayed for better health for Mahlon. We are happy together, as much as we can be under the circumstances."

Joash's wife, Deborah, handed her a package wrapped in cloth. "Here, take this fresh bread to Naomi with our greetings."

Ruth stood up. "Thank you, Deborah. I'm sure she will be glad to have this."

Deborah turned, lifted something out of a basket, and handed it to Ruth. It was a shawl woven of blue and purple threads. Ruth pressed its softness against her cheek. "Did you make this for me?"

"Something to remember me by."

There was a cry, and Deborah went to pick up her small son, Nashon, awakened from his afternoon nap. She had given birth to him ten months after her wedding, and while Ruth tried not to be envious, it grieved her that Deborah had produced a son so quickly, while she had no children at all. The sight of her nephew with his thumb in his mouth and his eyes droopy from sleep dispelled the negative thoughts. He was dear to her, and the thought of not seeing him again, and of never meeting any of Joash and Deborah's future children, caused tears to form in her eyes. She willed them back and put on a smile for her nephew, who reached out his arms for her. She held him against her, savoring his warmth, and silently prayed once again for the mercy of the Almighty, that He would grant her a child.

Joash came in from the fields and greeted her warmly. Her nephew suddenly lost interest in her and now reached for the father he adored. With a trembling smile, she gave the child up, realizing it was time to return home for the evening meal.

Her grandfather and Deborah embraced her briefly, and Joash walked with her a short way. "Be brave, sister, and trust the Almighty." He embraced her as well as he could while holding his small son and then turned back to the house.

She watched him retreat, and then she made her way through the fields as the tears dried on her cheeks.

When she entered the courtyard, she found one of the new herdsmen, greatly distressed, speaking with Mahlon and Chilion.

"My lord, there are strange sheep amongst the herd."

Mahlon frowned. "Where did they come from? When did they appear?"

"I'm not sure. We only noticed them when they wandered away from the rest of the flock. We did not recognize them, and so we counted the herd."

"Someone has given us some sheep?" Chilion asked.

The herdsman shook his head. "They are not good sheep, Master. They are acting strangely. They do not appear to be well."

The brothers looked at each other in alarm. A sick animal could infect the others.

Naomi hurried out of the storeroom. "What is this about, Daughter? Something is wrong with the flock?"

Before Ruth could respond, Chilion spoke up. "The shepherds say there are some strange sheep amidst our herd, *Imah*. I fear they are sick."

Naomi's hand flew to her chest. "What must be done?"

Mahlon picked up his cloak. "We must remove the sick animals before they infect the others."

The men left with the herdsmen, and Ruth, Naomi, and Orpah waited anxiously for them to return. It was nearly sundown when they did, and their faces were grave.

Chilion shook his head. "They were diseased, all right. We will need to watch the herds carefully, especially the lambs and kids."

Naomi stepped forward. "Mahlon, what did you do with the sick ones?"

"We killed them and covered the grave with stones so no animals could get to the carcasses. We must check each of the sheep carefully in the next days and weeks to see if whatever sickness afflicted those three has spread."

A pall seemed to hang over the evening meal as the men reclined around the low table in the courtyard. Ruth, Orpah, and

Naomi served in silence. Ruth realized each was worried about the future of the herds and the possibilities if the disease spread.

Chilion suddenly pounded his fist in his palm. "An enemy has done this!"

Naomi, pouring the wine, paused. "What enemy do you speak of?"

Mahlon glanced at Ruth, and she knew they had the same thought. *Abib.*

Mahlon turned to his mother. "There is one, *Imah,* who escaped when we caught the thieves stealing from our flock. You remember Abib, with whom Kezia ran away? That son of a camel driver thinks only of revenge. He was let go because of his carelessness with the herds."

Naomi shook her head. "May the Almighty avenge us this evil deed."

Chilion murmured, "I feel as though He has abandoned us."

Naomi put a hand on his shoulder for a moment, then looked at Ruth, giving a slight shake of her head and pursing her lips, before she resumed serving.

Orpah had not spoken all evening. Ruth glanced at her sister-in-law, but her face was unreadable. Ruth's heart ached for her friend, who went about her tasks in silence and had little to say these days. Ruth understood. Her own marriage was difficult, also.

Within two weeks, other sheep began exhibiting symptoms of the diseased animals. The entire family was put to work examining the rest of the flocks and herds. Some ewes began rubbing themselves on rocks and nearby trees, and some began to stagger slightly before they fell over. Four sheep had convulsions and were immediately killed and buried.

There was little sleep for anyone as the disease ran rampant through the flocks and herds. Many of the sheep were listless, hanging their heads. Others just bleated in distress. They appeared to eat well but were losing weight and becoming visibly thinner.

The young goats fared no better. Chilion found several lying dead on the ground one morning.

At night, the family fell into their beds, exhausted from their vigil. Naomi, accustomed to selling lambs in the marketplace, found the butcher would not take them. Fear of contamination caused their neighbors to be wary. The devastation continued, and the women began quietly selling their jewelry. They prayed for help from the Most High, and Mahlon was fortunate to find a buyer for their camels when a caravan passed near the town.

Just when they thought the worst was over, Chilion, weary from the long days and nights with the flocks and herds, came down with a raging fever. They called for Elisheba, but her healing herbs and potions seemed to make no difference.

Chilion tossed on his bed as perspiration rolled down his face. The elderly healer tried several different herb mixtures, to no avail. Ruth watched the woman's wrinkled but gentle hands lift Chilion's head to coax him to drink the last herb potion she had prepared. Chilion took a few swallows and turned away.

The woman shook her head. "His body is tired and too weak to fight the fever."

Naomi's eyes were pleading. "Is there nothing more you can do?"

Elisheba shook her head. "I have done all I can. I do not know the source of this fever, my lady."

The family gathered, and Mahlon stood silently at the foot of Chilion's bed, his face drawn and solemn. Orpah knelt by her husband's side, her eyes wide with fear.

Ruth watched as her mother-in-law put cool cloths on the forehead of her younger son, and joined in her whispered prayers for the Almighty to spare him.

The third day, Ruth noticed Chilion's breath was very shallow. He looked up at his wife, trying to speak. "Orpah" was all he managed to say, and he was gone.

Naomi flung herself across the body of her son, her weeping heartbreaking. Then Orpah cried out, and Ruth added her voice to the mourning. They prepared the body for burial, and when Chilion was placed in the burial cave beside his father, Naomi could not be comforted. Ruth put her arms around her mother-in-law and held her as she wept.

The family sat *shiva*, but as soon as it had passed, Mahlon had no choice but to continue to work day and night with the herdsmen to save their animals. The ewes were falling ill again, and one day they found fifteen lambs dead. By the time the crisis was over, there were fewer than twenty animals remaining of the large herds of sheep and goats.

Mahlon came home with his shoulders sagging and his face drawn with despair. "Twenty left. All our flocks and herds...." He sank down on the stone bench and wept, as did the women, overwhelmed by the enormity of all they had gone through in recent weeks.

Ruth gathered herself together. Her husband needed nourishment. He had eaten little for days. She brought him a savory broth, then fruit and date cakes, to tempt his appetite.

"Please, my husband, you must keep up your strength."

He only shook his head. "Strength for what? What is left to us? The Almighty has turned His face from us." He looked away from her and stared at the wall.

Ruth sought out Naomi. "What can I do, Mother? He won't eat anything I bring."

Naomi shook her head. "I have tried, also. He is weary from too many hours' work and too little rest. It has been too much for us all, Daughter."

"What will we do? He grows thinner by the month and at times grips his stomach in great pain."

Naomi looked out at the fields for a moment and then put her hand on Ruth's arm. "I am afraid, Daughter. I am almost sure it is the wasting disease." She hesitated. "There is no cure." With tears in her eyes, she turned her face heavenward. "Why has the Almighty afflicted us so? I do not understand. We never should have left Bethlehem." Then, as if realizing what she had said, she put a hand on her heart and bowed her head. "He gives and He takes away, blessed be His name. Who are we to question what He does?"

Naomi had spoken what Ruth feared was wrong with her husband. With a sob, she embraced her mother-in-law, and they wept.

Mahlon was growing weaker by the day. From the bench in the courtyard, he summoned the herdsmen, who had remained in their crude shelter on the hill, waiting to see what they should do.

"You must go and find other work. May the Almighty reward you for faithfully repaying your debt for the stolen sheep and prosper you in another field." He gave them what few coins he could spare.

"May He turn your sorrow into blessing once again," said one, as he put his coins in his waistband. The herdsmen bowed and hurried away.

When the men had gone, Mahlon turned to Ruth. "You and Orpah will take care of our small remnant. We can only hope the flock will grow and prosper again."

"You will see the flock grow again, my husband. Our fortunes will change, you will see. You must get better so you can oversee the increase of our flocks and herds."

Mahlon reached out and drew Ruth down onto the bench with him. "You must forgive me for not being the husband you thought you married. I have given you no sons to take my place when I am gone."

"Do not speak of leaving me." She lifted his hand to her cheek. "You will get better."

He shook his head. "The Almighty calls for me. My body is weary and my time is near."

Tears ran down her cheeks. "Do not leave me, my husband. What will I do if you are gone?"

"The Almighty will lead you and show you the path you are to take. May you find a husband who will give you sons."

She had no more words. For a long time, they sat together in silence. Finally, Ruth rose and, with a heavy heart, went to help prepare the evening meal.

Mahlon began to lose interest in the world around him. For long hours he would sit in the sun, staring at nothing. He did not bathe or change his clothing. Ruth was beside herself trying to encourage him. The stomach pains became more intense, and one day he was unable to rise from his bed. He moaned, crying out in agony. The healer came and gave him the one herb that dulled his senses, but even that did not totally alleviate the pain.

Then, one evening, as the sun set and shadows embraced the courtyard, Ruth and Naomi sat by his side as he struggled with pain-glazed eyes against the terrible thing that had invaded his body. He convulsed one last time and then lay still. Ruth cried out and tore her garment, then bowed her head on his chest, weeping for her loss. Could this family take any more? After almost ten years of marriage, she, too, was now a widow.

Her grandfather and other men from the village came to help carry Mahlon's body to the burial cave, and Ruth cried until she felt she had no more tears left. Naomi looked as though she had aged years in just a few months. Her hair was rapidly turning gray.

One week after *shiva*, Ruth sat with her grandfather on a bench in the courtyard.

"So, what will you do now?" he asked her.

"I don't know, *Sabba*. We have little to live on. I have seen Naomi looking toward the Jordan, and sometimes she walks in the fields to the cliffs and looks toward Canaan. I'm sure she is thinking of going back alone."

"Then return to us, Ruth. There is nothing of Elimelech's family left for you." He shook his head, his eyes full of sadness. "Who could know you would have such sorrow? The Almighty has cursed the family of Elimelech. Come back to your home."

"Oh, *Sabba*, I have considered that, but Naomi has been so good to me; I cannot leave her alone at this time. She speaks of a kinsman redeemer, but there is no one here of her family."

"Ah." Her grandfather pulled on his beard. "It is for the Almighty to decide. You must seek His will, child."

"I have prayed, *Sabba*. You have Joash and Deborah, and now a great-grandson. I would only be in the way. With *Savta* gone these last two years, Deborah is the woman of the household. She would not appreciate another woman there."

He nodded slowly. "Yes, that is true. She is a strong woman." He looked at her, his eyes moist. "I will miss you, Granddaughter, but you must do as you are led."

She walked him to the gate and hugged him tightly, then watched with tears in her eyes as he slowly trudged down the road.

Ruth looked toward the Plains of Moab. Past the plains was the escarpment overlooking the Jordan and, beyond that, Canaan.

When Ruth returned to the courtyard, she found Naomi sitting alone, her mending on her lap.

"Come, Daughter, sit awhile. My heart is anxious for the journey, but my body is weary."

Ruth sat down, and for a long moment, they were silent. The sun was going down, and the small courtyard was relinquishing its warmth to the shadows of late afternoon. Ruth's mind tumbled with thoughts and questions.

Finally, she turned to Naomi. "Tell me about Bethlehem."

Naomi got a wistful look on her face. "I remember the mountains where we could look down on the sea. The climate changed a great deal. From *Nisan* in early spring until *Sivan* in early summer, the hot, dry winds of *Khamaseen* blew in from the desert. It was hottest from Av to Elul, the end of summer, much like here. Then, around the time of Hanukkah, in the month of Kislev, it began to get very cold. Even through the barley harvest in *Nisan,* it was cold." She paused. "I liked the frosty air."

Ruth waited for her to continue.

"I was born in Bethlehem. My father was an elder. Like Elimelech, he sat in the seat of judgment for the affairs of the town. My marriage was arranged between my father and the father of Elimelech when I was only ten years old." Naomi smiled. "Of course, we did not marry until I was fourteen. I didn't know Elimelech very well. Our parents said we would learn to love each other, and we did." She paused, a pensive smile on her lips. "He was kind and gentle, and he told me I was beautiful. What young wife does not want to hear that?"

"He was a good husband to you."

"Yes, even after the loss of children and the difficulty of raising two sons who were not well." Naomi glanced up at Ruth. "You have had a difficult ten years of marriage, Daughter. I am sorry for the grief you've borne."

"Mahlon was not a bad husband, Mother. He did try, and he did not divorce me when I did not produce children. He felt it was somehow his fault."

"What can we know of the plans or will of the Almighty? He alone gives and takes away."

Ruth was thoughtful. "When you came here, everything seemed to go so well, and then we lost everything."

Naomi lifted her chin. "I begged Elimelech not to leave Bethlehem. I told him we must trust in the God of Abraham to take us through the drought and famine. He would not listen. He was convinced that our sons would be better off and healthier over here. We have paid the price for our disobedience. We are of the tribe of Judah, the line of the Messiah to come. We should have set an example."

Ruth reached over and put a hand on Naomi's arm. "You will be able to see your friends again, Mother. You will be able to return to your home. That should make you glad."

"Ah, dear Ruth. What a comfort and a blessing you have been to me. Yes, on the one hand, I long to see my friends, but I have no means to buy back my home. I return in disgrace. No husband, no sons. Nothing of what we left Bethlehem with. It will be a difficult homecoming."

It was then that Ruth knew what she must do. *Ha'Shem* had whispered to her heart.

Twenty-one

As Boaz walked from the fields toward home, the air felt cool, even as the sun shone down warmly on him. The first rains of *Tishri* had come again. The olive trees were ripe with fruit and ready for harvest. Soon the farmers would be sowing the barley and wheat fields in anticipation of the main rains that came near the time of Hanukkah. The drought had ended and life in Bethlehem flourished.

Feeling better about his crops, Boaz now worried about Miriam. She suffered frequent headaches, and sometimes the pain was so severe that her vision blurred. He knew of the potent herbs she had procured from Basmath, who had taken Zillah's place as town healer, for her headaches—though Miriam tried to keep them a secret. He watched her as she moved about the courtyard, sweeping. He tried to convince her to rest, to let the maidservants do more, but she insisted she was fine and could not just sit and do nothing all day.

Rachab had admonished her that morning, but Miriam only waved a hand and told her she was making too much out of nothing. Rachab sputtered but said no more.

As he walked, he wondered what the women would prepare for the evening meal. Jael, at fourteen, was as adept at preparing food as her mother and grandmother, for they had taught her well. Miriam and Boaz had spoken about a marriage contract for her, though Boaz was reluctant to do so. Jael, however, had her eye on a young man in the village by the name of Shelah. He worked in the shop of his father who was a carpenter. Jael badgered Boaz to speak with Shelah's father, and when Boaz finally realized he would have no peace until he did, he finally agreed. Before he had time to act on his decision, Zuriel, the father of Shelah, had called on him, and he had reluctantly negotiated the *ketubah*. Their betrothal was to last only six months, and then the young couple would marry. Boaz had groused around for weeks afterward, regretting that he had given in so easily to his only child.

Boaz shook his head. He knew Miriam lamented the way he indulged their daughter. After the wedding, Jael would leave them for the home of her husband. Shelah's father, a widower, would be more than willing to have Jael come to cook their meals and run the household.

Jael indeed had a mind of her own, and as he walked, Boaz wondered just how long she had been planning to marry Shelah. They seemed happy together, but they were both so young. Miriam had been only fifteen when he had married her.

When he arrived at home, his mother met him in the courtyard. "Have you seen Miriam? She should have been back by now to help prepare the evening meal."

Dread welled up inside of him. "No. Did she say where she was going?"

Rachab shook her head. "Only that she had something to take care of in town. I offered to go with her, but she refused."

There was a pounding at their gate, and Boaz quickly went to open it.

There stood their neighbors Dorcas and Levi. Their faces were grave.

Levi spoke. "Boaz, we were coming back from the marketplace and found her. She was lying by the side of the road, by that large rock." He glanced at his wife. "Dorcas had just seen her leaving town, so she was not there long…"

Dorcas wrung her hands. "I'm so sorry. We didn't know what else to do, so we put her in the cart."

Boaz glanced behind them at their cart, where he saw Miriam propped against some bags of grain.

He went and lifted his wife in his arms, his voice cracking as he thanked the couple for bringing her.

Rachab had come to the gate and gave a loud cry. She put her hand to her mouth. "Bring her into the house, Boaz. Lay her on her bed."

Dorcas and Levi stood there for a moment, looking uncertain, and then, with hasty farewells and expressions of sympathy, hurried on their way.

Boaz laid Miriam down carefully and bowed his head in grief. Her eyes were closed, and she appeared to be sleeping, but there was no sign of breathing. Miriam was dead.

"It must have happened suddenly, my son. At least she did not suffer." Rachab put a hand on his shoulder, which heaved with his sobs. "I will summon Jael."

Boaz felt as though his heart had been torn out of his chest. Miriam had been the light of his life, his loving companion, his wife. He tried to comfort Jael's hysterical sobs but had no solace of his own. Jael, Rachab, and the women of their neighborhood took up the cries of mourning, yet Jael would not be comforted.

Finally Rachab took her by the shoulders. "You must calm yourself. Can you help your father in his grief by being a burden to him? You must comfort each other in this loss."

Jael stopped weeping and looked up. "I am sorry, *Savta*." Still sniffing, but more contained, Jael wiped her face with her shawl. "Oh, *Savta*, I will miss her so."

"We will all miss her. You must console your father, for she was his wife, and he is beside himself with grief. You have Shelah and the prospect of marriage and children to come."

Jael nodded, her face stricken with remorse. She straightened. "I will be strong for my father, *Savta*."

She came to Boaz, seated on the stone bench in the courtyard, and put her arms around his neck. Boaz pressed a hand on her arm, acknowledging her attempt to comfort him.

Once again, Boaz found work to be his salvation. He strode the fields and called on the workers overseeing every aspect of the land. When he was not tending to his own property, he sat in the gate and heard the complaints and requests of the people of the town. Yet as months passed, his loneliness grew. He was almost fifty, an old man. What did he have to look forward to?

Twenty-two

Hearing insistent knocking at their gate, Ruth hurried to open it. Orpah's mother stood there. Evidently Rhoda had news.

"Ruth, I must speak with Naomi right away."

Naomi came out of the house and called Orpah, who had just returned with their small herd of sheep and goats.

Rhoda seemed about to burst as the three women gathered. "You asked me to tell you if any news came from Canaan about the famine. I had to come and tell you all. There is word that the famine is over and crops are growing again." She looked anxiously at Naomi.

Naomi dropped onto a bench. "Then I will indeed return to Bethlehem. I have sought the Almighty for wisdom, and this is my answer."

Ruth saw Orpah and her mother exchange glances. Her sister-in-law had been spending more and more time at her parents' home. Orpah had revealed to Ruth that her parents had finally told her plainly that her barrenness was Chilion's fault because he was not strong. They wanted her to marry again. Would Orpah go to Bethlehem or return to her parents?

Naomi's countenance brightened. "Thank you, Rhoda, for such good news."

After partaking of some sweet tea, bread, and cheese, Rhoda hurried off, no doubt to spread the word of Naomi's decision.

It took little time for Naomi to begin making preparations to leave. She called for Ruth's grandfather.

When he came, she gave him some wine and bread, and he waited patiently until she was ready to tell him what she wanted.

Finally Naomi looked him in the face. "We have few animals left. I am returning to my home in Bethlehem, and I cannot manage them on my journey. Will you buy them?"

"I will buy them."

He named an amount far above the animals' worth, which startled Ruth.

Naomi began to protest, but his stern face dared her to bargain for less.

Ruth gave her grandfather a grateful smile and watched as he counted out the coins. He had evidently anticipated Naomi's request. He then turned to Ruth with a lifted eyebrow.

"I will get my shawl."

They walked slowly, herding the animals ahead of them. The sheep seemed disoriented, but they followed the goats with Ruth's gentle encouragement.

She observed the fields. The barley was ready to be harvested, and after the wheat harvest, the dry season would begin. Coral vetchlings had attached themselves to some of the stalks of grain, and she knew the owner of the field would have to wait until the harvest to separate the herb from the grain stalk.

One field was surrounded by scarlet anemone, a red flower that grew in such abundance that it nearly encroached on the crops. The garland chrysanthemums that had bloomed profusely in March were fading out, making room for the field morning glory. As they walked, she absentmindedly wondered if these flowers grew in Canaan.

"You are going, then?"

"Yes, *Sabba*. I must go."

"I will miss you, Granddaughter."

She turned to him. "I will miss you, too, *Sabba*. I will miss your stories and your wise advice."

He smiled then. "Ah, I shall have to start all over again with my stories…now to a great-grandson."

Once again, Ruth's heart was pierced by the thought that Deborah had produced a child in her first year of marriage, while *Ha'Shem* had closed Ruth's own womb for these ten years.

She helped her grandfather drive the few animals into the familiar pens at the farm and closed the gate. He had paid far more for the sheep and goats than their worth, and she knew he had done it for her, so she would have money to travel to Bethlehem.

Ruth had a tearful good-bye with her family. They recognized, as she did, that they might never see each other again.

"You are sure, Ruth?" Joash put a hand on her shoulder and studied her face.

"I must do this, my brother. I feel *Ha'Shem* is leading me."

"Then you must do as He bids."

She held her small nephew, Nashon, who clung to her neck until Deborah gently took him.

"Go with our blessing, Ruth."

"Thank you, Deborah. I pray the Most High, blessed be His name, will bless you and Joash with many more children. May His peace rest on this house."

She turned and began the long walk home. She thought back to the first time she had seen Elimelech's caravan, and the hundreds of animals being driven along the trail. Now there was nothing left—no husband, no livestock. Naomi's beautiful rugs and furnishings had been sold. Since the men of the village had built the house for Elimelech, Naomi gave it back to the village. She could not, in good conscience, receive payment for it. She kept only the donkey, to carry their few worldly goods.

Naomi and Orpah were waiting when she returned. Ruth struggled to put away her sorrow and not place a heavier burden on Naomi than she already had.

"It is done, then?" Naomi asked.

"It is done. The animals are in my grandfather's pens."

Naomi nodded. "Dear daughters, let us have our evening meal and take our rest. Tomorrow will be a long day."

Orpah started to say something but closed her mouth. Tears rolled down her cheeks. She had wept a great deal lately. When Naomi had gone to her bed, Ruth took Orpah outside, and they sat on the stone bench as the shadows lengthened.

"You are sad, my sister. How can I help you?"

"You cannot help. My life has been a sad one so far. It started out so happy and joyful when I married Chilion. Now I have nothing, not even a babe to rock in my arms or to comfort me in my loneliness."

"It is the same with me. I share your sorrow. I can only hope there are better things ahead in Canaan."

"Oh, Ruth, I don't think I can go. I don't want to leave my parents. I don't want to leave our town and go so far away. There is...." She stopped speaking.

Ruth cast her a curious gaze. "Is there someone else? Someone in town you do not want to leave?"

When Orpah looked up, guilt was written across her face. She glanced down at her lap, studying her hands, clasping and unclasping them. "He is a widower. A merchant. We have spoken several times in the marketplace."

"He has children?"

Orpah's head jerked up. "Yes, how did you know?"

Ruth smiled. "I don't know. Perhaps I was guessing."

"He has three, and the youngest is only a year old. He needs a wife, and...."

"You must follow your heart, my sister. No one but *Ha'Shem* can tell you what to do."

Orpah nodded.

The sisters-in-law embraced and wept together before reluctantly seeking their beds. Ruth anticipated tomorrow with a heavy heart.

The next day, Ruth sat quietly with Naomi and Orpah, sharing their last morning meal in this courtyard. Orpah was brooding, her face drawn. Ruth saw Naomi studying the girl's countenance, and several times Ruth herself felt the contemplation of her mother-in-law's eyes. They put the dishes away a final time, and when everything was in order, they gathered their things from the house, packing the cooking brazier and bedding on the donkey and putting their clothing and basic necessities in bundles they could carry.

Naomi swept the courtyard as Ruth and Orpah prepared the bread, fruit, and as much other food as they could manage for the journey to Bethlehem.

Finally, with a last look at the house, the three women left the courtyard and started down the road. When they had gone a short distance, Naomi stopped and turned to Ruth and Orpah. She set her bundles down and took a deep breath.

"It is time for me to return to Judea, my daughters. There is nothing here for me anymore. Orpah, turn back. Go and return to your father's house. Ruth, your family will welcome you home, also. May the Lord deal kindly with you, as you have dealt with the dead and with me. May He grant you rest in the house of a husband."

Ruth looked at Naomi in alarm. "Surely we will return with you to your people."

Naomi shook her head. "You must stay here. Why will you go with me? Are there sons in my womb, that they may be your husbands? Turn away, my daughters, and go, for I am too old to have a husband. If I should say I have hope, if I should have a husband tonight and bear sons, would you wait for them until they were grown? Would you restrain yourselves from having husbands? No, my daughters; for it grieves me very much for your sakes that the hand of the Lord has gone out against me."

Orpah hesitated, looking first at Naomi and then at Ruth. With tears running down her cheeks, she nodded. Seeing her decision, Naomi kissed her and stepped back. Orpah waited for Ruth, but when Ruth gave an almost imperceptible shake of her head, Orpah's face fell.

"You have been my friend all my life. I shall miss you, Ruth." Wiping her eyes with her mantle, she turned and began walking quickly toward the village. She did not look back.

Naomi turned to Ruth. "Look, your sister-in-law has gone back to her people. The judges and her family will see to finding a husband for her. Return to your home also, my daughter."

Ruth smiled gently at the older woman she had come to love so much these past ten years and shook her head.

"Do not entreat me to leave you, or to turn back from following you; for wherever you go, I will go; and wherever you lodge, I will lodge. Your people are my people, and your God, my God." She took Naomi's hand. "Where you die, I will die, and there I will be buried. May Jehovah do so to me, and more also, if anything but death parts you and me."

Naomi opened her mouth but spoke no words. Her eyes glistened, and she nodded. Then, side by side, they began the long walk down the road to the Jordan River.

Twenty-three

As Ruth and Naomi approached the river, they met a family also traveling to Judea, two men and two women. At first, the man eyed them warily. "You travel alone? No man travels with you?"

Naomi shook her head. "We are widows, returning to my own home in Bethlehem. We have heard that the famine is past."

He rubbed his beard. "Ah, a long journey. I, too, have heard there is grain again in Judea." He turned and indicated the others with him. "I am Aaron. This is my wife, Hannah, my son, Seth, and my daughter, Jerusha. We travel to Jerusalem. My daughter is to be married."

Ruth smiled at the girl. "May *Ha'Shem* bless this union and give you many sons."

Aaron beamed at her blessing. After a glance at his son, he turned to Naomi. "It is safer if you do not travel alone. Join us as far as Jerusalem."

Catching Naomi's eye, Ruth breathed a sigh of relief and knew the older woman was thankful also. Naomi nodded. "May the Almighty bless you for your kindness."

In the winter months, the Jordan was easily forded, and Ruth recalled Naomi's reminiscences of wading in the river up to her knees. They had been forced to wait to travel until the month of *Nisan,* when the barley harvest had begun and the river level began to drop. As they approached the ford of Bethabara—The House of Crossing—a large wooden raft was being poled across the river, secured by ropes that had been strung across this narrow part. Simple wooden pulleys had been attached to the large trees on either side of the river. The travelers paid the ferryman his fare and stepped onto the raft. With soft words, Ruth urged the reluctant donkey onto the vessel. Aaron and his son helped pole because of the extra weight.

As she stared apprehensively at the river flowing around them, Ruth was reminded of poor Amon, who had tried to cross it at flood stage to get away from his pursuers and had perished. She was grateful when they safely reached the opposite shore.

Naomi and Ruth walked close to Hannah and Jerusha. Ruth glanced at the girl, who had not said a word so far. "Who is your betrothed?"

The girl looked at her mother, who answered for her.

"He is the son of my husband's cousin. We have not met him, but they have been betrothed since she was young. He has a small farm and is a hard worker." She beamed. "It will be a good match."

Ruth thought of her own wedding and the joy she felt when Mahlon first took her as his wife. He had not been a stranger. There had been a loving family, herds of sheep, and plenty of food on their table. Then, considering the troubles they'd had and the lack of a child, she sighed quietly. Strange years...years to be forgotten.

As they neared Jericho, Aaron turned to Naomi. "There is a caravansary just inside the walls of the city. We can stop there for the night. It is best not to camp in the open these days. I have heard rumors of bandits."

"We will do as you suggest, sir."

As they approached the city, Ruth looked carefully at the stone walls surrounding it, rebuilt again after being in ruin for many years. She wondered what the wall had been like before it fell. One of her favorite stories *Sabba* told was of her great-grandfather who had fought in the battle for Jericho. He and the other men of his tribe had followed the great leader Joshua as he led the armies of Israel and conquered the city. The fighting men from Gad and half of the tribe of Manasseh had also followed Joshua across the Jordan after the battle to overcome the Amorites in what was now Reubenite territory. The Reubenites conquered Canaan, as they and the leaders of Gad and Manasseh had promised Joshua. Then they returned to the Plains of Moab, where they had settled their families in villages left behind by the conquered Ammonites.

Ruth had marveled at the idea of a great troop of soldiers marching around the city, led by their singers and musicians, until the final day, when the army marched around the city in utter silence seven times, after which they gave a great shout, and their mighty God brought the walls tumbling down so they could conquer and kill all its pagan occupants.

As she walked, another name came to mind. Her grandfather had spoken of a brave woman named Ra'ab, a Canaanite woman who had hidden the Israelite spies and, trusting in the God of Abraham, saved herself and her family. Her grandfather said that she was a harlot and, though saved, had been placed with her family outside the perimeters of the Israelite encampment. Ruth thought she was indeed brave to take a chance on two strange men who came to her for lodging. How the people of the city must have trembled with fear as the Israelite army approached. Did they all know they were going to die?

She turned her mind from these morbid thoughts and looked around. Aaron waved a hand toward the city. "Ah, the 'City of Palms' awaits us."

Palm trees were certainly in evidence all around them, and flowers lined the road. Ruth was struck by the abundance of fields and groves of fruit trees they passed before they entered the city.

Naomi came alongside her. "It is also called the 'Key to Israel' because it is the entrance to Israel from the Jericho Road."

Ruth smiled at her. "I have much to learn about the land on this side of the Jordan."

The caravansary was a bustling place. The low moans of camels mingled with the neighing of horses and the murmur of many travelers moving to and fro, settling their animals. Aaron approached the innkeeper and arranged for a stall for his family. Ruth and Naomi hung back with uncertainty, and the innkeeper eyed them quizzically.

"There are six of us in my family...and one animal," Aaron announced firmly.

He was including them in his family? Noticing some unsavory-looking men near the camels, Ruth was glad for his foresight. No one need know she and Naomi were alone. Naomi thanked their wise benefactor for seeing to their safety.

They were given a stall, a room closed on three sides and open to the main courtyard. There was fresh straw, and Seth helped spread it out so that Ruth and Naomi would have a good place to sleep. Ruth tied the donkey to a ring in the wall, and the animal bent down to munch on the straw. She then helped Naomi settle their bedding in one corner. It was not the small, cozy room she had once shared with Mahlon, but they were poor, and she was grateful for shelter for the two of them. Naomi seemed to have no trouble falling asleep. It was no wonder, after a long day of walking.

Ruth was glad the older woman was able to get some rest. She wondered how they would be received in Bethlehem. Elimelech had been a man of great standing, from what Naomi had shared with her over the years, but Naomi was returning without any flocks, herds, or servants. She came alone, with only a daughter-in-law, and they had very little. How would they live? Surely there was something she could do to help Naomi. And what about her home? Naomi said it had been sold before they left Bethlehem. Could they buy it back? Did they have enough money to do so? If not, where would they stay? Questions bombarded her mind until she finally fell asleep out of sheer exhaustion.

Almost as soon as the sun came up, the caravansary bustled with the noise of the animals as a caravan was readied to leave Jericho for other cities, loaded with local goods for sale.

Ruth, rubbing the sleep from her eyes, stood at the opening of their shelter and watched the men handling the animals. There were shouts as camels were cajoled and urged to rise, and made ready to go. She had never seen such a sight, and her eyes lingered, taking in the excitement. Their own donkey brayed, anxious to be moving and spurred on by the sounds around him.

She found Seth at her side. Having discovered him watching her from time to time, she sensed the young man admired her. When she met his gaze, he quickly looked down at the ground.

"Did you ever have camels?" he asked.

She hesitated. "Yes, my father-in-law had many camels. We sold them when he died."

"You should have kept some. You would not have to walk all the way to Bethlehem." He blushed furiously. "You are very pretty."

Ruth refrained from smiling. It would do no good to try to explain the camels or to acknowledge the admiration of a young man.

"Daughter, will you not help?"

Ruth turned quickly and joined Naomi in setting up the small brazier they had brought to heat their tea. As the pot was warming, Ruth pulled some bread from one of their bags and broke it in pieces for their breakfast. She looked over at the family of Aaron, where Seth hurriedly occupied himself with their goods. She was prepared to share what they had, but Aaron shook his head, as if anticipating her offer. "We have plenty."

When they had packed up their things and the donkey was ready, Ruth and Naomi waited quietly for Aaron's family, and then the small group left Jericho and traveled on toward Jerusalem.

Leading the donkey, which for the moment plodded along docilely, Ruth walked next to Hannah. "How far is the city?"

"My husband told me it is around fifteen miles, but the mountain road we must travel on can be dangerous with many bandits. I am afraid."

Naomi spoke up. "We must pray for the protection of the Almighty to see us safely through." The women paused and quietly did so.

Ruth glanced at the young girl, Jerusha. She seldom spoke, except to her mother, and most of the time she walked in silence. Could it be she was not looking forward to her wedding? Most young women rejoiced to be a bride, but Jerusha seemed to be dragging her feet.

"Is your daughter not well?" Ruth asked Hannah. "She seems sad."

Hannah gave a small snort. "She is moping over a young man in our village, who was totally unsuitable. She will get over it when she is busy being a wife and mother." Hannah turned to Ruth and eyed her curiously. "You have no children?"

Ruth cringed. "I'm sure you are right," she said, ignoring the question and instead responding to the woman's former comment.

Suddenly there were shouts and a large commotion in the road ahead. Aaron, Seth, and the women hurried around a bend in the road and found the caravan that had left the caravansary earlier. One camel lay wounded, and the driver tended to him with cries of dismay. A smaller group of men was disappearing into the hills.

Aaron strode forward. "What has happened here?"

One of the men in the caravan shook his fist at the departing band of marauders.

"Bandits!" said another. "We drove them off. They didn't know we had skilled fighters among us, and we sent them running back into the hills. Unfortunately one of the camels was wounded. We will have to kill the poor beast and distribute his load among the others." The man glanced at the group. "You had best travel with us to Jerusalem. They might return. You are not safe alone."

"Thank you for your kindness. May the Most High reward you, my friend." Aaron turned to his family and Ruth and Naomi. "We will join them for our safety."

The small group stayed close to the caravan. Ruth almost wept for the poor camel. The driver had unloaded the bundles from the animal's back. He stood for a moment, knife in hand, and then leaned forward and made one quick stroke. The camel died instantly.

Naomi stood by Ruth, clicking her tongue. "They have no choice but to leave it by the side of the road. There is nothing they can do here."

Ruth sighed. The jackals and scavengers would make short work of the carcass. It was the way of all creatures. The death of one benefited others.

"You are all right, Mother?"

Naomi sighed. "Yes, Daughter, I am all right. I must confess I am anxious about returning home. But it will be good to see my neighbors and friends again."

Ruth didn't answer. She was happy for Naomi, but the neighbors, friends, and family she'd known all her life were back across the Jordan. She would never see them again. With a heavy heart, she turned her eyes to look ahead—to Jerusalem.

Twenty-four

Finally the time came for Jael's marriage to Shelah. Boaz could not fault her choice. The young man was a carpenter, and a good one. He had learned his trade well from his grandfather and father. Boaz only hoped no one would know that his daughter had made the choice herself instead of her father. Still, it would be a good match.

Rachab had given up on Boaz's marrying again, and while it grieved her that she had no more grandchildren, she spoke of the great-grandchildren she hoped Jael and Shelah would provide—and soon.

"I pray you will be fruitful, Jael," she said, "and provide me with grandchildren before I die."

Jael only smiled enigmatically. "We will certainly do our best, *Savta*."

Boaz knew Jael and Shelah had been meeting secretly during their betrothal. They didn't think he knew, but he had followed her and remained at a distance, hidden in the shadows of the trees, watching, hoping to protect her from herself and prevent any gossip that would stain their family. Fortunately, the young couple only talked. Shelah did not touch her.

Boaz wistfully remembered his own secret meetings with Miriam so many years ago. The thought of her did not bring the same sorrow it had for so long, and he realized he could think of her without pain. Now, with Jael getting married and his mother growing older, the reality that he would one day be alone sank in. The prospect brought a sense of melancholy.

When he went into the house and saw his daughter coming toward him, dressed as a bride, his heart turned over as he remembered how lovely Miriam looked at their wedding. How much Jael looked like her mother.

He smiled at his daughter. "You are a beautiful bride. I hope your Shelah realizes how fortunate he is."

She put a hand on his arm, and probably would have kissed him on the cheek, as she usually did, but for the veil she wore. "I am fortunate to have you for a father."

Around midnight, just when Boaz was beginning to think his daughter's bridegroom had forgotten her, Shelah came for Jael. With laughter and tambourines, Shelah had led his bride to the home of his parents, then back again through the streets to the home of Boaz.

The moments under the canopy seemed a blur to Boaz. He led Jael to her bridegroom and listened as the rabbi intoned the familiar liturgy. Jael circled the canopy seven times and spoke the words that were part of every wedding ceremony. Boaz could almost recite them all from memory. Finally, when it was over, Boaz and Rachab led their guests to the marriage feast.

He had contributed three lambs for the meal, along with other foods from his storage. Shelah's father was not wealthy, and Boaz had been tactful with his gifts.

"Jael is my only child," he had said to Zuriel. "It would give her grandmother and me great pleasure, and temper our sadness at losing her, to contribute to this joyous occasion."

Shelah's father had gratefully accepted, for most of the town attended the wedding.

Along with lamb stew with squash and olives, they provided a bitter herb salad, saffron millet with raisins and walnuts, and moist date cakes. Some of the women had baked special bread with wheat, barley, beans, lentils, and millet and sweetened with honey. Adding to the mixture of aromas that wafted in the air were herb-flavored goat cheese and honey-almond-stuffed dates.

The wine flowed freely, and Jael's eyes were alight with happiness. Boaz rejoiced for her, but, like most fathers through the ages, he watched his daughter and her groom with mixed emotions, remembering her as a baby.

Even now, the memories of moments with his wife and daughter sifted through his mind—watching them knead the bread dough together for the first time; Jael's small hand in his as they walked among the grapevines. He paused a moment in his musing. Though memories flooded his mind, and the faces of Miriam and his son wedged their way into his thoughts, he confirmed that he could consider them with less pain. This was not a day for sadness. Soon enough, in the quiet of his house, the pictures would form in his mind again, and the loneliness would overwhelm him, but he would not allow it to do so on his daughter's wedding day. He turned to watch a line of men who had gotten carried away with the music and were performing a traditional dance, bending and swaying and kicking their feet in the air, and he joined in their exuberance.

Hannah turned to Naomi. "Do you have property in Bethlehem?"

She shook her head. "My husband sold it when we left."

To Ruth's surprise, Hannah beamed. "Then it shall be returned to you."

Naomi frowned at her. "What do you mean?"

"Naomi, it is the Year of Jubilee. The land must be returned to the original owner. That is the law."

Naomi's eyes widened. "I had forgotten. That is true."

Naomi glanced back at Ruth and smiled for the first time since they'd left the Plains of Moab.

Hannah chattered on about the upcoming wedding—what food the family would provide, what Jerusha would wear. Ruth listened, thinking of her own wedding, but she let the words flow over her. She was wondering how she could help Naomi when they returned to Bethlehem and what their welcome would be.

Ruth could see the stone walls of Jerusalem when they were still a long way off. The sun shone over the city like a benevolent angel. Her grandfather had described Jerusalem to her one time, and it sounded like a magical place. She never believed she would see it. The road they traveled would pass by the city walls, but she longed to go inside the gates.

"Thank you so much for all you have done for us, Aaron," Naomi said. "We feel we made it this far because of your care." She smiled up at the big man, and Ruth nodded her head to him in agreement. He beamed with pleasure. Then Naomi turned to Hannah and Jerusha.

"May the Most High smile on your wedding and bring you many sons."

Ruth was sure she saw tears in the girl's eyes, but Jerusha only murmured, "Thank you."

Hannah shrugged and rolled her eyes at her daughter's response, then turned to follow her husband into the city.

Seth gave Ruth a bright look. "Perhaps I will see you again one day."

"Perhaps, Seth."

Hannah paused with her hands on her hips. "Come, Jerusha and Seth, we do not have all day!" Her daughter and son hurried to catch up with her.

Ruth and Naomi watched them go, and then Naomi turned and looked down the road. "It is fifteen miles to Bethlehem. I fear we shall not reach there before dark. Let us go into Jerusalem and find an inn for the night. I have enough money."

They found a small inn just inside the city gates. The innkeeper gave them a questioning look, but Naomi drew herself up with all the dignity she possessed and looked him in the eye. "We parted from our family here and must travel on to Bethlehem, our home. Surely you would not wish two widows to spend the night in the fields."

The donkey was left in the small stable, which looked to Ruth as if it had not been cleaned out for some time. Even the donkey seemed reluctant to remain. Naomi paid a young man to watch their goods. The innkeeper was sullen as he showed them to a small room with a straw mattress. The room was not clean, by Naomi's standards, but they spread a covering on the mattress and covered themselves with their cloaks. They were so tired that sleep came easily.

The next morning, they left the inn as soon as possible. The breakfast fare provided by the inn looked less than appetizing, so they purchased a small loaf of fresh bread and some fruit in the marketplace. Retrieving their donkey, Ruth noted with relief that all their goods appeared to still be there. Naomi paid the boy another coin, and he gave them a wide grin before running off with his treasure.

A few travelers passed them on the road, but Ruth and Naomi looked ahead and kept a steady pace. It was as if Naomi had renewed energy as she neared her home.

As they walked, Ruth observed the barley stalks waving in the afternoon breeze. Men were reaping in the fields. She was sorry their journey did not take place in the spring, when it was cooler, but the river would have been too high. The summer heat was hard on Naomi.

Ruth watched the reapers for a moment longer, and an idea formed in her head. She realized there was a way she could provide food for Naomi and herself.

Flocks of sheep grazed on the hillsides, and she could see the herdsmen walking back and forth, keeping them from wandering off. By the side of the road, purple cornflowers pushed their way into the fields, and pink Cistus vied for space with Scarlet

Anemones. Vines were laden with new grapes growing for the fall harvest, and there were many women picking figs.

As they entered the town, two women with baskets balanced on their heads stopped and stared at them. One lifted the basket down and approached them.

"Naomi? Is that truly you?"

Naomi nodded. "It is I, returned after this long time away." The two women embraced. "It is good to see you again, Sarah."

The other woman ran ahead into the town, crying out, "Naomi, wife of Elimelech, has returned to us."

People gathered around Naomi. Not knowing what to do, Ruth just stood quietly.

An elder by the city gate approached. "The wife of Elimelech, prince of Judah, returns? Welcome home, Naomi." He looked past her. "And where is Elimelech?"

Naomi hung her head. "Do not call me Naomi, Micah. Call me Mara, for the Almighty has dealt bitterly with me. I went out full and have returned empty." She looked up, tears in her eyes. "Why do you call me Naomi, 'pleasant,' since the Lord has testified against me and the Almighty has afflicted me?"

Micah shook his head slowly. "Our friend Elimelech is dead, then?"

Naomi nodded. "And also my sons. I have only my daughter-in-law, Ruth, Mahlon's widow, who in kindness accompanied me."

Micah studied Ruth keenly. "Where are you from?"

"I am from the Plains of Moab, where my grandfather has a small farm. We are…I was a Reubenite."

"There are no sons?"

Ruth hung her head. "No, my lord, no sons."

She could hear the tsks of the women as they murmured to themselves. No children.

Naomi straightened her shoulders. "Is there an inn where my daughter-in-law and I can stay?"

Micah smiled. "For my friend Elimelech's family, there is a house. It is small, but my tenants have left. You are welcome as long as you need it. There is a small courtyard for your animal."

"And what of my own house?"

"I have kept an eye on it since you left. It was sold a second time. There is a family living there now, but the house has weathered some neglect. I have not been inside since you left."

"How can I return to it, Micah?"

His brows knit together in contemplation. "With no men to work the fields and provide income, perhaps it would be best to dwell elsewhere for a while until you are able to buy the property back."

"Returning to my own home was the wish of my heart, Micah, but I see it is not possible. You know what I must do for Ruth."

He nodded. "I understand. May the Most High grant you mercy in your quest."

He gave them directions to the house he had mentioned, and the two women started through the city, anxious to be settled before nightfall. As they walked, to Ruth's amazement, women began to come up to them.

"I baked too much bread; it will go to waste. Take this extra loaf, Naomi."

"These figs are so ripe, you must try them."

"These date cakes are nothing, I have so many. They will be good for you after your long journey." A woman pressed a cloth bag into Ruth's hand.

"We have this extra bottle of wine."

"It will be cold. You don't have enough to cover you," said one woman, handing them two coverings. They draped the coverings over the donkey.

"Lamb stew should be eaten while it is warm. The small pot is nothing. Do not worry about it."

Surprised speechless, Naomi could only nod her head in thanks. By the time they found the small house of Micah's, the two women could hardly carry all they had been given. Then, as they went to enter the house, Ruth had to put down what she was carrying just to open the door.

The house was clean, but little remained from the tenants who had been there before. The dirt floor was swept, and there was a small clay brazier to cook on. To Ruth's surprise, a small bundle of sticks for fuel had been left behind. A clay lamp sat on a rough-hewn table. Ruth shook her head. At least it was shelter. And she had noticed a clay oven for baking bread in the small courtyard. She surveyed the food that had been given to them.

"You are well thought of still, Mother," she ventured.

"At least we will not starve, if only for the first few days. After that, I don't know what we'll do."

Ruth lifted the covering on the pot of lamb stew. The savory smell had made her stomach growl.

After giving thanks to the Almighty for a safe journey, they dug into the food like children. They hadn't had a feast in some time.

As they ate, Ruth decided to bring up her idea. "Mother, there is an oven outside, but we need grain for bread. I saw the barley fields being harvested. Tomorrow let me go into the field and glean heads of grain after the one in whose sight I find favor."

Naomi reached out and put a hand on Ruth's arm. "What a blessing you are. Go, my daughter."

They settled themselves on the dirt floor for the night, grateful for the extra rugs from another caring woman.

When she was sure Naomi was asleep, Ruth rose and looked out through the small opening in the wall. The house reminded her of the room she'd shared with Mahlon, except that the floor had been stone, and there were soft rugs to keep her feet warm. She listened to the bird calls for a while, and then, realizing she had work to do the next day, she turned back to her bed. She had herded sheep and goats, worked in a garden, cared for a husband, washed clothes, turned fresh wool into fine thread on her spindle, and made fabric on a loom. She had never gleaned in a field—a task left to the poor and widowed.

Twenty-five

Ruth shivered in the chill of the morning air. She'd eaten only a little of the bread and hadn't taken time to heat water for tea. She prayed fervently for favor as she hurried to the fields. When she reached them, she paused in indecision. Which field should she start in? She went to the nearest field and saw several women gleaning. Taking a deep breath to bolster her courage, she approached the overseer.

"Sir, my mother-in-law and I are widows. According to the law, may I glean and gather after the reapers?" She stood quietly, hopefully, awaiting his answer.

He studied her a moment and then waved toward the field. "You may glean."

"Thank you, sir."

She quickly joined the other women and spread her apron like a bowl to put the heads of grain in. The women glanced at her, and one spoke. "Aren't you the woman who came with Naomi yesterday?"

"Yes, I'm her daughter-in-law."

"Her husband was one of the elders who sat in the gate. You are without means, then? You must glean?"

Ruth smiled a little sadly. "Who knows the ways of the Most High? Is it not His world to do as He chooses?"

The woman shrugged. "That is so. Stay in this field to glean. It belongs to a wealthy landowner named Boaz. On his orders, his men do not bother us."

"You are bothered in other fields?"

"Women have been raped in the shelter of the barley or wheat. I myself barely escaped last harvest. Boaz will not allow that in his field. He is a godly and honorable man."

Ruth nodded and began to glean. After a couple of hours, the woman next to her straightened. "Come with us to the shed reserved for the workers. We are permitted to rest a short time there."

Having worked hard in the intense heat, Ruth was glad for the rest. She drank from a dipper of water and sat quietly, stretching her back.

"You are a widow?" a tall woman asked. "I have not seen you before. Where are you from?"

"My husband died. My mother-in-law, Naomi, is from Bethlehem, but I am from across the Jordan, the Plains of Moab."

Two of the women whispered among themselves, and then one of them spoke. "You are from the Plains of Moab. Is it not true that you are a Moabitess?"

Ruth smiled at the woman. "The Plains of Moab are in the territory of Reuben. My family are Reubenites."

The women frowned, then shrugged.

Another woman, called Basmath, shook her head. "We knew Naomi's family. Which son were you married to?"

"Mahlon." Ruth wanted to be polite, since she was a stranger in their town, but she wished they would not question her so.

"Ah, I remember he was not well." She gave Ruth an impudent look. "He must have thrived in the new land, to have married. Do you have children?"

Ruth took a deep breath and rose. "No," she murmured. She left the shed and started back to the field, pondering Basmath's comment. Why would she say such a thing? They did not even know each other.

She worked steadily, keeping to herself. Before she realized it, the sun was reaching its zenith, and she felt perspiration running down her back.

Just then, she heard one of the other women say, "There is Boaz now."

Ruth straightened and turned. She saw a man striding through the fields toward his men. He was tall and trim, his hair graying slightly above his ears. She could not see his face clearly, but he walked like a king, surveying his domain. About his shoulders was the red cloak designating him as a chief in his tribe. Boaz spoke to one of his men and then turned and glanced her way. He regarded her thoughtfully for a moment, then spoke to the overseer. She felt the blood rise to her face and hid her crimson countenance from the other women as she began to work harder. He was asking about her. Her heart pounded. Would he order her out of his field since she was not of this town? She turned and began to glean furiously, hoping he would go about his business and ignore her.

Boaz had risen that morning sensing that the Most High had something for him to do, and it concerned his fields of barley. When he reached the first field, he saw a strange woman gleaning by the side of the field that had been reaped. Her slender body moved gracefully as she gathered into her cloak the grain left behind. Even her head scarf could not conceal the luxury of her hair. He could not see her face, but he felt a stirring he had not felt for some time. Who was she? Still keeping an eye on her as she worked, he called a familiar greeting to his men.

"The Lord be with you!"

They answered, "The Lord bless you."

He motioned to the servant in charge of the reapers. "Who is the new young woman who gleans in my field? I don't recognize her."

The servant seemed hesitant to answer. "She came to me this morning and told me she was a widow and, according to the law, asked to glean in your field. I gave her permission." The servant watched Boaz anxiously. "Should I have said no?"

Boaz stroked his beard. "I believe this is the young woman the town is talking about. Her mother-in-law is a kinswoman. How has she behaved since she came here?"

"She has continued from morning until now, though she rested awhile in the house. She was courteous, not brazen, as some."

Boaz put a hand on the man's shoulder. "You did well. Instruct the men according to my rules."

The servant nodded, obviously pleased he had not angered his master.

Boaz watched the woman for a few moments. Curious to see more of her, he approached where she was gleaning.

He waited until she looked up, then felt a shock. Her face was beautiful, but, to his dismay, her dark eyes were fearful. He needed to reassure her. He remembered his kinswoman Naomi and was touched that she had been blessed with such a daughter-in-law.

"You will listen, my daughter, will you not? Do not go to glean in another field, nor go from here, but stay close by my young women. Let your eyes be on this field in which they reap, and go after them. I have commanded the young men not to touch you. When you are thirsty, go to the vessels and drink from what the young men have drawn."

Her relief was almost tangible. She fell on her knees before him and bowed down to the ground. "Why have I found favor in your eyes, that you should take notice of me, since I am a stranger in your land?"

"It has been fully reported to me all that you have done for your mother-in-law since the death of your husband, and how you have left your home and the place of your birth and have come to a strange city and people you did not know before. May the Lord repay your work, and a full reward be given you by the Lord God of Israel, under whose wings you have come for refuge."

"Let me find favor in your sight, my lord, for you have comforted me and have spoken kindly to your maidservant, though I am not one of your maidservants."

He studied her a moment, touched by her sincerity. And then, still puzzled at the emotions that flooded him, he turned and walked quickly away.

Ruth watched him go, examining the strange feelings his words and presence had stirred within her. She was also confused by his sudden departure. When he had smiled at her, small crinkles formed at the edges of his eyes. She decided he must smile a great deal. She wondered at his age. Nearing fifty, perhaps? He had a rugged face that some would not call handsome, but kindness shone from eyes that were like dark pools, shaded by heavy brows. His was a face one could trust. What was it about him that awakened long-forgotten emotions? She shook her head to clear the odd thoughts and bent to continue her gleaning.

At mealtime, Ruth hesitantly followed the other women to the low tables and benches situated by the side of the field. Boaz was there, and she stood still a moment, wondering where to sit.

Once again, Boaz smiled at her. "Come here, and eat of the bread and dip it in the vinegar." He nodded to the space across from him.

Boaz was inviting her to his table? She quickly sat, ignoring the other gleaners who looked at her with raised eyebrows. Boaz passed parched grain to her, and she ate until her hunger was lessened. Not wanting to appear greedy, she kept some back. She would take it home to Naomi.

Once or twice while she was eating, she felt Boaz's eyes on her, yet she felt no fear. It was not a look of lust but of curiosity. When the workers rose up to return to the fields, Ruth followed the other women. As she walked, she glanced up and saw that one woman had paused and was looking at her with narrowed eyes, her lips pursed in disfavor. It was Basmath.

When Ruth was out of earshot, Boaz turned to his reapers. "Let her glean even among the sheaves, and do not reproach her. Also, let some of the grain from the bundles fall purposefully for her and do not rebuke her."

"Yes, my lord, it shall be as you say." The overseer raised his eyebrows briefly but did not question.

Ruth gleaned until the sun began its descent beyond the mountains. Her back ached, and her hands were red and rough. The skin had broken open on two of her fingers. She wrapped her hands resolutely and kept working until the overseer came and released them to return to their homes.

She beat the sheaves she had gleaned against a wooden board and was surprised to find she had almost filled the small wooden tub with the grain. Elated, she emptied the contents of the tub into her cloak and then, balancing the bundle on her hip, hurried home to Naomi.

Naomi's eyes widened when she saw the large sack of grain Ruth brought home. Ruth also gave her the food she had saved from her lunch.

"Where have you gleaned today, Daughter? Blessed be the one who took notice of you."

"I gleaned in the field of a man called Boaz."

Naomi clapped her hands. "Blessed be he of the Lord, who has not forsaken His kindness to the living and the dead."

Ruth stared at her. "You know this man?"

"He is a relation of Elimelech's, and one of our close relatives." Naomi's face became contemplative. "Yes, a near relative," she murmured.

"Then perhaps that is why he was so kind. He told me to stay close by his young men until they have finished all the harvest."

Naomi looked to the heavens. "Nothing could be better. It is good, my daughter, that you go out with his young women, and that people do not meet you in any other field."

When Naomi saw Ruth's hands, she searched among her things and produced a small jar of balm, which she gently applied to the sore places. Her ministrations were tender, and Ruth felt a great love rise up in her heart for this woman who was a mother to her.

The evening shadows crept over the house as Ruth, weary, lay down for the night, keeping her hands free so that the balm could do its work. She would have a long day tomorrow and many long days after that.

Twenty-six

Ruth had gleaned in the fields of Boaz all through the barley harvest. When it was over and the wheat harvest began, she returned to glean again. Boaz made it a point to see that she joined the reapers at his table for mealtimes. While his manner was casual, he was diligent in seeing that she had enough to eat and that water was available to her.

Many days during the harvest, he did not speak to her, keeping to his men. Yet Ruth was aware of him as he came and went, and one time, looking up, she realized he was covertly watching her as she worked. Rather than fearing his perusal, she felt comforted that he seemed to be looking out for her. Gleaning was hard work, but his presence made the task seem lighter.

The house Naomi and Ruth occupied was on the edge of the town and therefore within a Sabbath day's journey of the house of Boaz. One Sabbath afternoon, Naomi was not feeling well, and she shooed Ruth out of the house so she could rest.

Not long after Ruth had left on a walk, Naomi heard a soft knocking at the door. She frowned. Who could it be? She rose and answered. There stood her old friend Rachab before her.

The two women fell into each other's arms. Rachab spoke first. "My friend, tell me how it is with you. I have heard of your return with only your daughter-in-law, Ruth. My son, Boaz, speaks well of her and how hard she works. All of Bethlehem is talking about the virtuous young woman who accompanied you home. What happened to you?"

Naomi waved an arm to welcome her in and then closed the door. "It is a sad tale, Rachab. Come, sit with me, and I will tell you of my journey."

Naomi brewed a pot of tea on the brazier and placed some fruit on the table. When the tea was ready, she sat down and sighed heavily. As the shadows lengthened, Naomi shared all that had happened since she and her family had left Bethlehem. Rachab listened without interrupting, except for making small sounds of sympathy and emitting a gasp upon hearing about the small herd of animals left after the disease had run its course.

"Oh, Naomi. You have truly lost everything." She leaned forward with an air of confidentiality. "You are aware, are you not, of the rumors in the town that Ruth is a Moabitess?"

"I overheard two women speaking about it at the well. Who would start such a rumor?"

Rachab pursed her lips. "There is one who has coveted my son since the death of his wife. He thought of marrying her as a mother to Jael, and to appease my insistence that he marry again. But he did not find her acceptable, and I think she felt shamed. She had spoken freely about her belief that they would marry."

"This woman is...?"

"She is called Basmath. A widow, she has taken Zillah's place as the town healer and midwife."

Naomi shook her head. "I'm sorry she feels she must say those things. Ruth is a good daughter-in-law and a kind woman. She is a true daughter of Israel."

"Then you must find a kinsman who can redeem your property and marry Ruth."

Naomi almost spoke of Boaz, but, knowing there was one closer in line, she guarded her words. "There is indeed a relative close to us, but I need to speak with him to find out if he is willing to do the part of a kinsman to us. I have no man to speak for me."

"Then you must do so as soon as possible. You cannot live like this, in this small house. Think of the home he could buy back for you. You could have grandchildren to sit on your knees." Rachab suddenly stopped. "Is Ruth barren?"

Naomi looked toward the small window opening in the wall, through which sunbeams were streaming down to a circle on the floor. "Though it grieves me to say so, I do not believe the problem lay with Ruth. Neither Mahlon nor Chilion was well in body. I believe the Almighty closed Ruth's womb for a reason. Though I do not understand, I cannot question His ways."

Rachab nodded thoughtfully. "Who is the kinsman you have in mind?"

"Tobias."

Rachab's eyes widened. "He is the closest?"

"Why do you say it in that manner?"

"My friend, the reputation of that man is known. He is stingy with his money and not kind to the merchants he deals with. I grieve that you must go to such a one for your daughter."

"I have no choice. I need my home and property back, but I cannot redeem them myself. Even if I could, I have no funds to do so."

The sun had begun its downward swing, and Rachab rose slowly. "I must return home to prepare for the Sabbath meal. Boaz will be concerned to find me gone." She took Naomi's hands in hers and looked into her eyes. "Come and share the Sabbath meal with us, dear Naomi. I have not been well and have been remiss in waiting so long to see you."

Naomi thought of the simple meal she was going to prepare and nodded her head. "I thank you for your kindness. Ruth went for a short walk. When she returns, we will refresh ourselves and join you."

Rachab's face lit up with a smile. "I will tell Boaz to expect you."

As Naomi watched her friend move slowly down the road, she felt a sense of anxiety over the disconcerting details she had shared about Tobias. Naomi could only pray he was not the man he appeared to be. Ruth would be obedient for Naomi's sake, and for the sake of the house and land, but could she wish such a man on the precious daughter who cared for her so kindly?

Naomi bent her head and beseeched her God for wisdom. As she did, a sense of peace flowed into her heart. She could trust the Almighty with her cares.

A tall figure was walking toward Ruth on the road, and she immediately recognized her benefactor. She thought of his name, Boaz—"strength is within him." The name suited him. She had watched him many times as he came and went in the fields and always found her heart lifting at the sight of him. Now, seeing him approach, she was embarrassed to feel it beating faster as he drew near.

When they faced each other, Boaz seemed to search for words. "The Almighty has given us a small respite from the heat."

"He has, my lord." She searched for another topic. "Your mother is well, my lord?"

"She is well." He looked past her. "How is it that you walk alone today?"

"Naomi was not feeling well. I'm afraid I was too anxious for her health." She smiled. "I believe she wanted some respite."

He laughed then, his dark eyes dancing with tiny lights.

"I believe my mother was going to call on her. I came to escort her home." He frowned. "If Naomi is not well, perhaps they did not visit. My mother was going to invite you to share our Sabbath meal. I have been remiss as a relative in that I have not invited you both to my home to welcome Naomi back."

She hesitated. A meal at his home? What would she wear? Her clothes were growing thin from being washed so many times. She and Naomi had brought only as much as they could carry. Suddenly conscious of her appearance, she felt a flush of shame. With her rough hands, how could she sit with his family? Then another thought intruded. Who would be there besides the three of them? She had heard of his daughter's marriage from a woman at the town well who was prone to gossip.

"I will speak with Naomi, my lord."

"It would give me great pleasure to have you meet my family. My daughter, Jael, and her husband, Shelah, will also join us. Your mother-in-law was a great friend of my mother's in earlier years. Rachab has not been well and has been longing to see her. This is the first time she has left the house in a few weeks."

"In that case, I will accept for both of us."

He looked past her, and as she turned, she saw an older woman approaching, walking slowly up the road. Boaz hurried to meet her and gave her his arm.

"Your visit with Naomi went well, *Imah*?"

"It went well." She smiled at Ruth. "You will both join us for our Sabbath meal. She waits only for you to return home."

"Thank you, my lady. I will go quickly." Ruth ventured a glance at Boaz, and the warmth in his eyes as he smiled at her flooded her being. It was not lost on his mother. She looked from one to the other, and the corners of her mouth turned up briefly.

Twenty-seven

Naomi was waiting anxiously for Ruth's return.

"I met Boaz and Rachab on the road, Mother. They have—"

"Yes, yes, I know. We must choose our best clothes and dress quickly."

Dressed in their best garments, Ruth and Naomi hurried down the road to the home of Boaz. Ruth was impressed by the abundance of flowers that grew around the house. A servant opened the gate and beckoned them in as though they were royalty, and Ruth was overwhelmed by the splendor of their surroundings. The home was larger than any she had seen. A building nearby housed workrooms and storage areas, and there were pens for animals and chickens along the outermost wall.

What was she doing here, surrounded by such wealth and abundance? Then she remembered that she had been married to a prince of Judah; whatever their circumstances now, she was of the tribe of Boaz. She lifted her head slightly as they moved forward into the courtyard.

Boaz came to meet them, followed by a young couple. The girl was tall and very beautiful. It was easy to see that her young husband doted on her.

"My daughter, Jael, newly married, and her husband, Shelah."

Ruth and Naomi acknowledged them with a nod and a smile. Boaz beamed at his daughter, and as the girl smiled back, Ruth sensed the close bond between them.

Their surroundings must have reminded Naomi of her own home, for she seemed to stand taller and act more like the woman Ruth had met at the tents of Elimelech.

"I am happy to meet you." Jael's voice was almost musical. Ruth hoped she was as gracious as she was beautiful, but then, how could she be otherwise, with Boaz for her father?

They entered the house itself, and Ruth noticed a striking wall mural depicting the battle of Jericho and the courageous leader Joshua. The doors and windows were framed with warm, rich wood, and Boaz pointed out that it was Lebanese cedar. There were chests and comfortable chairs, and the stone floors were covered with an abundance of thick rugs, as she had first seen in the tent of Elimelech years before.

A hallway led to the private family rooms, and she wondered for a moment what the room of Boaz looked like. Just then, Rachab came slowly down the hall, leaning on a walking stick. She wore clothing like Ruth had seen on Naomi when she first went to the tent of Elimelech with Orpah. Her robe was embroidered with intricate handwork of silver and purple threads, and she wore a red silk head covering. "Welcome," she said, her bright, dark eyes seeming to penetrate Ruth's very being.

Ruth smiled. "Greetings, my lady."

"Rachab, it was so good of you and Boaz to invite us," Naomi said. "I have missed proper Sabbath meals."

"Ah, then we shall see that you have a meal to enjoy," said Boaz. "Come, sit by me. Our family eats together."

This surprised Ruth, who was used to eating after the men had finished.

They gathered around a low dining table in the cooler part of the courtyard. Boaz seated Naomi next to his mother and Ruth next to Naomi, across from him. His daughter and son-in-law sat on his other side.

A servant presented wet cloths to them for washing their hands. Then Rachab drew her mantle over her head and welcomed *Shabbat* by lighting the candles. Moving her hands slowly over the Sabbath candles, she murmured, "Blessed are You, Lord our God, sovereign of the universe, who has sanctified us with His commandments and commanded us to light the lights of *Shabbat*."

For some reason, as Ruth watched the older woman, she was reminded of her grandmother, Eunice, and unbidden tears rose to her eyes. Longing for her family—her brother and grandfather—filled her heart, and it was all she could do to set the feelings aside, lest she embarrass Naomi with her emotions.

Sensing she was being watched, she turned to Jael. The girl was observing her with a look Ruth couldn't define, yet she could tell she was curious. Ruth smiled at her. "I am happy for you, Jael. May your marriage be blessed with many children."

Jael gave her a brief nod of acknowledgment, then turned to speak to her husband. Ruth was startled at the deliberate snub. Not wishing to cause concern to Boaz, she bowed her head. Hearing her name spoken softly, she looked up into his eyes and saw a puzzled look on his face. He raised his eyebrows in question. She gave a slight shake of her head, smiled at him briefly, and turned her attention to Rachab and the Sabbath meal.

"When our child is born, you will have your hands full, *Abba,* with taking care of the land and being a grandfather," Jael said. "*Savta,* you will be a great-grandmother. You must come and see us more often."

Rachab, who had been conversing with Naomi, nodded her head. "Yes, Jael, a child will be a blessing. *Ha'Shem* be praised that I should live to be a great-grandmother." She studied her granddaughter shrewdly. "Is there something you wish to tell us?"

Jael blushed. "I am with child."

Boaz raised his eyebrows. "You have not wasted any time, Daughter." He glanced at Shelah, whose face colored with embarrassment. "I look forward to a grandson."

Jael sat proudly, looking pleased with herself, and Ruth thought about her comment that Boaz would not have time for anything else. It was clear the girl was jealous of her father's time and friendships. She sighed to herself. Perhaps he had indulged the girl too much. She caught the eye of her mother-in-law, and the warmth in Naomi's face encouraged her. Ruth wondered why Jael would go out of her way to make their guests uncomfortable. She glanced again at Boaz and saw he was watching his daughter with a thoughtful expression on his face.

They ate a wonderful meal of lamb; lentil and coriander stew; squash with capers and mint; and leeks with olive oil and vinegar; along with leavened griddle bread. For dessert, Rachab served pomegranate seeds and poached apricots in honey syrup. For the two women who had done with so little for so long, it was a feast.

As Boaz reached out for a piece of bread, Ruth could not help but notice the strength of his arm and his hand. They were large and muscular, showing the evidence of hard work. He did not have the soft hands of a man of leisure. Everything about him spoke of virility. Why had he not married again? Surely there were women in town who would be more than willing to marry such a man.

When she realized where her thoughts were going, she brought herself up sharply and concentrated on Jael, who was speaking.

"The baby will be here in the spring. We are hoping *Ha'Shem* will bless us with a son."

How fortunate Boaz was to be having a grandchild. She turned and looked at Naomi, only to see a wistful acceptance on her mother-in-law's face. She experienced the old sadness. *If I marry again, will I be able to have children? Will the Almighty open my womb?*

Shelah beamed at his wife and then returned to his conversation with Boaz concerning the crops and his own work in the carpentry shop.

The women spoke of many things, but no one mentioned Ruth's gleaning in the fields, for which she was grateful. She realized they would not mention her station to embarrass her.

She and Naomi were treated as special guests, and Ruth wondered how often they would be invited here. She sensed Boaz's eyes on her from time to time during the meal, and whenever she looked up, she met his glance without guile. He was her benefactor. She could not allow her feelings to show.

As they prepared to leave, Rachab embraced Naomi. "Be our guest again soon, dear friend."

"We will do that. Thank you for a wonderful Sabbath meal."

Boaz accompanied them home, his servant holding a lamp to light their way after the Sabbath had ended. He saw them to their door.

"May your sleep be peaceful, Naomi and Ruth."

"And yours, my lord," they answered.

They thanked him again, and Naomi turned into the house. As Ruth watched Boaz walk away, she felt a sense of melancholy and realized her sleep would not be a peaceful one at all.

After Ruth left the house for the wheat fields, Naomi watched through the window until she was out of sight. Then she gathered her shawl, slipped out of the house, and headed quickly for the center of the town, intent on finding out all she could about Tobias. As their closest relative, he was in a position to take the role of kinsman redeemer. How fortunate that the Almighty had instituted the command for a close relative, if not a brother, to marry his brother's widow and raise up sons in the name of the deceased. Yet she was disturbed by what she had heard about Tobias from Rachab. She remembered little of Tobias from their earlier years in Bethlehem. He'd been just a young man then, but she vaguely recalled a pinched face and eyes that did not look directly at you when he spoke. No doubt he had married while she was gone. Would he take a second wife? Would he be good to Ruth? She loved her daughter-in-law, but for Ruth to remain a widow was unthinkable. She was still of an age to marry. Naomi pursed her lips. It was up to her to do what must be done.

"Lord, please lead and guide me, that I may know if this close relative is worthy of my daughter-in-law."

When she reached the town, she inquired about Tobias as tactfully as possible. She merely stated that he was a relative whose acquaintance she would make when time permitted.

One of the vegetable vendors offered an earful. "A sorry relative he might be, my lady—a man with a tight coin purse, that Tobias," the merchant said with a frown. "Don't expect him to be glad to see you. All he thinks about is his own gain. His servant usually asks to purchase vegetables that are not fresh so he may pay me the least amount possible."

Naomi raised her eyebrows but did not reply. She merely shrugged and pretended to peruse the vegetables. She selected some fava beans and squash. The small leeks looked fresh, and she took a few of those, as well. The squash would go nicely with some capers and mint for their dinner. She paid the man carefully from her small reserve, placed her purchases in her cloth bag, and, with a smile, moved on.

Tobias didn't seem to be very popular. She wondered what kind of a wife he had chosen. It would be better for her cause if he was unmarried, but it would be best to call on him and judge for herself.

She asked directions, and when she knocked on the gate, a dour-faced servant answered. "If you are seeking alms, you must go elsewhere."

Taken aback, Naomi gave the servant one of her sternest looks. "I am the wife of Elimelech, a relative of your master's, recently returned to Bethlehem. I merely wished to pay my respects."

The servant eyed her skeptically, surveying her worn clothing. "You will have to come another time. My master is on a business trip. He returns tomorrow."

"Is his wife at home? I have not met her."

"The mistress died two years ago." After this statement, he closed the gate in her face.

Naomi was torn between unbelief and outrage. Never had one of her servants treated a guest in that manner. Strangers were always welcomed at the home of Elimelech.

She strode quickly away, her steps fueled by her anger. This relative would hear from her about his servant's treatment. On the way home, she also pondered what she had heard in the marketplace. Uneasiness settled over her spirit. She could only pray for the will of the Almighty to be done. If Tobias was willing to marry Ruth, then she had no choice. At least her dear daughter-in-law would be provided for.

Then another thought struck her. What if Ruth was still barren and produced no children with Tobias, either? What if her failure to bear children with Mahlon had not been due to a curse on the family of Elimelech for leaving their homeland and not trusting the Almighty to see them through the famine? Would things be different if Ruth married again? Round and round the questions circled her mind.

She stopped and sank down onto a large rock beneath a sycamore tree. As she gazed out across the fields where she knew Ruth was gleaning, she pondered the question. Neither Mahlon nor Chilion had produced children. Would the curse be lifted now that they were back in Bethlehem? She covered her face with her hands and prayed for wisdom. At a chirping sound, she peeked through her fingers and saw a small, brown sparrow standing in the road, watching her. As they observed each other, the thought came to her that she was as small in the eyes of the Almighty as this sparrow was to her, yet did He not feed the sparrow?

She considered Boaz and sighed. Why could not that good man be the closer relative? "O God Who Sees, hear my prayer for Ruth. Give me wisdom and discernment to know in which direction to go." She bowed her head and was filled with wonder as a sense of peace swept over her. The Almighty had put the answer on her heart.

Her steps were firm with determination as she hurried to reach home. Tonight she would tell Ruth what she must do. It had to work. She could not—would not—consider the alternative.

Twenty-eight

That morning, as Ruth had left to go glean in the fields, her mother-in-law had given her an enigmatic smile. When Ruth had asked what she was up to, Naomi had been almost secretive, saying only that there was someone she needed to meet. Ruth couldn't imagine who it was.

She found herself hurrying in the early morning chill to reach the fields. Gleaning was hard work, and she didn't look forward to it. She also dreaded seeing Basmath, who whispered among the other women. Ruth found them turning to stare at her from time to time. When it became public knowledge that she and Naomi had shared a Sabbath meal at the home of Boaz, the look Basmath sent her was pure hatred.

Yet Ruth felt she could manage as long as she had to. She could treat the women with kindness, for it was her nature. It was the man who owned the field that she found herself looking for. Some days, he came to the fields; some days, his business took him to other places. She learned that he also sat at the gate of the town, as one of the elders, judging cases that were brought to him.

An important man like Boaz would not look twice at her. She was nothing in his sight, and a stranger in the town. While the tribe of Reuben was a tribe of Israel, they had seldom come across the Jordan to mingle with their fellow Israelites. Ruth remembered the first time she saw Naomi and noticed how beautiful her clothes were—so different from what Ruth and the women of their small village wore. Over the years, as their losses had compounded and money for fabric had become scarce, Naomi had begun wearing homespun clothing herself.

Ruth tried to imagine how Naomi felt, having left her home in Bethlehem with a husband, two sons, servants, and the wealth of flocks and herds; over the years, losing everything, little by little; and finally returning to her hometown nearly a pauper. It grieved Ruth's tender heart to consider all Naomi had endured, and she resolved to take care of her as long as she was needed, even if it meant never marrying again.

As she worked alongside the other women, she looked up and saw Boaz striding into the fields. He spoke with his men, encouraging them, and then, to her embarrassment, he suddenly looked her way and found her staring at him. She felt her face flush and quickly bent to her task.

"Ruth." His deep voice was gentle as he spoke her name.

She stood before him, her eyes modestly on the ground.

"Are you and your mother-in-law well?"

She hesitated, her heart beating erratically. Why did this man affect her so? "Yes, my lord, we are well, thanks to your kindness."

"I am glad you were able to join us for that Sabbath meal."

"We were honored, my lord."

He looked around and cleared his throat. "No one has, uh, bothered you?"

"No, my lord."

He stood there a moment, then said, "That is good." Then he was gone.

Anna, one of the women who had befriended Ruth, whispered, "It is fortunate that Boaz has noticed you and seen to your welfare. He looks on you with favor."

"Why should he favor me, a stranger to your town?"

"You are of the tribe of Judah now, by your marriage to the son of Naomi." The woman smiled. "He likes you."

Ruth was taken aback, but the woman added, "I see how he looks at you."

"You must be mistaken, Anna. Why should he take notice of me? He is kind for Naomi's sake."

Anna gave her a knowing smile, shook her head, and went on gleaning. They had neared the other women, and nothing more was said.

That afternoon, Basmath bumped her, causing her to drop her basket of grain. Ruth was tempted to comment, feeling it was done on purpose, but she refrained. She was grateful when Anna and another woman helped her to scoop the grain back into her basket.

At the end of the day, Ruth started home, her feet moving but her body rebelling. Boaz had joined them for the noon meal, and although he did not speak to her, she caught his gaze from time to time and trembled inwardly. He was just being kind to her, a distant relative. She could not bring herself to speak, lest she offend her benefactor in some way.

When Ruth at last reached the small house, Naomi was waiting eagerly for her return. They put the grain in a large basket and settled down to the simple meal Naomi had prepared. After Naomi asked the blessing of the Most High, Ruth, famished, dipped her bread anxiously into the fava bean stew. Naomi said little during the meal, but when they had finished and were cleaning the wooden platters, she broke her silence.

"My daughter, you were a good wife to my son Mahlon, but he is gone now. You have been a joy to my heart and a worthy companion, but shall I not now seek security for you, that it may be well with you? You must seek shelter in the home of a husband. I have considered this well, and Boaz, whose young women you were with, is our relative. Tonight he will be winnowing at the threshing floor. This is what you must do. Wash and anoint yourself, and put on your best garment. You must go down to the threshing floor, but do not make yourself known to the man until he has finished eating and drinking."

Ruth's heart pounded at the thought of what her mother-in-law was asking of her. What would she say to Boaz? Would he be angry at her boldness? Would he be filled with drink and laugh at her? She stared in disbelief at Naomi, who continued on, heedless of the look on her face.

"Then it shall be, when he lies down, that you shall notice the place where he lies; and you shall go in, uncover his feet, and lie down; you will ask him to be your kinsman redeemer, and he will then tell you what you should do."

Ruth hesitated, but the determined look on Naomi's face told her that her mother-in-law was adamant.

With her fear rising, all she could do was nod her head and whisper, "All that you say to me I will do."

"You are an obedient daughter. You shall see that it will come out well. Boaz is a widower with a grown daughter, but he needs a wife."

Ruth did as Naomi asked and prepared herself as best she could. As she walked in the gathering darkness, she looked fearfully about her and jumped at every strange sound. She could not light a lantern. Would she find the right person in the dark? What if she approached the wrong man, and he was drunk? She shivered, suddenly remembering the incident with Amon those many years ago.

She made her way quietly to the threshing shed, where she removed her sandals and glided noiselessly over the floor. There was a man, about the shape and size of Boaz, and he was sleeping. She peered at his face in the semidarkness. Just then, the moon came out from behind a cloud, briefly giving soft light to the room. It was Boaz. She put a hand on her heart as if to still the beating. Trembling with anticipation of the outcome, she did as Naomi had instructed her. As Ruth listened to his gentle snoring, she was satisfied that he was still asleep, and she crept up softly, uncovered his feet, carefully lay down, and wrapped her mantle around herself. Now all she could do was wait.

Twenty-nine

In the middle of the night, Boaz turned over and, with a sharp intake of breath, peered at her in the shadows. "Who are you?"

She tried to keep her voice from quavering as she answered bravely, "I am Ruth, your maidservant. Please, spread your cloak over me, for you are a close relative."

He was silent so long, she feared his displeasure. Then he reached out and gently put a hand on her shoulder. "Ah, Ruth, blessed are you of the Lord, my daughter! You have shown more kindness at the end than at the beginning, in that you did not go after young men, whether poor or rich."

She trembled slightly at his hand on her shoulder.

"Do not fear me, Ruth. I will do for you all that you request, for all the people of Bethlehem know that you are a virtuous woman." He sighed. "I had hoped, Ruth. It has been years since my wife died. Before the day when you first appeared in my field, I did not seriously look at another woman."

"I could see you were a good man, Boaz, the way your workers looked up to you with respect," she responded. "I admired you, but then, as time went on, I began to more than admire you."

"Is it possible, Ruth? I am years older than you. I hid my feelings, thinking you would not be interested in a man like me."

"Oh, Boaz, how could a woman not admire a man as kind and gentle as yourself?"

He leaned closer, and the moon slipped again from behind a cloud, briefly lighting his face, and his eyes that looked into her heart. He murmured, "The thought of love was buried so long, I never knew I would have feelings for a woman again."

He was silent for a moment, and then he spoke again. "Ruth, there is one complication. It is true that I am a close relative; however, there is a relative closer than I."

"He has the right to redeem me? But I thought...." She felt a tear slide down her cheek. "It is you I want to marry."

"He has the right, according to the law, but I will think of something, Ruth. Trust me in this. Stay this night, and in the morning I shall find out if he will perform the duty of a close relative for you—and if he will, good, let him do it. But if he does not want to perform that duty for you, then I will, as the Lord lives."

He added the latter comment with such emphasis that Ruth's heart lifted. She was glad that in the darkness he could not see her face, which filled with such joy at his words.

"Lie back down until morning, Ruth."

She lay back down but scarcely slept until the first grayness of the dawn appeared. It was still too dark for anyone to recognize her.

Boaz stirred and said softly, "Do not let it be known that a woman came to the threshing floor. Quickly, hold out your shawl." She did as told, and he measured six *ephahs* of grain, which she laid on her shoulder. She tiptoed from the threshing floor and looked around. Seeing no one, she felt a rush of relief and hurried home to report to Naomi.

She knew the door would be bolted for the night, so she knocked softly.

"Is that you, my daughter?" Naomi answered immediately. Ruth felt she had stayed up all night just waiting for her return.

"It is I, Mother, and I have news."

Naomi opened the door. "Quickly, tell me what happened."

When Ruth had deposited the grain in their container, she turned to Naomi and told her everything Boaz had spoken to her.

"He gave me this six *ephahs* and told me not to go empty-handed to my mother-in-law."

Naomi clasped one hand to her heart. "It is as I hoped, Daughter. We must wait patiently to see how this matter will turn out. I am positive Boaz will not rest until he has concluded the matter this very day."

Ruth sat down at their small table and yawned. Her body was exhausted from her anxiety over how Boaz would respond.

Naomi patted her on the shoulder. "Rest, child. Do not go to the fields today. You will need to be at your best for what lies ahead."

Ruth did not need further urging. She sank down on her pallet and was instantly asleep.

When Naomi was certain Ruth slept, she gathered her shawl and slipped out the door. As she neared the town gate, she saw a group of elders gathered there. Among them was Boaz. She blended into the crowd nearby to listen.

As his kinsman Tobias came by, Boaz motioned to him. "Come aside, friend, and sit down here."

Tobias frowned but did as asked and sat down.

Boaz glanced at the elders gathered around them before speaking. "Naomi, who has come back from the Plains of Moab, sold the piece of land which belonged to our brother Elimelech. I thought it best to inform you that you are the one eligible to buy it back. You may do so in the presence of the inhabitants and the elders of my people. If you will redeem it, do so, but if you will not redeem it, then tell me, that I may know, for there is no one but you to redeem it, and I am next after you."

Tobias almost licked his lips, and Naomi could see he was anxious to add to his land. He did not hesitate. "I will redeem it."

Boaz appeared to consider his answer, and then he answered almost too casually, "Oh, in addition, on the day you buy the field from the hand of Naomi, you must also buy it from Ruth, the Reubenite, who returned with her mother-in-law, as the widow of her dead son Mahlon. You must perpetuate the name of the dead through his inheritance."

Tobias rose immediately. "I cannot redeem it for myself. Would you have me ruin my own inheritance? You go ahead and redeem my right of redemption. You are next in line." As was the custom, he took off his sandal and gave it to Boaz to confirm his words.

Boaz held up the sandal and spoke clearly so that everyone could hear. "You are witnesses this day that I have bought all that was Elimelech's, and all that was Chilion's and Mahlon's, from the hand of Naomi. Moreover, Ruth, the Reubenite, joined to the house of Judah through her marriage to Mahlon, I have acquired as my wife, to perpetuate the name of the dead through his inheritance, that the name of the dead may not be cut off from among his brethren and from his position at the gate. You are witnesses this day."

And all the people who were at the gate, including the elders, said in unison, "We are witnesses."

Micah stepped forward and spoke. "The Lord make the woman who is coming to your house like Rachel and Leah, the two who built the house of Israel, and may you prosper in Ephrathah and be famous in Bethlehem. May your house be like the house of Perez, whom Tamar bore to Judah, because of the offspring which the Lord will give you from this young woman."

Boaz handed the sandal back to Tobias, who was obviously relieved at the outcome. He hurried away.

Naomi slipped away from the crowd and walked as quickly as she could to her home. She smiled to herself, thanking the Almighty for all He had done on behalf of Ruth.

Ruth awakened as the door opened and sat up with a start as Naomi entered. "My daughter, I have such news."

~

Ruth eyed her mother-in-law apprehensively. "What news?"

"Boaz has purchased the property of my husband, Elimelech. He has redeemed it for us."

"For us?"

"Daughter, he will take you as his wife, that you may raise up children in the name of my son."

Ruth stood up slowly. "Boaz will be my kinsman redeemer?"

Naomi beamed and put a gentle hand on her arm. "I, too, am glad it will be Boaz. There was another who was closer to us, but he chose not to redeem it."

"Because he would have to marry me?"

"He was not the man I chose for you. I knew he had the right over Boaz, but I saw the way Boaz looked at you. He loves you, Ruth. I prayed, and I felt the Almighty directing me. That is why I told you to go to Boaz on the threshing floor. He would think you were too young for him and not do a thing." She waved a hand with a knowing smile. "It was necessary to nudge him a little. After all, he is only a man, and sometimes they do not see the obvious."

Ruth began to feel the impact of Naomi's words. She was to marry Boaz. A warmth began in her heart and radiated through her body. That good and gentle man, that very lonely man, had redeemed her. She turned to Naomi.

"What do I do next, Mother?"

Naomi smiled broadly. "I do not believe you have to do anything other than plan a wedding. I believe we will have a caller very soon."

Her mother-in-law's words proved true, for in less than two hours, Boaz was knocking at their gate.

"May the Lord bless those in this house."

"The Lord bless you, Boaz," Naomi replied. "Welcome to our small home."

He glanced around at their meager surroundings. "This is where you have been living since you returned?"

"With the kindness of Micah our friend, who owns the house."

He turned to Ruth. "You know why I have come?" His eyes glistened, and there was a smile playing about his lips.

She moved closer and looked up into his face. "You are my kinsman redeemer."

He took her hands. "Will that make you happy, Ruth?"

She reached up and touched his cheek. "Yes, Boaz, that will make me very happy."

Naomi watched them both, her hands clasped. "Then it is done. We can plan the wedding."

He waggled a finger at her. "You are a very wise woman, Naomi. I understand now what you did, and I am grateful."

She faced him. "I know what you went through, Boaz, and how long you have been lonely. May the love I see between the two of you be blessed by the Almighty, and may you have a son to walk in your footsteps."

His eyes showed his thanks as he nodded his head. "You may not only plan the wedding, but you may do so from your own house, Naomi. As kinsman redeemer, I have purchased the property belonging to your husband for you. My men will work your fields and vineyards. The present tenants are leaving, and you may enter the house in two days' time."

Ruth and Naomi hugged each other, and Naomi cried, "Truly the Almighty has blessed me and turned my sorrow into joy. Thank you, Boaz."

Again the corners of his mouth twitched in a smile. "I have also given word to the merchants that whatever you purchase in the way of clothing, food, or household items to restore your home and attend to your personal needs are to be charged to me. My steward shall oversee those matters."

Ruth let her eyes say all that was in her heart, and it was returned tenfold in the face of her intended. "And how much time will I have to prepare, my lord?"

He thought a moment. "Does the date harvest in the month of Elul, two months from now, give you enough time?"

She nodded. "I will look forward to Elul with all my heart."

"And I, also. I am a fortunate man indeed." As he looked at her, his face was that of a man in love, but only for a moment. He then resumed his bearing as chief. "I must go. There are matters to attend to. Plan whatever you wish to celebrate our marriage, Ruth." He turned to Naomi again. "You will wish to consult with my mother."

"We will do that."

He paused a moment, as if reluctant to go, and then turned and hurried out the gate.

Ruth and Naomi watched him leave, and Ruth felt her heart would burst with happiness. She thought of the time when she was betrothed to Mahlon and the joy she felt as she became his wife. She was not fifteen anymore but a mature woman of twenty-seven. She was ready to assume the duties of the wife of Boaz. Then a thought came to her with crushing intensity. She had not borne a child for Mahlon in ten years. Would she still be barren? Or would her coming to Bethlehem with Naomi break the curse of the Most High?

Thirty

Boaz eyed his daughter, Jael, as she sat with him for the evening meal. Her young husband, Shelah, sighed and rolled his eyes upward but kept still.

"You do not approve of Ruth, Daughter?"

"*Abba,* she is not from our town. I was just thinking that Basmath would suit you so much better."

"And where would that have left Naomi, your grandmother's friend?"

She picked an imaginary piece of lint off her garment and then smiled sweetly up at him. "Can you not buy the land without marrying that Moabite woman? Surely our God forbids this."

"Jael, she is not a Moabite; she and her family lived on the Plains of Moab, as did others of our brethren who sought good pastures for their flocks. She is a Reubenite."

"But she is not of the tribe of Judah. Basmath says…."

She was belaboring the point, and he felt his anger rising that she should try to tell him what he should or shouldn't do.

"Her former husband was Naomi's son, of the tribe of Judah. You are aware of this, Jael, so why do you speak of it? What is this that Basmath is saying?"

"Only what I have said."

"The woman interferes and is spreading false statements. I suggest you listen no more to her." Then a glimmer of an idea surfaced. "Do you fear for your own inheritance?"

"If she has children, which, from what I hear, may be impossible, would they not share in my inheritance?"

"You know the laws of our people. A child born to Ruth and me would inherit the property of Elimelech. It will not touch your inheritance...that is, if I do not decide to give it to someone else more worthy." He glowered at her, even as he realized his temper had gotten the best of him.

Jael shrank back. "You would do that, *Abba*?" Fear rose in her eyes.

"Not unless you give me good reason to do so."

"But, *Abba*, you are nearly fifty. You are older. Must you marry again, and in only three weeks?"

Now he began to understand what was troubling her. Jael had been the center of his attention all her life. She was jealous of Ruth, as was Basmath. He did not regret his decision not to marry her.

His anger dissipated as he studied his daughter. "You are soon to have a child, Jael, for which I rejoice. Surely you have enough to do with your own household. I appreciate your concern, but I am not too old to desire the comfort of a wife. Ruth is a kind and virtuous woman."

She lifted her chin. "I believe you have feelings for that woman."

"I would not marry her if I didn't. And her name is Ruth. Do not refer to her in my presence again as 'that woman.'" In his exasperation, he managed a chuckle. "Passion does not die when one is fifty, my daughter. Perhaps, should I reach double that age, I might still be as our lawgiver, Moses, whose natural strength was not abated."

She opened her mouth to answer but closed it again.

Boaz broke off a piece of bread and dipped it into the lamb stew. "Let us leave this subject and enjoy our meal." He turned to his son-in-law. "Tell me, how are things in the carpentry shop?"

Shelah's face showed relief to move on from his wife's stubborn protest of her father's wedding. "It goes well. We have enough business. Right now I am working on a cradle for our child."

Jael smiled and leaned forward. "It is beautiful, *Abba*. My husband is gifted when he works with wood. You must come and see it."

"I will do that."

The two men discussed crops, ending with the grape harvest that was quickly approaching.

"There is a good crop this year," Boaz said. "I will be able to store more wine than last year. A time of rejoicing."

Shelah grinned. "A good time for a wedding. Your guests will not run out of wine."

Boaz returned the smile. "Yes, a good time for a wedding."

Jael pursed her lips.

After the meal, Boaz slowly walked them to the gate, for the sake of his pregnant daughter. When they had gone, he sat brooding on a bench in the courtyard. It bothered him that Jael was not happy about his wedding. She was used to speaking her mind. He hoped she understood him. He would not have Ruth feel unwelcome.

At the thought of Ruth, his heart warmed, and he allowed himself to contemplate their upcoming wedding. His daughter was young and, though married and expecting a child, still naïve about the thoughts of men. He stood and stretched, filling his lungs with a deep breath. Then, nodding to his steward, who watched nearby, to light the evening candle, he went to his bed. He was alone, but in a few weeks, his beautiful Ruth would be at his side.

Naomi was like a young girl as she waited anxiously for the tenants to vacate her former home. Ruth helped her to clean the small house belonging to Micah and to pack up their few belongings. When they left, she had to urge the donkey to walk faster to keep up with the older woman, so eager was she to be home.

The gate to the courtyard was opened by a servant. "Welcome to your home, my lady. I am Eli, your steward. I have been sent by my master, Boaz, to see to your needs and the needs of the household."

Naomi was once again the gracious lady as she nodded to Eli. "Thank you. It is good to be home again."

Ruth looked around the courtyard, amazed. Just like in the courtyard of Boaz, the water from a small fountain tinkled merrily, and many flowers bloomed, both in the ground and in clay pots. Didn't Micah tell them when they first arrived that the house had been neglected? Then she smiled. *Boaz.*

The house itself was two stories, with a staircase leading up to the second story and another set of steps leading to the roof.

Under the house, Eli showed her the good condition of the storerooms and the pens for the animals. The previous occupants had taken their animals with them, but Ruth knew that they would be replaced, thanks to the generosity of Boaz.

Another servant had unloaded their donkey, put him in a stall, and given him hay. A young woman came out of the house and bowed to Naomi. "Most gracious lady, I am Phebe, your maidservant. Welcome to your home."

"Thank you, Phebe. I will be glad for your help."

Ruth marveled at how quickly Boaz had seen to their needs.

As Ruth and Naomi ascended the steps to the second story of the house, Naomi clasped her hands in pleasure. "My furnishings are still here. They have been good stewards of my house." She put one finger to her cheek. "I will need new rugs on the floors. I took my old ones with me, and it looks like the previous tenants have taken theirs."

Ruth could see Naomi mentally deciding what she would need to restore the inside of her house.

Phebe took their bundles from them on the patio, but when she joined them again, Ruth noted she did not bring their clothing.

"You may do with our old things as you will, Phebe. We will not need those things any longer."

"Yes, my lady, as you wish."

Naomi put her finger to her chin as she voiced a list of things for Eli to purchase in the marketplace. Then, with a last look around, Naomi hurried Ruth from the house to the marketplace, where they found the sandal maker and sellers of fabric. The word of Boaz was all Ruth and Naomi needed as they chose new robes, belts, head coverings, and sandals more in keeping with their status.

The women of the town once again flocked around Naomi and embraced her with blessings and tears. They congratulated Ruth on her upcoming wedding to Boaz. Basmath stood a short distance away and watched, her eyes appraising Ruth, her countenance downcast. Finally she came forward and congratulated Ruth, then hurried away. One of the women leaned closer to Ruth and whispered, "Basmath has been trying to entice Boaz for years. You are a fortunate woman, Ruth. Boaz is a wealthy man, and not ugly or fat. There are several women who would have been glad to share his home...and his bed."

Ruth blushed. "I'm sorry for Basmath, but I am very happy to be chosen."

When they had purchased all they needed, Eli suddenly appeared with another servant and gathered their purchases to be taken to the house. Rugs were selected and arrangements made to deliver them.

The women of the town went on with their various tasks, but Ruth knew that word of her marriage to Boaz, and all the information they had gleaned from her, was spreading from woman to woman. She felt like she was being examined by each set of curious eyes, and she found herself wondering about Basmath. The woman was older than Ruth yet very attractive. Why had Boaz not chosen her? Then she knew. Boaz did not want just a wife. He wanted more. She remembered the words he spoke to her at the house two days before. He wanted a wife he loved.

When at last they returned to the house, they entered the patio and were welcomed again by Eli, who had hurried home ahead of them. They were also greeted by delicious smells coming from the kitchen area.

They feasted on a goat stew with squash and olives, and Ruth remembered the dish they ate often on the Plains of Moab at the tent and then the house of Elimelech. She dipped fresh bread in the stew and felt the warmth of contentment steal over her. Her eyes became heavy with fatigue.

There was a knock at the gate. The men had come to deliver the rugs Naomi had chosen. As they were laid down, one by one, in the areas Naomi indicated, the house began to take on a warmer feel. Naomi looked around, her eyes bright with pleasure.

The men left, and Ruth felt the weariness of the long day. She and Naomi followed Phebe to a room. It was furnished with a wide bed covered with multicolored woven rugs. Flowers graced the chest of drawers, and soft white curtains moved softly with the breeze coming in through the small window. Ruth noticed that the frames of the windows and doorways were of a wood similar to those in the house of Boaz.

Naomi waited until Ruth had looked around.

"I will bid you good night, Daughter. Phebe will show you to the room that used to be my son's. You will find it comfortable. I will see you in the morning." She smiled. "We have much to plan and do."

Ruth embraced Naomi briefly and then followed Phebe a few steps to another room. When the carved wooden door was opened, Ruth almost gasped. It had been furnished almost as splendidly as Naomi's room, with thick woven carpets, a chest of drawers for her clothing, and a comfortable-looking chair in the corner by a wooden-shuttered window overlooking the garden. There were two beds in the large room, one with a rug over it and a few cushions, the other made up with a sleeping rug and pillows. She said good night to Phebe, who lit the small clay lamp by the bed and excused herself, closing the door softly behind her.

Ruth looked around again, and then, still feeling the weariness of the day, dropped her clothes on the floor, slipped on the soft sleeping shift of fine wool she'd purchased that afternoon, crawled into her bed, and gave herself to sleep.

Thirty-one

Ruth awoke to the sun streaming in through the window. It was late. She rose quickly. Seeing that the clothes she had dropped on the floor last night were gone, she pulled a simple robe from the small chest and found a sash and a head covering of soft blue. Her new everyday sandals waited at the end of her bed, and she slipped them on.

Hearing voices in the courtyard, she hurried down to find Naomi. She stopped suddenly when she saw Naomi talking to Boaz.

He smiled at her, his eyes twinkling. "You rested well?"

She had never slept so late. She felt the heat rise in her face. "I rested well, my lord."

He stood quietly, taking in all of her, and she moved toward him. She touched her new mantle, remembering all they had purchased the day before. "Thank you, my lord, for everything you have done for us."

"It gave me pleasure to restore what Naomi had lost. I cannot restore her husband and sons, but I could bring her once again to the home she knew and loved."

Naomi touched his arm. "Come and see what you have allowed us to choose, Boaz." They mounted the stairs, Naomi leading, and Ruth conscious of the man who followed behind her. He radiated energy and virility, and she, having been a wife and then endured the pain of widowhood, found herself looking forward to the joys of marriage again. Mahlon, though handsome, was never strong, and she was young then. Now she longed for a man to hold her... to feel his strength and his love.

As they entered the house, they brushed arms, and she felt a tingle go through her body. She realized she loved this man with all her heart.

Boaz looked around the newly decorated space and nodded his head in approval. "You have chosen well, Naomi."

"Will you sit and refresh yourself?"

"I can stay but a short time, as there are things I must take care of. My mother bids you both come to her." He chuckled. "I believe she wants to help plan the wedding."

Naomi called Phebe. Like a good guest, Boaz sipped a cup of wine and spoke to them about his orchards and the fields, which were still doing well after the drought and famine.

Ruth was content to listen and watch Boaz, and he glanced at her from time to time, longing evident in his eyes.

Naomi had been observing both of them. "Boaz, I wonder if you had considered moving the wedding date closer. You are both widowed, and surely you do not need a long betrothal. Why not marry as soon as possible?"

He hesitated. "It had crossed my mind. I did not wish to hurry Ruth." His eyes sought Ruth's as his eyebrows raised in question.

"My lord, I have little to prepare. It shall be whenever you wish."

His shoulders relaxed in an apparent show of relief. "My family is prepared to embrace you, Ruth." She heard the words he didn't utter. *As am I.*

"In three weeks, the month of Av will be upon us, as will the grape harvest. It is a time of celebration. Would that suit you, Ruth?"

She looked into the face that had become so dear to her and nodded her head. "That will suit me, my lord."

When Boaz left the house, Naomi remained behind, while Ruth walked with him to the courtyard.

He took her small hands in his and examined the calluses and the places where blisters had formed. "Never again, my beloved, will you have to glean in the fields. With my mother getting wearier by the day, you shall have enough to oversee in my household and...and raise our children."

An arrow of fear pierced her heart as she sought to answer him. Perhaps *Ha'Shem* would lift the curse from her. If it continued, all her hopes, and those of Boaz, were in vain.

He tipped her chin with his finger. "The Most High, blessed be His name, has assured me that His blessing will not only be over our marriage, but over our children, as well. Fear not, my beloved."

She could only stare at him, bewildered. Surely the Most High God did not speak to mere men. Yet Boaz seemed so sure. She didn't answer.

"I must go, or I shall be tempted to do more than hold your hands." With a wry smile, Boaz turned and left the courtyard.

With her head full of questions, she hurried up the steps to seek Naomi.

Boaz walked quickly from the house of Naomi, feeling a sense of euphoria. He had found the one who could make him forget Miriam; and while the office of kinsman redeemer was a duty, he rejoiced that his love for Ruth was returned. He would no longer sleep alone, nor would he suffer the pining looks of the single women and widows in Bethlehem. He felt a slight twinge of guilt over Basmath. She was a good woman, pleasant to look at, and he knew she cared for him. But when he thought of taking her as a wife, he felt a check in his spirit, and the Lord whispered, *She is not the one.*

He could not even put into words the shock that pierced his heart like an arrow the first day he saw Ruth gleaning in the fields. There was something in her demeanor that showed strength and determination. He watched her every time he came to the fields, appreciating, as men did, the lithe form that moved beneath her tunic. Yet she did not flaunt her beauty or spend her time gossiping. She was a woman of integrity. She worked hard, was kind to the other women, and seemed to have the care of Naomi as her first thought. He found he not only cared for her but also respected her devotion to her mother-in-law. The one thing that was most impressive was that she did not flirt with him, though she had more than one opportunity.

He mused on the day he finally saw in her eyes what he had longed for these many years. Ruth loved him. It was in her face and manner, though she tried to hide it.

As he approached his home, he recalled the night on the threshing floor when she had implored him to be her kinsman redeemer. How his heart leaped that she obeyed Naomi and did as her mother-in-law must have instructed her to do.

He opened the gate just as Rachab was preparing to leave with a servant.

"Ah, *Imah,* you are going to the home of Naomi? I have news for you. We have agreed to be married in three weeks' time." He kept a straight face and watched her expression of astonishment and then dismay.

"Boaz, how am I to get everything ready in such a short time? You are like a bull in his rutting season. What am I to do with you?"

He laughed. "I have every confidence that you will complete all the preparations in plenty of time. You have fed large crowds before, during Passover. You and Naomi are capable women. Go now and commiserate with her on the unreasonableness of men."

She waved a hand in exasperation and left the courtyard.

He entered the room he used for a study and sighed at the pile of scrolls that were spread out on the heavy wooden table. Some were from his steward, to pay the wages of the men who worked in the fields and the orchards. He noted the bills from Naomi and Ruth's shopping trip to the marketplace and nodded with pleasure. Naomi had been thrifty and chosen her purchases carefully, as had Ruth. That was a good sign that Ruth would be careful with her household money.

He sat down on a leather chair and reflected on the fear he saw in Ruth's eyes when he mentioned children. He understood her anxiety, since her marriage to Mahlon had produced no children. But he had the promise, whispered to him in the night, that *Ha'Shem* would bless their marriage. He was of the direct line of the Messiah. Would their son—and he was sure there would be one—be the promised Redeemer? Every woman in the tribe of Judah who bore a son carried that hope, yet the Redeemer had not come. He sighed. The Almighty worked in His own time, and it was not for mere man to question Him.

A knock sounded on the doorpost. He glanced up and saw his steward. "Come in, Nadab."

"You are prepared to go over the accounts, my lord?"

"Yes, let us get the business done. It is too nice a day to remain inside."

"You have other thoughts on your mind, my lord?" He was smiling.

"Of course, you old fox. I am getting married in three weeks' time."

The steward raised his eyebrows. "You have changed the date, my lord. You are eager for this marriage." He smiled at Boaz with the familiarity of one who has been in his master's service a long time. "I am happy that you have found a woman worthy of you."

Boaz raised an eyebrow and grinned back. "I think we best set to work here."

They spent more than an hour going over the business of the land and vineyards, and Nadab listed the funds to be paid to each worker. Lists of provisions needed for the animals and the household were made.

"My mother will inform you of the foods needed from the marketplace for the wedding. We can select some produce from the gardens, so see what will be available."

"Very well, master." Nadab picked up the billings. "These shall be taken care of at once."

When his steward had gone, Boaz opened the door leading to the side of the house and wandered into the courtyard. He was restless and realized his mother was right. He was like a young man eager for his wedding and everything that it entailed. The face of Miriam came to mind, but it did not cause him sorrow. He remembered only the sweetness of their union and all that she had been to him. Miriam would be happy for him. She always thought of others more than herself.

Then there was Jael. He sighed. She continued to be reserved in her comments concerning Ruth, and though he suspected her of a little jealousy, he felt she would come around. He was certain Ruth's gentle manner would win over his daughter.

Looking up at the sun, which was beginning its descent, he roused himself. It was time to walk in the orchards and, as was his custom, encourage those who had worked through the heat of the day.

Recalling his mother's ribald comment, he smiled to himself and strode forth, feeling younger with each step.

Thirty-two

Will Rachab come here today, or will we go to the home of Boaz?" Ruth asked her mother-in-law.

"She is coming here to discuss the food," Naomi replied. "Both our households will provide for the wedding feast. Eli and Phebe can take our provisions over there on the day of the wedding."

Ruth smiled. Naomi and Rachab had been deep in plans. It was to be an important wedding, as befitted Boaz's station and standing in the town. Naomi said that she and Rachab had no idea how many guests would come, but Ruth suspected half the town had been invited and knew all would come, if not for the ceremony, then for the food.

The first figs, plump and juicy, were being harvested. Women picked them by the basketfuls for storage in large crocks. Over the year, the fruit would be made into cakes and other delicacies. Figs were also placed on the tables of homes throughout Bethlehem to enhance family meals. Ruth bit into one, enjoying the sweetness.

She was glad to have finished her work on the loom. Using very fine linen thread, she had woven the material for her wedding dress, and now she would work on the gold embroidery for the sleeves and hem. Since she was no longer working in the fields, she was able to concentrate on her wedding garment. Yet, with the change in the wedding date, she had less time than she had expected to finish her preparations.

Boaz's wedding gift to her—a pair of finely jeweled sandals and a set of gold earrings—waited in her room, along with a sheer mantle and the ring of coins for her forehead.

When she considered what it would be like to be taken into the arms of Boaz, the thought caused her some sleeplessness. She found it best to occupy her hands and her mind.

The needle flew in and out of the material as the patterns took shape. She smiled to herself with pleasure. It was to be a beautiful wedding robe.

Rachab arrived, as expected, leaning on the arm of her handmaid. She inspected Ruth's work and nodded in approval, patting Ruth on the shoulder.

"My son has chosen well. Only the Almighty knows how long I have waited for him to marry again."

Ruth smiled up at her, grateful that she had favor in the eyes of her future mother-in-law. For now, Naomi was all the family she had, and she thought of her more as her mother than her mother-in-law.

Ruth continued stitching as Naomi and Rachab discussed the food, deciding what they could make the most of beforehand and what needed to wait until the day before the wedding. The two elderly women sounded as excited as young girls to her.

"The baklava…Naomi, there must be plenty. That could be made ahead. And the date and fig cakes…."

Naomi threw up her hands in mock despair. "I do believe we are feeding the whole town. How many has Boaz invited?"

Rachab rolled her eyes. "Too many, I fear. Was there ever such a man? He has no idea of the work it will take."

Naomi frowned. "The saffron millet with raisins and walnuts will go far. We should include that, and, of course, fried sardines with capers."

"The quail are plentiful in the fields; let us have grilled quail. Oh, and Boaz has set aside five lambs for roasting."

The voices became a hum as Ruth's mind wandered from her sewing to the years that had gone so quickly. She never expected to be a bride again. Her only plan was to take care of Naomi. The thought of a kinsman redeemer had crossed her mind, but Naomi had no immediate family back in the Plains of Moab. It wasn't until they reached Bethlehem that Ruth understood how much Naomi had been thinking about providing for her future, as well as reclaiming the property of Elimelech. When Mahlon promised his father on his deathbed to bring his mother home, no one anticipated that Mahlon and Chilion would not return with her.

In her mind, Ruth crossed the Jordan and saw the escarpments that protected the Plains of Moab. She saw herself driving the goats to their grazing places; she pictured the underground streams that made their way to the escarpment and cascaded down into small patches of green.

The face of Mahlon came to mind, and she remembered how he had shocked her by coming to the fields alone and proposing marriage. Then, in her mind's eye, she saw the young girl she had been, dancing in happiness to the music of her flute. How long ago that seemed. Now she was to be married to Boaz, chief of the tribe of Judah, and live in a house larger than any she'd known. Boaz had a steward and a servant. And she would be in charge of the household.

In spite of her fears, her mind lingered on the thought of children. She had prayed and begged *Ha'Shem* to open her womb. To at least grant her a son to raise up for Naomi and Mahlon. She pushed those anxious thoughts aside to concentrate on finishing the last few inches of her hem.

She had not heard from Orpah. Though they had known each other all their lives and had been sisters-in-law together, Ruth had felt a burden of sorrow when Orpah left her and Naomi and began to walk back to the town. She sensed she would never see her friend and sister, nor her own family, again. Did Orpah marry again and bear children? Ruth would never know.

"Ruth!"

The impatience in Naomi's voice told her she had been addressing her for some time.

"Yes, Mother?"

"Did you wish to add anything to the wedding feast?"

Both older women contemplated her with questioning eyes.

"Everything you have planned sounds wonderful. How could I possibly improve on your expertise?"

The women sat back, looking pleased with themselves.

Then she couldn't resist. "Perhaps some stuffed dates? They would be ready for harvest by then. Of course, I'm sure you already thought of that," she added quickly.

Rachab raised her eyebrows, then nodded vigorously and glanced at Naomi. "Oh yes, of course we planned on those."

Ruth suppressed a smile.

They had tea and some fig cakes before Rachab rose to return home. As arranged, her servant waited at the door to assist her.

When Rachab had gone, Naomi sighed. "She and I are both getting older. If you and Boaz delay in having a grandchild for me, I may not be around to see it."

Ruth laid a gentle hand on her arm. "Do not be concerned, Mother. Boaz has told me that *Ha'Shem* has spoken to his heart and will bless our marriage, and I believe that includes children. We must trust in the Lord." She hoped she sounded more confident than she felt. Yet, as her wedding day drew near, her hopes of children occupied her mind more and more.

Thirty-three

On her wedding day, Ruth opened her eyes. The morning was clear and bright—a good omen. A rooster had already crowed, but she stretched and remained in her bed for a little longer, daydreaming. Today she was to marry Boaz, her redeemer. Would he prove to be a tender lover? He walked with the stride of a much younger man and was handsome still. She shivered in anticipation of their wedding night. How different it would be from her first night with Mahlon. She was so young then, so inexperienced.

In the pen below the house, the sheep and goats moved restlessly and complained loudly, letting all know they were hungry. Then she heard heavy footfalls descending the stone steps to the stable. Eli would make sure the animals were fed.

Still, this was not a day to be lazy. She rose, stretched again, and walked to the window, looking out over the fields and orchards. Workers were already moving through the vineyards with their pruning knives, harvesting the grapes. She pictured baskets full of the lush fruit being emptied into the stone wine vats. It reminded her of the times at her grandfather's farm when she would tread the new grapes in his small winepress. The rich juice would run into a stone holding area, where it was scooped out to be placed in large storage crocks.

A tear slipped down her cheek as she realized none of her family would be able to share this happy occasion with her. She wiped the tear away. A new life was ahead of her, and she would thank *Ha'Shem* for this wonderful blessing.

When Ruth entered the main room of the house, she found Naomi waiting for her.

"I was beginning to wonder if you were going to sleep through your wedding day, Daughter." The twinkle in her eyes softened the gentle rebuke.

"Watching the harvesters from my window reminded me of when I used to tread the grapes for my grandparents. It seems so long ago."

"Indeed it was, Ruth. But those times are past, and we have a glorious day ahead of us. Come. Phebe and I will accompany you to the *mikveh,* to purify yourself for your wedding."

Ruth smiled. She remembered her first *mikveh* as she prepared to marry Mahlon. No bride would consider facing her wedding day without the cleansing bath.

Ruth did not eat breakfast; she and Boaz both followed custom by fasting before the wedding. She walked with Naomi and Phebe to the local pond used by the women. With Phebe holding a large linen cloth around her, she dropped her robe and stepped nude into the pool, which was enclosed with a wall for privacy. A clay pipe brought water from a nearby stream, keeping the pool fresh. She spread her arms and sank down until the water covered her head. Then she rose partially, raising her arms to heaven, and recited, "Praised are You, *Adonai,* God of all creation, who sanctifies us with Your commandments and commanded us concerning immersion."

Twice more she dipped herself, then stepped up out of the water and was wrapped in the linen cloth. Another robe was wrapped around her for modesty, and the three women returned to the house. Ruth dried her hair, and Phebe entwined flowers in it.

Next, Ruth put on her wedding robe, and Naomi tied the beautiful multicolored sash she had purchased as a gift to her daughter-in-law. Ruth inserted the gold earrings from Boaz into her ears. Since she was a widow, she would not wear the bridal veil but a linen mantle of soft blue. And, this time, the bridegroom would not come at night but would meet her in the daylight and walk with her to his home.

As Ruth descended the steps and entered the courtyard, she saw not only Boaz waiting to meet her but also Jael, who stood by his side. The expression on the young woman's face was unreadable. She glanced at her father and then stepped forward.

"May the Lord bless you on your wedding day. Would you like me to stand by you at your wedding, since there is no one you know well enough to be your bridesmaid?"

Jael's eyes bored into hers, and her smile, which held no warmth, belied the kindness of her words. Ruth swallowed her first impulse to refuse. It would only spoil the day, and she had no intention of allowing Jael's animosity to do that. She smiled. "You are so kind, Jael. I would be honored."

Boaz, apparently oblivious to the tension between them, took Ruth's arm in his and gave her a tender smile. "Let us go, then."

Naomi, Phebe, and the other members of the household followed as they started for the home of Boaz for the wedding. Jael, moving slowly due to her pregnancy, trailed them, holding on to her husband.

It was a glorious procession. They were joined next by Micah and the elders with their wives and children, along with others who would be guests at the wedding. People from the town lined the streets, tossing flower petals at them and calling out good wishes.

They reached the gate of the house of Boaz and entered the courtyard. It was strung with garlands of green, and flowers in pots lined the walls. Micah, as the head elder and judge, went over to the *chuppah,* since he would oversee the wedding ceremony.

Ruth stopped suddenly, her mouth open in astonishment. Standing just inside the courtyard was her grandfather, Misha. By his side was her brother, Joash, his wife, Deborah, and their young son, Nashon. To her added delight, she saw a small girl standing unsteadily, holding Joash's hand.

Joash stepped forward and lifted his daughter up in his arms. "Her name is Priscilla."

Ruth smiled at the little girl, then turned to Boaz, her heart overflowing. "You did this?"

"I thought you should have family near to share in our joy."

"What have I done that *Ha'Shem* should bless me with such a man? Thank you, Boaz."

Tears filled her eyes as she embraced each of her family members. She had feared never seeing them again.

Then Boaz took her hand and they stood under the *chuppah*. Deborah and Jael stepped back, and Naomi led Ruth around the *chuppah* seven times, representing the number of completion, as well as the days of creation, then handed her to Boaz.

When the words of the ceremony had been spoken, Ruth looked up at her new husband and saw the light shining in his eyes. Could her heart contain such happiness?

As the servants began to carry the food out to the tables that had been set up, Ruth took a deep breath. The smell of roasted lamb with garlic and cumin filled the house, and there were pungent fried sardines with capers and fried fava beans. There was a basket filled with loaves of fresh bread next to a bowl of dip made from ground sesame seeds. Another bowl held dilled cucumbers with olives and goat cheese, while still another contained lentil salad with watercress and goat cheese. Platters held sweet baklava, date cakes, and stuffed fresh dates. The wine flowed freely as cask after cask was brought out to refill the wooden goblets. Musicians played flutes and lyres, and Deborah joined the women playing their tambourines. Some of the men, warmed by the libations, formed a line and began to dance the *Horah*. The spectators clapped and cheered as the dancers placed goblets of wine on their heads and in slow movements continued the dance without spilling a drop.

Boaz and Ruth sat in special chairs as the guests presented them with wedding gifts—linen table coverings, a menorah, pillows, wine, and more.

She looked over at her grandfather and saw him keeping time to the music and enjoying himself. Then Joash was at her elbow, holding Priscilla. Nashon clung to his father's leg.

Joash nodded at Misha. "He didn't think he had the strength for the journey, but look at him now."

"Oh, Joash, I cannot contain my happiness at seeing you all again. How did Boaz do this?"

"He sent word of the wedding, along with wedding garments. And, considering the age of your grandfather and the possibility of small children, he sent donkeys for our journey. He also sent armed protectors to travel with us on the Jericho Road."

Ruth shook her head in amazement at the kindness of her husband. Then she stooped down and spoke with her young nephew.

"Are you having a good time, Nashon?"

He nodded. "I like the music."

"I like it, too. I'm glad you could come and share this special day."

Priscilla looked at her with wide eyes, her thumb in her mouth.

"Are you having fun, Priscilla?"

She nodded, too, and then buried her head in her father's shoulder.

Boaz was speaking to some of the elders, and Ruth scanned the room for Jael. She stood near her husband, Shelah, and watched her father with a look of sadness and longing on her face. Ruth wanted to go and put her arms around her stepdaughter, to assure her that she still had her father's love and that he was not abandoning her. But Jael must have noticed Ruth looking at her, for she quickly dropped her eyes and turned away. The moment had passed. Yet Ruth vowed to do everything she could in the days to come to win Jael. If not for her own sake, then for Boaz.

She caught her grandfather's eye, and he beamed at her.

The celebration went on into the evening until finally the guests, mindful there were still grapes to harvest, began to drift back to their homes.

Ruth stood quietly by her new husband. Micah put a hand on Boaz's shoulder and said, "A fine wedding, Boaz. The best we have seen in Bethlehem in years."

The other elders nodded their heads in agreement, and Micah pronounced one last blessing before departing with his family.

Boaz embraced Jael and clapped Shelah on the shoulder. "I shall await news of my grandson."

"We will send word the moment the time comes, Father."

Naomi would take Ruth's family home with her and provide lodging during their stay. Ruth was reluctant to let them go. With tears, she embraced each one, her heart so full of happiness that she felt it would burst in her chest.

"We will see you tomorrow, dear sister." Joash carried his sleeping son, while Deborah held their small daughter. "We will visit then."

"How soon must you return home?"

Her grandfather put a hand to her cheek. "We can stay for two days. Neighbors are watching the animals, but we, too, have harvesting to do. You have my blessing, Granddaughter, for the Almighty has brought you to a new place. You will have a good life with this man who is so well respected."

"I understand. I am so grateful you could come, even if for only a short time. I have missed you all so."

He sighed. "It is good to know that you are well and in the care of a good husband. That will sustain us in the years to come."

She and Boaz watched them leave with Naomi and Phebe. Eli held a lamp to guide their way through the darkness.

When they were out of sight, Boaz turned her to face him, lifted her chin with his finger, and kissed her soundly. They looked into each other's eyes, and laughter bubbled up between them.

Boaz surprised her by picking her up, and as he carried her into the house, she felt his strength, which had not abated with age. She wrapped her arms round his neck and put her head on his shoulder, and he murmured, "I believe we have some celebrating to do…in private."

Thirty-four

The first rains of *Tishri* had come, bringing a refreshing to the air of Judea. The parched ground drank in the welcome moisture, and soon the farmers were able to drive their oxen and till the ground in preparation for the sowing of the barley and wheat seeds. The olives hung like black jewels on the trees, and workers were hired to help harvest the crop. Already the olive presses were producing the oil used in every home in Bethlehem. Ruth made sure the casks were sealed properly after they were filled. She was pleased. The storage rooms of her husband would be amply stocked. She made sure some of the olives were packed in brine to keep them for household use during the year. She went over the household accounts regularly with Nadab, the steward, who in turn consulted her diligently.

As she contemplated their stores in order to determine what they needed from the marketplace, she heard footsteps behind her, and two large hands settled gently on her shoulders.

"My husband, I thought you were in the fields." She turned and was gathered in his arms.

"The planting is going well. I came for the noon meal."

She shook her head. "The time flows by like a rushing river. I hadn't realized the sun was at its zenith."

He kissed her on the forehead. "If I am not to die of starvation, let us go and see what has been prepared."

"Will Rachab join us?"

"She does not wish to leave her room. It is getting harder for her to walk. Her handmaid has taken her meal to her." He sighed. "She grows weaker. I fear she will not be with us much longer."

Ruth reached out and put her hand over his. Rachab was nearing her seventieth year. She was tired a great deal, and her eyesight was dimming.

"It is hard to see her thus, Boaz."

"It is a time that comes to all of us, sooner or later. It is life, like the sun that rises in the morning, when everything is fresh and new, reaches its peak, and then gradually lowers until it sinks out of sight. So the Almighty has given us our days and numbered them."

She nodded and followed him to the courtyard. As they ate the meal, she studied Boaz from across the table. They had been married two months, and she could not be happier. Boaz was a gentle husband and a considerate, if not passionate, lover. She was not with child yet, but hope had risen in her heart, and she felt *Ha'Shem* was asking her to trust Him. Boaz was anxious for a child, but he would not embarrass her by discussing it. He would know when the time came.

She put another piece of bread in her mouth, and when she looked up again, Boaz was watching her. His dark eyes, shaded by heavy brows, filled her with warmth. He took her hand, rubbing his thumb across the back of it.

"You are so beautiful."

"You spoil me, my husband. I am not a young girl anymore. When Jael has her child, I shall be a grandmother."

At the mention of his daughter's name, Boaz became serious. "And how is it with the two of you now?"

"I think we shall be friends. I told her I did not intend to be her mother."

"I think with *Imah* losing her strength, Jael will need you more than ever. They are very close, and I dread the day my mother is no longer with us."

He turned those dark eyes on her again, and the corners of his mouth twitched. "It is the time of noonday rest, Beloved."

She rose with a smile. Taking her hand, Boaz led her down the hall to their chamber.

When Boaz returned to his fields, Ruth went to her loom and continued to work on a shawl of soft blue she was making for Jael's baby. Her fingers were nimble as she sent the shuttle through the threads. She pressed the thread down to make sure it was tight and then moved the shuttle again.

She looked up as Nadab entered the weaving room. "The baskets have been prepared as you requested, Mistress."

"Good. I will get my shawl and join you." She knew of some families in Bethlehem that were struggling. In one, the father had injured his leg while plowing and could not provide for his family until he was able to work again. In another family, the father had died, leaving his wife and children destitute. Ruth put together baskets of grain, olive oil, bread, and honey, along with platters of date cakes and bottles of wine. With the help of another servant, she would deliver them today. The staples—enough to feed each family for a couple of weeks—were always received gratefully.

Boaz had helped, as well, by sending the healer to see to the injured man and assuring him he could return to his fields as soon as his leg was healed. Ruth learned that Boaz had also contacted the town matchmaker quietly and asked her to look for a husband for the widow, at his own expense.

When Ruth returned home after making the deliveries, she found a flurry of activity. "Nadab, what is happening?"

"It is the master's daughter, mistress. She bears her child. I have sent for the master."

Ruth hurried to Jael's home, without Rachab, who was too weak to travel.

Basmath was already there, tending Jael, who was crying in pain. Boaz had come in from the fields. He, Shelah, and Shelah's father, Zuriel, waited in the small courtyard.

Ruth put cool cloths on Jael's forehead and spoke comfortingly to her as the girl alternately whimpered that she was dying and screamed with each contraction.

"The head has crowned," Basmath announced, and in moments the baby slid into her hands. Jael appeared to have fainted from the exertion but soon recovered.

"It is a daughter, my lady," Basmath murmured as she cleaned the baby and wrapped her in the soft wool cloths that had been prepared. Then she handed the tiny girl to Ruth.

A grandchild by marriage, but a grandchild nonetheless. Ruth could hardly bear the love that rose up within her for this baby. She held the child to her heart and carried her out to the courtyard, where the men waited.

"You have a daughter, Shelah." She turned to Boaz. "And you have a granddaughter."

She handed the baby to Shelah, who stared at his daughter in wonder.

Zuriel contemplated the baby and gingerly touched one of her small hands. When the baby grasped his forefinger, Zuriel hastily pulled his hand away.

Both Boaz and Shelah laughed.

"She will wrap you around her finger, Father," Shelah said. "Be prepared."

Zuriel huffed but looked pleased.

"Jael, she is doing well?" This from Boaz.

"Yes, Boaz, your daughter is doing well." Ruth smiled at her husband and saw relief flood his countenance.

When Ruth went back inside the house and laid the baby in Jael's arms, Jael looked up at her with no animosity in her gaze. "You were here when I needed the comfort of a mother. I have been so unkind, Ruth. Forgive me."

Ruth smiled down at her stepdaughter. "You are forgiven. I am glad it went well. Have you thought of a name for her?"

Just then, Shelah entered with Boaz and Zuriel. Shelah looked at Boaz. "We had thought to name a daughter Miriam, after her grandmother."

Boaz nodded, his eyes glistening with tears. "Thank you, Shelah. She would have liked that."

Basmath looked at the family gathered round and then said quietly, "My work here is done. I must go. I congratulate you, Boaz, on your granddaughter." She nodded to the rest of them, glanced briefly at Ruth, and hurried away.

Jael needed to rest, so Ruth remained. She would tend Jael until the young woman was able to resume her own household duties.

Boaz needed to return to the fields, and Ruth walked with him a short distance, both of them silently pondering their own thoughts. Was Boaz thinking of a child of their own? Ruth felt her anxiety return, but he said nothing.

As he turned in the direction of the fields, he looked at her with a gaze full of love. "You are all I could hope for, Beloved."

He walked away, and she looked heavenward. "O God Who Sees, may You show me grace and be merciful. Grant us what we desire most, I pray."

Thirty-five

When the rooster crowed to announce the morning, Ruth opened her eyes but lay quiet and still. Soft snores told her Boaz still slept. She was filled with wonder when she remembered that the time of women had not come, and it had been six weeks. She was sure Boaz had noticed she had not set herself apart, as was required by the law of Moses. Dare she hope? In the past, each time she allowed herself to hope, those dreams were dashed. But now she was sure. The Almighty had answered her fervent prayers at last.

She sat up, waiting for the nausea to pass, and reached inside the basket she kept by the bed for a small chunk of bread. She ate it slowly.

As she rose and walked to the window, the first light of dawn slipped through the lattice, pushing the shadows from the room. She wrapped her arms around herself, as if to contain the happiness that bubbled up inside her.

A sound behind her caused her to turn, and she found herself in the arms of her husband. She leaned against him, glad for his strength and warmth.

"I didn't hear you rise, my husband."

"When were you going to tell me?" His eyes sought hers, and she detected a slight twinkle, as a smile twitched the corners of his mouth.

"I just wanted to be sure. I have been disappointed so many times."

"You have not separated yourself from me according to the law of Moses."

"There has been no reason to separate. Oh, Boaz, I thought never to experience the wonder of this time. I still can hardly believe it."

"Ah, the town of Bethlehem will be talking for weeks. A woman barren for ten years, married to a man who is a grandfather? We shall be as our ancestors Abraham and Sarah."

She laughed then. "You are not an old man, my husband—certainly not the age of Abraham."

Boaz chuckled. "I look at you and feel the fire of my youth, Beloved."

"You have loved me well." She pushed him away with a smile and an arched eyebrow. "I have work to do to run this household of yours."

"I must be on my way into Bethlehem. It is my turn as judge for the people's grievances. Promise me you will rest today."

"I will rest." She smiled up at him, and his dark eyes again sought hers.

He leaned down to kiss her. "We will continue this discussion when I return this evening."

When he had dressed and gone, her handmaid, Bilhah, came in quietly, carrying a small tray. "I have brought a little wine and bread for your stomach. How are you feeling, Mistress?"

"It is slight, Bilhah. I will be all right. It is wonderful, yet hard to believe after so long. I cannot get over the wonder that I am carrying a child at last."

Bilhah gathered a robe and sash and handed them to Ruth. "*Ha'Shem* has heard your prayers. Have you told the lady Rachab?"

Ruth smiled at her. "If she is not already aware, I shall tell her. She misses little that goes on in this house. I have a feeling she is waiting for me to confirm her suspicions."

When Bilhah was ready to go down to the kitchen to prepare the morning meal, Ruth decided it was time to talk with her mother-in-law—and Naomi.

"Please send for the lady Naomi. I wish to discuss something with her. Invite her to stay for the evening meal."

"Yes, Mistress."

When Bilhah had gone, Ruth knocked on Rachab's door.

"Come in."

The elderly woman sat by the window. When Ruth entered, her mother-in-law's sharp eyes studied her. "You do not look well. Have you been ill?"

"What afflicts me shall last for some time, *Imah*. Probably until around the time of the date harvest."

"The Almighty be praised. I thought so. You did not set yourself apart." Tears sprang to her eyes. "It is true then, Daughter? You are with child?"

"It is so, though I can hardly believe it. I have sent for Naomi to join us and stay for the evening meal. She can rejoice with us."

Rachab pursed her lips. "If my son knew, he has not said a word to me."

"He, like you, was waiting for me to confirm his suspicions, *Imah*."

"If I know my son, his joy is unbounded. Praise to the Almighty for this great gift. I feel revived in that I shall know your child before I leave this life." She took one of Ruth's hands. "You are a blessing, Ruth. I praise the Almighty for the day Boaz found you. Come, I have stayed in this room long enough. I am ready to partake of some breakfast."

Rachab leaned on Ruth's arm, her step lighter than it had been in past weeks.

When the bread for the day was in the clay oven, and the kitchen garden tended, Ruth spent time at her loom. The baby would need soft swaddling clothes, and she chose her woolen thread carefully.

Naomi arrived two hours after the midday meal.

"I am sorry to take so much time answering your invitation, Ruth. I had the household to see to, and there was a problem with one of the sheep, and it was only recently Eli was free to accompany me." She waved a hand. "I promised Boaz that I would not go anywhere alone these days." She sank down on a bench in the courtyard, her eyes widening as she realized Ruth and Rachab were standing there, watching her, with smiles on their faces.

"Rachab, you are looking well. I heard that you were ailing, and I was making plans to call on you."

"I have been strengthened this day in many ways, Naomi."

Ruth came and knelt at Naomi's feet. She looked up into her face. "I called you here to tell you our good news. The Almighty has heard our prayers. Dear Naomi, I am with child at last. Your family line has truly been redeemed. You will have a child to raise up in Mahlon's name."

Naomi's eyes widened, and her mouth opened, but no words came forth. Then, finally, she sputtered, "It is true? Oh, my dear daughter, you have blessed me beyond anything I could imagine." She reached out and cupped Ruth's chin in her hand. "I have waited for this news for so long. I shall have a grandchild at last."

Naomi rose and embraced Ruth and then her dear friend.

Rachab clapped her hands, and Bilhah appeared. "Call Nadab. We are to have a celebration feast tonight. It is to be a special meal."

"Yes, Mistress." From the smile on Bilhah's face, Ruth knew she had been listening. Did the neighbors know? Surely they did, for the servants talked among themselves. She sighed. This kind of news could not be kept quiet. Soon every woman in Bethlehem would be gossiping to her neighbor about the miracle that had taken place. She considered her husband's words that morning. Yes, a woman barren for ten years of marriage, married to a man over twenty years her senior, and a grandfather, was expecting a child. She almost laughed out loud. What did it matter if everyone knew? Nothing could spoil her joy this day.

Ruth stood with Boaz at their bedroom window, looking out at the orchards. The almond trees, now in bloom, dotted the landscape like clouds of pink froth. The spring rains had come, the flax had been harvested, and soon the barley would be ready for harvest and threshing.

"The Almighty has been generous with His blessings," Boaz murmured behind her. "The barley will be abundant this year."

"Oh, my husband, truly it seems the dark days of the famine and drought are a thing of the past."

"It was Naomi...and you, Beloved, returning to Bethlehem, that brought the change."

She turned in his arms, smiling. "There was a change, wasn't there? Yet the Almighty does what He pleases. I would not credit Naomi or me."

Just then, the child within her moved and gave its father a sharp kick. Boaz looked down at her stomach, his eyes wide. "I had forgotten this part. Does he do this often?"

She put a hand on his cheek. "Just like a man to assume it will be a boy," she said saucily. "And, yes, your *son* is very active."

Ruth had prayed for a son, not only to inherit the land and house of Elimelech, but for the sake of Boaz. Perhaps he felt he needed to prove his manhood, or maybe he wanted to accomplish what he intended when he redeemed the child's inheritance. Whatever his thoughts, she knew his hopes for a son occupied his mind a great deal.

"I must go, Beloved. I will be in the fields this day but will return for the evening meal. You will be careful?"

She nodded with a sigh. "Yes, dear husband. You have obviously spoken to the servants. I can hardly move without their watching and asking if there is something they can do for me. Carrying a child is a normal thing. Most women in the town are doing their daily tasks up until the day their baby is born."

"You are not just any woman in the town, Ruth. I will not have you taking any chances. We will not lose this child."

At the vehemence in his voice, she remembered the story Boaz had told her of the losses of babies years before. Her heart filled with compassion.

"I will be careful, Boaz."

He kissed her forehead and left the room.

When he had gone, she turned back to the window. There were tasks for her, also, but she could not grind the grain with the grinding stone, nor was she allowed to lift anything of consequence. The handmaid took the clothes to the stream to wash and beat clean. At least her overly anxious husband had not forbidden her to weave. It was fortunate that she loved creating fabric for their home. Perhaps she could go into the town. It was market day, and the merchants would be setting up their booths. There would be fresh produce. Yet her anticipation was tempered by the need to ask if Nadab was free to accompany her. Rachab, though stronger than they'd seen her in recent months, could no longer make the trip. Ruth brightened when she remembered she had not seen Naomi for a week or so. She knew the older woman was lonely sometimes. "I will tell Nadab I wish to visit the lady Naomi. Surely he must make time for that," she murmured to herself.

Bilhah came in to help her select clothing for the day and to comb her hair. "You are in good spirits this morning, Mistress."

"I am going to visit the lady Naomi today. It has been a while, and I know she likes company."

"Nadab will accompany you?"

Ruth gave her a knowing glance. "I will ask him, but Boaz keeps him busy. I hope he is free."

"Perhaps I could go with you, Mistress. I would love the walk, and I would like to see my friend Phebe."

Ruth had forgotten that her handmaid and Naomi's knew each other. She smiled to herself. The day was shaping up well.

As the two women descended to the courtyard, Bilhah whispered, "This has been an unusual morning."

Ruth stopped at the bottom of the steps and stared at Rachab, who was kneading bread dough with a smile on her face. She glanced up, her expression daring them to comment, and went on with her task.

"Don't look so surprised. I just wanted to see if I could still tell when the dough was ready to rise."

Ruth shook her head in amazement and sat at the simple wooden table. Bilhah brought her a cup of fresh goat's milk and a chunk of bread, along with a wedge of cheese. She wondered what Boaz would say if he saw his aging mother making their bread for the day.

Leaving the dough to rise, Rachab settled herself with a smug look of satisfaction and began to dip her bread in a small bowl of olive oil.

"I had thought to visit Naomi today," Ruth told her. "Shall I bring your greetings to her?"

"Certainly, Daughter. I'm sure she will be glad to see you." She waved a hand. "Though I'm surprised Boaz lets you walk anywhere. You'd think you were the first woman to bear a child."

"It is a little wearying, Mother, but then, I know he just wants me to be careful. What will you do this day?"

"Besides drive everyone frantic by making the bread?"

Ruth laughed. "It is a good sign, Mother, that you are feeling well."

They sat together, enjoying the warmth of the morning, until Nadab hurried in the gate and approached Rachab. "Mistress, the master bids me send food and anything else they might need to the home of Ramiah, his foreman. His wife, Rebekah, is in labor, and her mother-in-law is ill."

Ruth rose. "Let us gather some things, and I will stop on my way to Naomi's to see if there is anything I can do."

Rachab went with her to the storeroom. They filled a basket with a bag of wheat, cheese, a few raisin cakes, a clay jar of olive oil, and some fava beans. Then Ruth went to the weaving room and gathered some soft linen cloths.

Nadab eyed the items. "I shall have to accompany you, Mistress. The master—"

Ruth shook her head. "I know what my husband said, but he merely didn't want me to go alone. You have work to do, so Bilhah shall go with me."

Nadab looked from her to Bilhah and shrugged. "As you say, Mistress."

The coolness of the morning made for a pleasant walk, and as they passed the fields of ripening barley, Ruth was reminded of the first day she came to the fields to glean. How could she have foreseen the events that would unfold from that day? She had sought only to find food for herself and Naomi, and then she'd met Boaz. The years on her grandfather's farm, taking the goats out each morning, leading them down the path through the escarpment to the small spring that flowed from under the abundant fields; the close call with Amon; the terrible disease that devastated their flocks; the deaths of her grandmother and her husband…it seemed another lifetime. She considered again. It was another lifetime.

The God Who Sees ordered her life. What plan did He have for her? Her grandfather had pointed out that she had married into the tribe of Judah, the line chosen by the Almighty, through which the Messiah would come. She knew each mother of Israel who bore a son hoped that he would be their deliverer. Ruth wondered to herself, *Could I be the one chosen to bear the Messiah?* No one knew the time or place, only that one day the Messiah would come. She felt the child move within her, and she rested her hand over the place where the small foot made an arc across her belly. It was a wondrous thought to contemplate.

When Ruth and Bilhah reached the home of Ramiah, they found the household buzzing. Basmath was there with Rebekah, who sat in bed, breathing heavily. Across the room, Rebekah's mother lay on her pallet, her face flushed with fever.

Bilhah placed the food they had brought in the kitchen area. Then there was a sharp cry as the child came into the world. Basmath cut the cord, and Ruth handed her the cloths she had brought to swaddle the baby in.

"It is a boy," Basmath murmured. "Ramiah will be pleased."

Rebekah sighed with relief. "We have two daughters. My husband will be more than pleased."

As Basmath took the cloths, she glanced at Ruth. "You should not be here, my lady. I do not know what ails Rebekah's mother. Please, you should go."

Basmath's voice was harsh, but Ruth understood her concern. Things were well in hand here, and they had brought the things Boaz had asked them to bring the family.

"You are wise, Basmath. I did not consider that. Bilhah and I will go. I'm sure you and the other women can take care of things here."

Basmath's face softened. "Forgive me for my abruptness, my lady. I hope the fever will pass and be nothing, but I cannot be sure."

Ruth smiled at her. "You are a blessing to all of us, Basmath. I, too, shall rely on your skill when my time comes."

Basmath nodded. "I will be there."

When Ruth and Bilhah came out of the house, the neighbor women gathered around them with questions.

Ruth beamed. "Ramiah has a son."

The women exclaimed among themselves, and then one named Tamar turned to Ruth.

"You are well, Ruth?"

She nodded.

"We are happy for you. *Ha'Shem* has blessed you at last."

"Indeed He has."

Just then, Ramiah rushed up to them, breathing heavily. His face was red. He must have run all the way from the fields.

He looked at Ruth. "My wife is...?"

She nodded. "You have a son, Ramiah. A fine boy."

"A son. I have a son!" The man beamed from ear to ear, as if he'd given birth himself, then turned and hurried for the house.

With a shake of her head, Ruth left with Bilhah for Naomi's. Rebekah was in good hands; her needs would be taken care of.

When they entered the courtyard, Naomi's handmaid, Phebe, looked distressed. In Naomi's hands were the pieces of a broken pot, and she sounded frustrated.

"This is the third thing that has been broken this week, Phebe. What can you tell me?"

"I don't know, Mistress. I don't mean to break anything. It just happens."

When Naomi noticed her visitors, she waved a hand at her maidservant. "We will discuss this later. Bring some refreshments for the lady Ruth." She gave a nod to Bilhah, who hurried into the house with Phebe.

Naomi and Ruth embraced. "My dear daughter, it is good to see you. How are you feeling?"

"Very well and very normal, but you wouldn't know it at my home."

Naomi smiled. "Boaz is being overprotective?"

"Yes, a little."

"Come, sit by me here on this bench and tell me the news."

"Well, Boaz's overseer, Ramiah, has a son. We stopped by the house on our way. He has two small daughters, so he should be overjoyed."

"It was good of you to see to them, but how is Rebekah's mother? I hear she is ill."

"She has a fever, and Basmath sent me away, rather quickly, too. She doesn't know the source of the fever."

Naomi's brows knit together. "She was right to send you away. I pray the fever is nothing serious. You took a chance going there in your condition."

"I know. We stopped only briefly, with some food and other things they might need. Boaz always takes care of his workers."

"Yes, that is good, but you must be careful, Daughter. You are past the most crucial months, but still, you must be wise."

Ruth needed to change the subject. She was fussed over enough. "Have you not seen the almond trees in bloom? The pink blossoms are everywhere."

Naomi took the hint. "All of the nut and fruit trees are beautiful when they are in bloom. I look forward to replenishing our supply of almonds. Boaz is well?"

"He is well. He is sure we are going to have a son. He always refers to the baby as a 'he.'"

"The way of men." Naomi's face turned serious. "It must be a son, Ruth, as you know. I pray every day that the property of my husband will be secure for future generations."

"I pray for that also, Mother Naomi."

Phebe brought out wine and cheese, which she set on a small table in front of them. She glanced at her mistress, as if to gauge her mood. Naomi did not appear cross at the moment, and Phebe quickly returned to the house.

Naomi looked after her. "I'm worried about Phebe. Her mind seems to be on other things these days. She has broken several pots while sweeping or cleaning. I'm not sure what to do about her."

"Does she seem distracted?" Ruth inquired. "Does she seem not to hear you the first time you speak?"

"Why, yes, come to think of it, that's just what is happening. And her humming has been driving me to distraction lately."

A suspicion formed in Ruth's mind. "Does she seem to smile all the time?"

"Ah. Do you think there is a young man involved?"

"Phebe is young, somewhat past the marriageable age, since her parents died before arrangements could be made. But I would guess that you have discerned the problem. Do you know of anyone she might be thinking of?"

"I am an old woman, nearly half blind. It has been so long since I experienced those feelings, as I did so only with Elimelech." She considered the question and then tapped her forehead. "The sandal maker's son has delivered some things from the marketplace for me. He has lingered to speak to Phebe a time or two."

"Then, there is your problem. She is in love, and her mind is not on her work. Perhaps you should question her, to discern if we are right. If so, Boaz could arrange a marriage for her."

"Oh, Ruth, what would I do without your tender and discerning heart? I've indeed been blind."

The two women talked until the sun began to descend on its afternoon path. Ruth rose to go.

"Be sure to tell me what you find out from Phebe."

"I will do that. Come again soon."

Bilhah appeared, and as they left, Ruth glanced back over her shoulder and saw the two servants smile at each other. It was the furtive grin of a shared secret. Had Phebe told her heart to her friend? Ruth was going to find out.

Thirty-six

Boaz was not pleased. His face was stern as he spoke. "You tell me you will rest, and then you walk to the home of Naomi. I wished to send Nadab to Ramiah's home with the supplies, but you went instead. Do you think I did not know Rebekah's mother was ill with a fever? Why did you disregard my wishes?"

It was the first time in their marriage that Boaz had been angry with her, and she was puzzled as to how to deal with it.

"My lord, forgive me if I misunderstood you. I am healthy and have months to go. The walk was good for me, and it was a beautiful morning. I cannot sit and do nothing until the babe is born. And I didn't go alone. Bilhah went with me."

"But you went to Ramiah's when her mother was ill with an unknown fever."

"I am sorry, my husband. I do know that you take care of your workers with great kindness, and I sought only to represent you." She gave him her most innocent smile.

Boaz sighed and gathered her to him. "Am I being foolish in my old age?"

"You are not old, my Boaz, and I understand your concern. I will be more careful from now on."

He stepped back, his hands on her shoulders. "I cannot remain angry with you, Beloved, but I pray the fever of Rebekah's mother is neither serious nor contagious."

"I'm sure it is not. I have seen the fever that devastates a village, and the symptoms of it were not there."

He nodded, his dark eyes on her a moment, and then he turned. "I must get back to the vineyards. We are pruning the vines. We should have some good grape wood for the cooking ovens."

"There will be a good harvest this year."

"A good harvest, indeed."

As he opened the door of their room, she ventured, "Ramiah has a son. A healthy boy."

He turned, a smile twitching about his mouth. "I know that, too." And he closed the door behind him.

Ruth sighed. Boaz had his fields and the days of judgment at the gates of the town. And herself? She could weave, check the kitchen garden, and walk. With a huff of frustration, she went downstairs to see what was being prepared for dinner.

As she approached the kitchen area, which was outside now thanks to the pleasant weather, she saw Bilhah cutting up vegetables. Ruth took up a knife and began to help her. The girl opened her mouth to say something, but a sharp look from Ruth kept her quiet.

Ruth worked for a few moments, trying to decide how to approach Bilhah about Phebe.

"It was good of you to accompany me to Naomi's, Bilhah," she began.

"It was a beautiful day, was it not, Mistress? I love to see the flowers blooming by the side of the road and hear the birds chirping in the sycamore trees."

"I do, too. I'm glad you enjoyed your visit with Phebe." At the mention of Naomi's maidservant, Bilhah's face took on a cautious look.

"The lady Naomi is concerned that Phebe is not herself lately," Ruth continued. "Would you happen to know the reason why?"

"I...I'm not sure, Mistress."

"Would it have anything to do with a sandal maker's son?"

Bilhah's eyes widened. "How did you know?"

"She has all the symptoms of a young woman in love. I told the lady Naomi so."

"Was she angry?"

"Oh, Bilhah, she does not have a heart of stone. Do you think Phebe would be interested in having my husband arrange a marriage for her?"

"That is possible, Mistress?"

"Of course. She has no parents. My husband could speak for her."

"Oh, Mistress, they do want to marry. They just didn't think there was a way."

"I will have the lady Naomi talk to Phebe, and if it is true and she is willing, Boaz will call on the young man's father."

Bilhah covered her heart with her hand. "You are kind, Mistress. May the God Who Sees bless you as you bless others."

As Ruth walked to the kitchen garden, she felt pleased with herself. She had solved the problem, and more quickly than she'd hoped. She paused. Now she had only to convince Boaz.

"What news do you have, *Imah*? You are well?"

Jael had brought her young daughter, Miriam, with her to spend the day. Ruth rejoiced that Jael had accepted her. Still amazed at being a grandmother, Ruth cuddled little Miriam in her lap. Bilhah had helped Rachab from the house so she could sit in the shade with the women. Then she'd brought them some diluted wine, some fresh goat cheese, and some dried figs.

Ruth knew Jael would want to hear about her idea of arranging a marriage for Phebe and Levi, so she shared.

"Do you think my father is willing to do that?"

"He is interested in the lives of all his people, Granddaughter," Rachab assured her. "I'm sure Ruth will choose the right time to inform him of his duty."

There was a brief silence, and the three women began to laugh.

"Oh, how I wish I could somehow be a bird at the house of Amos and Dorcas to hear that conversation." Jael chuckled.

The baby began to cry, and Ruth handed the child to her mother, who started nursing her.

Jael suddenly looked up and asked, "Do you fear bearing a child at your age?"

Ruth pondered the question a moment. "I am in the hands of *Ha'Shem*. Somehow I feel this child is destined for things I cannot fathom. Your father feels the same way. He believes *Ha'Shem* has told him it will be a son."

Jael frowned. "Then his inheritance will be the property of Elimelech, now Naomi's."

"Yes, Jael. And your children will inherit all that belongs to Boaz. I am sure your next child will be a boy. Though I doubt your father will dote on a son more than this little one. He is delighted with her."

Jael sighed, seeming somewhat pacified. "I know. His eyes light up whenever he sees her. I think she reminds him of my mother."

Rachab put a hand on Jael's arm. "You do that every time you come, Jael. You are the image of your mother. It was hard for him at first. He loved your mother so. You remember how he was after she died. Then he realized how much you needed him, and he began to come out of his grief."

"Forgive me, *Savta*." Jael glanced quickly at Ruth before turning back to Rachab. "Why did my father wait so long to marry again? Surely there were women in the town who would have been willing."

Ruth understood her question but felt a small stab of jealousy that Jael would bring this up now.

Rachab looked into the eyes of her granddaughter. "Your question is not appropriate, Jael, with your father's wife sitting here expecting a child, yet I will answer. I know you are friends with

Basmath, but she was not the one. Only when one has loved greatly does one seek that love again. Your father did not wish to marry just to provide you with a mother. His need went deeper. He wanted a wife he could love as much as he loved Miriam. He was willing to wait until *Ha'Shem* showed him the one He had chosen for him."

It was a long speech for Rachab, and Ruth was touched that the older woman had spoken thus. That Boaz loved her, Ruth knew with all her heart. She was not just a woman chosen to soothe his loneliness.

Shelah came from the town to join them for the evening meal, arriving almost at the same time as Boaz.

Boaz gave Ruth one of his warm, intimate smiles, and then, as little Miriam began to make noises, he strode over to his daughter, kissed the top of her head, and gathered his granddaughter in his arms. The baby cooed and smiled up at him.

He beamed. "I think she knows me."

"Of course, *Abba,*" Jael murmured. "She will start speaking and call you *Sabba* any day." Her eyes twinkled.

"I am nothing but a statue in the courtyard when his granddaughter is around," Rachab said, a slight reproof in her voice.

Boaz handed the baby back to Jael and turned to his mother. "Ah, *Imah,* you are up and about. I'm glad you are feeling well today."

"As if you noticed."

It wasn't like Rachab to be so cross or to show self-pity, but Ruth had noticed the changes over the last year. Her mother-in-law wept easily and complained often. Maybe this was the way of old women, but Ruth had not seen those symptoms in Naomi. Perhaps, since she didn't see her as often, she had not noticed. She resolved to be more aware of the needs of her two aging mothers-in-law.

For the meal, they served saffron millet with raisins and walnuts, along with a lentil salad of watercress and goat cheese. Ruth had helped Bilhah cook, since Rachab was no longer able. She'd soaked the lentils and thrown out any that surfaced. When the lentils were drained, she had cooked them until tender, then taken a small bowl and blended red wine vinegar, olive oil, minced garlic, mustard seeds, and salt. The mixture was poured over the lentils and watercress and tossed. She added fresh goat cheese. Some olives marinated in brine were also placed in a bowl on the table.

Shelah ate hungrily. "You must show my mother how to make this meal, my lady," he said to Ruth.

Ruth wondered about his comment. She knew Jael was a good cook, for Rachab had taught her well.

Frowning, Rachab turned to her granddaughter. "Do you help your mother-in-law with the cooking, Jael?"

Jael glanced quickly at her husband and seemed to choose her words. "There are other things for me to do, and I must look after the baby."

Boaz looked up, his brows knit together in question. "You do none of the cooking, Daughter?"

"No, *Abba*."

"Because you choose not to, or...." The question hung in the air.

Jael glanced again at Shelah. "My husband's mother prefers to cook, *Abba*."

Boaz's frown deepened. He gave Shelah a pointed look but said nothing. The young man shrugged and looked uncomfortable.

To Shelah's obvious relief, Boaz began to discuss the upcoming grape harvest with him, while the women turned to discuss various happenings in the town.

Rachab, weary from the exertion of the afternoon and evening, soon bid all good night and retired. Jael held the baby close so she could brush her lips across the child's forehead.

Boaz held his peace until the young couple had gone, then turned to Ruth as Bilhah cleared the table. "Why would the mother of Shelah not allow Jael to do any of the cooking? I wonder what they are eating."

"Perhaps they are not able to provide some of the herbs and spices I can use, my husband. Shelah certainly enjoyed his meal."

Boaz drew her close. "Perhaps we can find a way to help?"

"You mean, make a gift to them from our abundance? I don't know how she would take it."

"You will find a way, Beloved. I am quite sure of that." He bent down and kissed her. "The shadows fall, my love, and the evening grows late," he whispered.

Soon Ruth lay next to her husband, and the moon shed its soft light into the room as they talked quietly. Boaz was concerned about Rachab but knew that there was nothing he could do to stop the advances of old age.

"She waits for our child, my husband," Ruth told him. "She has said as much."

He nodded and settled down for sleep, but Ruth decided it was as good a time as any to ask about Phebe.

"My husband, when we were visiting Naomi, I learned that her maidservant, Phebe, and Levi, the son of the sandal maker, are interested in each other. I believe they care for each other but don't have any hope of marriage. Phebe has no family to speak for her."

That got a "Hmm" from Boaz. His eyes were closed. "Why can they not marry?"

"As you know, her parents are dead. She has no one to arrange the marriage."

Boaz opened one eye. "And?"

"And, if they are truly interested in each other and wish to marry, I was hoping you would call on the sandal maker."

"Ah, to arrange the *ketubah*."

"Phebe has no dowry, but I...."

He chuckled. "But you have already arranged things in your mind. Just like a woman."

She laid her head on his chest. "I have found such happiness. Why would I not wish it for others?"

"You are indeed persuasive, Beloved, as always. If the two of them wish to marry, I shall speak for her. Now may I get some sleep?"

He kissed the top of her head, rolled on his side, and in a moment was lost in slumber.

Ruth allowed herself a pleased smile. And tomorrow? Tomorrow she would send Bilhah for Phebe and Naomi, and they would plan.

Thirty-seven

When Naomi and Phebe arrived, Naomi settled herself next to Ruth on a bench in the courtyard. Phebe hovered nearby, her face anxious.

Naomi inclined her head toward her maidservant. "The girl said she has been speaking to young Levi, the son of the sandal maker...."

"We have done nothing wrong, Mistress. We have only talked. He has not touched me. Please believe me. Do not send me before the judges."

Ruth reached out and put a hand on her arm. "No one is planning to judge you, Phebe. We merely wish to know if you and Levi desire to marry."

The girl's eyes widened. "Marry? We have talked, but I have no dowry, and we are both poor. It did not seem like a possibility."

Naomi waved a hand. "All is possible, child. The question is, do you wish to marry?"

Phebe nodded her head slowly. "Yes, Mistress."

"Then it is settled," Ruth put in. "My husband will speak to the father of Levi on your behalf. If he is agreeable, we will arrange the *ketubah*."

Phebe's eyes filled with tears. "You would do that for us?"

Ruth nodded. "We would do that."

Naomi raised one eyebrow. "You have, of course, spoken to Boaz about this?"

"Of course, Mother Naomi, and he has agreed."

The older woman just shook her head. "I'm going in to visit Rachab." She got up and entered the house.

The two young maidservants hugged each other. "I told you it was possible," Bilhah crowed.

Boaz walked toward town with Nadab in the cool of the early evening, wondering how he had gotten himself into this. As the chief of their tribe, he had participated in betrothals, but here he was, on his way to serve in the capacity of a father and speak on behalf of Naomi's maidservant. And his object was the home of the local sandal maker. He shook his head and smiled to himself. He was doing this for Ruth.

As he neared the town, he turned down one of the side streets. "This is the right street, Nadab?"

His steward nodded. "It is the one, Master. The third house on the right belongs to the sandal maker."

Boaz scratched his head and straightened his shoulders. They stood in front of the rough gate, and Nadab knocked firmly.

A woman came to the gate. She wore no shoes, but her clothes of simple homespun were neat and clean. When she saw who was standing at her gate, she put her hand to her mouth and stepped back, bowing her head and indicating they should enter.

"Has my husband done something wrong, my lord?"

Boaz smiled. "No, I come on a more pleasant errand. But I would speak with your husband."

The small courtyard had a clay oven for baking. A goat was tied in a nearby stall, and three scrawny chickens scratched in the dirt. A stone mortar, filled with grain in the process of being ground by the pestle resting nearby, sat on a straw mat near the oven. The woman must have been working on it when they came.

"Your husband is home?"

"He has just arrived from his shop, my lord. I will call him."

"No need, Dorcas. I am here."

Boaz turned to the sandal maker and smiled. "May I speak with you, Amos? It concerns your son."

He nodded, his face apprehensive, then turned and called out, "Levi, come and greet our guest."

The young man stepped from the house, his arms full of bedding. He moved slowly toward them and laid the pile down on a mat. "Yes?"

Amos's wife spread the blankets across the mat, and Amos gestured for Boaz and Nadab to be seated. When they were settled, Amos and Levi sat also.

Boaz smiled at Levi. "You are learning your father's trade. It goes well?"

"Yes, my lord."

Boaz asked Amos a series of questions about the process of making sandals. He then talked about the weather. When the amenities had been observed, and Boaz had partaken of a small cup of wine, he got to the point.

"Amos, I am here as your leader, but I have been asked to intercede on behalf of your son and a young woman of the town who works for Naomi, the widow of Elimelech. It is my understanding that your son is interested in Phebe, and I came to discuss the matter of their marriage."

At the mention of Phebe's name, Levi's face lit up. "She is a virtuous maiden, *Abba*, a hard worker."

Amos frowned. "Where is her father, that our chief must speak for her?"

Levi opened his mouth to reply, but Boaz raised a hand and answered instead. "Her parents died in the fever that swept the town years ago. She was raised by an aunt and now serves Naomi. She is indeed a worthy young maiden, and that is why I agreed to come. Would you consider accepting her as a wife for your son?"

Amos turned to Levi. "This is the maiden you have chosen?"

"Yes, *Abba,* she is the one."

Amos nodded slowly, pondering a moment. Then he straightened his shoulders. "I am honored that you have come, my lord, and upon your recommendation, I shall agree to the marriage."

The look of joy that crossed the young man's face was well worth Boaz's time and effort in making the trip here.

Levi's mother stood nearby, her eyes alight and her hands clasped over her heart. It was not her place to speak, but her eyes caught the gaze of her husband, and Boaz did not miss the look of wonder that passed between them.

Amos put a hand on his son's shoulder. "We never had a daughter, but the Almighty has blessed us with a son to be proud of. He would not choose an unworthy maiden, and we will welcome this young woman into our home."

The arrangements were discussed. The betrothal would occur in three days, and the most auspicious date for the wedding was selected. His business thus concluded, Boaz rose from the mat.

Levi spoke up. "Would you wait just a moment, my lord? It is customary to give a gift to the bride as a sign of my intentions." He went into the house and returned with a small, intricately carved leather box, covered with flowers and birds.

Boaz examined the box. "You made this?"

"Yes, my lord. I hope Phebe will accept it."

"I'm sure she will, my son. I'm sure she will." Boaz turned to Amos. "I will inform the young woman of the arrangements and tell her the betrothal ceremony will take place at the home of Naomi in three days."

Nadab waited by the gate. When it had closed behind them, he grinned at Boaz.

"That went well, Master, did it not?"

"Yes, I believe it did. The family is poor, but the mother keeps a good house, and I believe Phebe will be welcome." He had noted that there was little space where a room could be added to the house for the young couple, but they had a solid roof with a small rooftop shelter accessed by a set of stairs. Levi and Phebe would have a place of their own, even if it was a tiny shelter on the roof. Phebe would not expect more.

They walked quickly through the gathering darkness, Nadab holding a lamp to light their way. Boaz knew Ruth would be waiting anxiously to hear how his errand had gone. Thinking of Ruth caused his heart to lift, and he quickened his footsteps.

Thirty-eight

The barley was harvested and then the wheat. The dry season began as the first figs ripened. In the orchards of Boaz, and all around Bethlehem, workers climbed wooden ladders to pick the plump, juicy fruits that threatened to burst their skins. The women of Ruth's household, like the other women of the town, busied themselves with making various cakes and compotes used as sweeteners during the year. Nadab and his helpers carried the full crocks to the storage room after they were sealed.

Ruth moved slowly as the babe within her grew. The baby seemed more active at night, and so she slept little. Still, she felt well and continually thanked *Ha'Shem* for the blessing of carrying a child at last. The swaddling clothes were ready, and there was little more she could do but wait.

She sat in the shade of a sycamore tree in the courtyard and watched the work taking place. Boaz did not have to admonish her to rest; she rested every chance she got. She worried about Rachab, for her mother-in-law's mind had begun to slip, and she bent over slightly as she walked. The disease that had first enlarged the knuckles of her hands ran rampant throughout her body. She knew Rachab was determined to see her grandson into the world, and, as she'd told Boaz, she believed that was all that was keeping Rachab alive.

Bilhah went about with a smile on her face, happy for her friend Phebe, whose marriage would take place in just a few months. Young Levi had been making the rooftop shelter into something more substantial, and Naomi had been helping Phebe prepare some household items to take with her. Ruth and Naomi taught Phebe how to weave, and Nadab hung lengths of yarn from the crossbeam of the weaving room to create a second loom. He anchored the yarn with heavy clay weights on the free ends, with the warping stick separating the warp into two parts. Phebe learned to push the shuttle through the weft with different colored threads and push it tight against the fabric being formed. Naomi was also teaching her how to dye the yard using different plants. By the end of the first month of lessons, Phebe was weaving fabric as if she had done it all her life.

As harvest time neared, the overseer and some of the men who worked for Boaz built shelters by the grapevines where they would stay throughout the harvest season. Ramiah, the overseer, occupied a round stone tower with a storeroom on the ground level. There were simple living quarters above and an outside stairway to the roof. He moved his family there, and his wife, Rebekah, cooked their flat bread on stones heated in a fire pit.

Ruth entered her ninth month as the grape harvest began. The month of Silvan was warm, and she could only stay in the shade and watch as the workers carried basket after basket of the ripe fruit to the vat. There Bilhah and other young maidens trod the fruit, letting the dark juice flow down into the holding area, where other workers scooped it up to transfer into new wineskins, where it would ferment into wine. The skins were then sewn closed for storage. The workers were allowed to eat the grapes during harvest but were not allowed to take any home. Some of the grapes were set aside to dry on cloths to make raisins. As in the time of the barley and wheat harvests, gleaners were allowed to help themselves to whatever was left on the vines.

The babe within her was so active, Ruth felt every part of her insides had been kicked in one way or another, and she longed for the time of delivery. Rachab did little but move from her bed to a bench in the courtyard, where she remained most of the day. After the evening meal, she retired early and was not seen again until late morning the following day.

Bilhah was full of news of her friend Phebe and of all that was being prepared at the home of Naomi for the wedding.

Boaz, overseeing the grape harvest and attending to his duties at the city gate, left early in the morning and didn't return until evening. He made sure he was home before the sun went down, especially on the Sabbath, and now Ruth instead of Rachab covered her head and moved her hands over the Sabbath candles, saying the time-honored prayers.

Ruth had gathered some herbs and spices and put them in a basket as a gift for Shelah's mother, Salome, whose eyes lit up at the unexpected treasures. When Ruth saw her kitchen shelves, she realized the woman knew only how to cook simple meals that filled the stomach but did not satisfy the soul. She tactfully brought up the subject of letting Jael do some of the cooking.

The woman's eyes widened. "I thought that our daughter-in-law was used to someone else doing the cooking. She is from the family of the chief of our tribe."

Realizing the woman did not know her daughter-in-law had been taught the rudiments of keeping a home, including cooking, Ruth sought an answer.

"Jael is a good cook. Perhaps there are days you are weary when she could be of help to you. She could share some of the meals she likes and recipes she loves, and you would be able to spend more time with your granddaughter."

From the way the woman's face brightened, Ruth knew she had identified the problem and discovered a solution. Jael beamed at her, also, and Ruth could almost hear her small sigh of relief.

Finally, Boaz forbade her to leave the house with her time so near. She sat now in the shade, waiting for the moment *Ha'Shem* had set for her child to be born.

When Boaz returned home late that afternoon, he had a strange look of wonder and awe on his face.

"Boaz, what has happened?" she inquired. "You look like you have seen an angel."

He sat down next to her, slowly shaking his head. "I did not see an angel, Beloved, but for the third time in my life, I heard the voice of the Almighty."

She put a hand to her heart, which began to beat faster in anticipation. "What did the Lord say to you?"

"That from my loins shall come one who will lead His people."

And the first pain radiated from her womb and arched her back.

Boaz saw Ruth wince in pain and stood quickly. "Bilhah, your mistress needs you."

The girl took one look at Ruth's face and turned to Boaz. "Master, you must send for the midwife. The babe is coming."

"Nadab, fetch the midwife and alert the lady Naomi."

"Yes, Master." He was almost running when he left the courtyard for the town.

Boaz scooped Ruth up in his arms and carried her into the house, placing her on their bed. By now she was crying out in pain.

Rachab had seen them pass, and for one who seemed in her final days, she moved rather swiftly to Ruth's bedside, waving a hand at her son.

"Boaz, leave us alone. This is no place for the husband. Bilhah and I will tend to her until Basmath arrives."

Boaz stood uncertainly for a moment, then turned and strode out to the courtyard. Word spread quickly, and soon women of the neighborhood were gathering, bringing linen cloths and food. They murmured among themselves, casting covert glances at Boaz, who sat on the stone bench feeling extremely uncomfortable.

Basmath arrived and soon was urging Ruth to breathe between the contractions. Ruth was aware of voices around her, but the pain obliterated most of what they were saying. All she knew was a voice in her ear telling her to push.

Naomi came into the room, and Ruth, between contractions, saw her and Rachab grasp hands, their faces hopeful and anxious. Then Basmath checked her.

"The head is crowning. Push, Ruth, push."

Basmath and Bilhah raised her up over the birthing stool, and as she gave one last scream of pain, the child entered the world, crying lustily. Basmath caught the baby and wrapped it in the waiting cloths.

Smiling, Basmath laid the crying baby in Ruth's arms. "You have a healthy son."

Naomi moved forward, brushing Ruth's forehead with her hand. "A grandson. Oh, Ruth, a grandson." She reached down and, with a smile of triumph, carried the baby outside to the waiting crowd and Boaz.

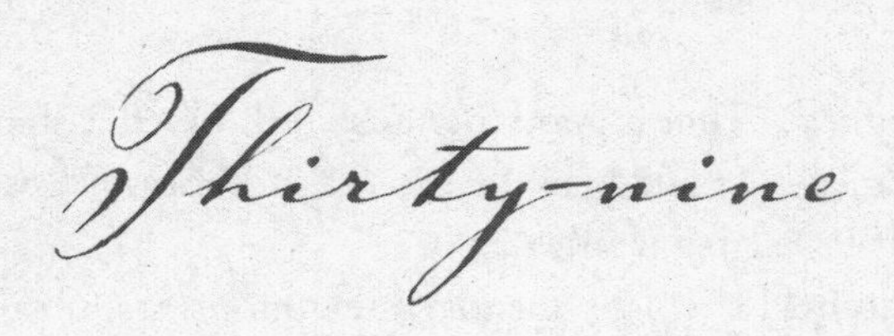

Boaz stood, filled with anticipation, as Naomi approached.

"You have a son. A strong, healthy son."

He gazed down at the small bundle in her arms and ran his finger down the baby's cheek. "A son. I have a son!"

The crowd erupted in exclamations of praise and good wishes. The women gathered around Boaz and Naomi, gazing at the new life that had come to the family.

One woman turned to Naomi. "Blessed be the Lord, who has not left you this day without a close relative; and may his name be famous in Israel!"

Another woman spoke up. "And may he be to you a restorer of life and a nourisher of your old age; for your daughter-in-law, who loves you and who is better to you than seven sons, has borne him."

Another offered, "A son is born to Naomi at last. How will you name him?"

Naomi turned to Boaz and waited.

He looked around at those gathered and said, "My son shall be called Obed, 'servant,' for he shall be a servant of the Most High, blessed be His name."

The women nodded all around, pleased at his choice. Then Boaz and Naomi returned to the house so Rachab could hold her grandson and Boaz could kneel at Ruth's bedside.

"Beloved, you have blessed me beyond my greatest imagination. Thank you for my son."

She smiled up at him with tired eyes. "And his name?"

"Obed, servant of the Lord."

She sighed. "That is good, my husband. Obed it shall be."

He leaned over and kissed her on the forehead. "Rest, my dear one. You have earned it this day."

Rachab held the baby for just a few moments, until her arms became tired. "I have lived to see the son of my son born." She turned to Bilhah. "Help me to my room. I must lie down now."

Basmath gathered her bag of herbs and medicines and was preparing to leave when Jael hurried into the room.

"*Abba*, I have a brother?"

"Yes, Daughter, you have a brother."

Jael went to look at the baby, now back in Naomi's arms. "He is beautiful." The baby grabbed her finger and held on as she laughed. "He is strong, too. You will have him in the fields soon, *Abba*."

Boaz grinned. "Perhaps not too soon."

Jael sat by the side of the bed. "I shall help you, Ruth, as you helped me when my daughter was born."

"And I shall tend the baby," Naomi spoke up, almost fiercely. "I have waited so long for this moment."

Jael squeezed the water out of the rag in the basin nearby, then put the cool cloth on Ruth's forehead.

Naomi gently laid Obed in Ruth's arms to nurse for the first time, and the baby let all in the room know he was hungry.

When Obed was fed, Naomi placed him in the cradle nearby, and Ruth gave her husband a weary smile before giving herself to sleep.

Boaz stood at the edge of the field, which was ripe with grain. His son Obed was in his arms, and Ruth at his side.

"The crops show the promise of abundance."

"No more famine, my husband. The Almighty has blessed us again at last."

Boaz thought of the day so long ago when he had stood here with his son Jacob and his father, Salmon, looking out over the parched fields.

"May your mother, Rachab, rest in peace. I pray Naomi will be with us much longer."

They had mourned for Rachab, who had lived long enough to see her grandson circumcised on his eighth day of life. They had buried her in the cave next to Salmon. The sorrow at her loss was tempered by the joy of their son, who was growing into a sturdy, happy child. At the invitation of Boaz, Naomi rented her house to tenants and came to stay with him and Ruth. She tended her grandson with joy, teaching him stories and songs.

Ruth could only marvel at the past years and how far she had come from her grandfather's small farm on the Plains of Moab.

"There will be a good harvest again this year, my husband."

He smiled down at her. "Yes, again we will have plenty to share." For Boaz was ever mindful of his responsibility to his people.

"I miss Rachab."

Boaz nodded. "She lived a long time, my beloved, longer than most women of our town. Obed was the joy of her heart, and I'm glad she lived to see him."

Obed squirmed in his arms, and Boaz set him on his feet. The child wobbled back and forth, clinging to his father's hand. "I believe he will be walking soon."

"He will be into everything in the house."

Boaz chuckled, and then they shared a companionable moment of silence.

Finally Ruth murmured, "Jael is with child again."

"Ah. Perhaps it will be a boy this time."

"You men. Always it will be a son."

He didn't answer. At the thought of Jael expecting another child, Ruth became silent again. She was glad for her stepdaughter, but there had been no sign of another child this year for herself. Perhaps, at her age, there would be no more children. At least *Ha'Shem* had taken away the disgrace of her barrenness with the birth of Obed.

Ruth glanced at Boaz, and her heart swelled with love for him. He still stood straight and tall in his later years, respected by the other elders and the people of Bethlehem. She had the joy of motherhood and a child to raise.

She looked down at Obed, who was examining a trail of ants, and picked him up to brush the dirt from his small, grubby hands.

As the shadows of the sycamore trees stretched over the road, Ruth and Boaz turned toward home. Naomi would be waiting for her grandson, and there was the evening meal to prepare. She handed Obed to Boaz and mused on what path their son would take. He was destined to take his father's place as chief one day, just as Boaz had done in succeeding his own father. Would she and Boaz live to see him married? Would they bounce grandchildren on their knees, as Naomi did now? She looked down the road, as if to see into the coming years, but then shook her head at her foolishness. All things would come in the time the Almighty had set, for He alone knew the paths they would take.

And Obed begat Jesse; and Jesse begat David the king....

In generations to come, Mary,
who was of the house and lineage of David,
gave birth to the Christ.

Background Information

When the Israelites left Egypt, they traveled along the borders of Edom and Moab until they reached the Arnon River. The land they now entered was formerly occupied by the Moabites, but the land had been conquered by the Amorite King, Sihon. Every man, woman, and child of Moab had been driven out of the land and confined to the territory below the Arnon River. The Israelites conquered King Sihon and took possession of the land. Then they conquered Og, King of Bashan, who ruled the territories east of the Sea of Galilee and the northeastern portion of the valley of the Jordan. The Israelites were now in possession of all the territory from the Arnon River (see map, bottom of Reuben Territory) to Mt. Hermon (see map, top of East Manasseh Territory) in the north. The Arnon River was now the dividing line between the territory of racial Moab and that of Israel. Of the territory south of the Arnon River, the Lord had declared through Moses, "I will not give thee of their land for a possession" (Deuteronomy 2:9 KJV). (They were descendants of Lot, Abraham's nephew.)

Because this new territory, still called the "Land of Moab," was so fertile, three tribes desired to settle there: the tribe of Reuben, the tribe of Gad, and half of the tribe of Manasseh. They were given permission to have the land, provided the warriors of those tribes continued on with Joshua to conquer the land of Canaan, which they did. They left their families, flocks, and herds behind and kept their promise to their leader.

The land had continued under its ancient name "Land of Moab" during the Amorite occupation, and when, by conquest, it became the possession of the Israelites, the name was not altered by the new owners. Racial Moabites remained below the Arnon River. (Over the years, the Moabites had to be subdued by Israelite armies time after time to keep them within their own boundaries.)

At the time of the Judges, a famine occurred in Canaan, now in the possession of the Israelites. A family of Bethlehem-Judah, Elimelech, Naomi, and their two boys, Mahlon and Chilion, who were evidently of delicate health, crossed the Jordan River into the "Land of Moab." Elimelech was a member of the princely House of Pharez-Judah, and so he sought refuge from the famine among their own kith and kin. It is not logical, given the evidence presented, to suppose that this family of Israelites would cross the Jordan to their own "land," occupied by their fellow Israelites, which was well watered and where there were no famine conditions, and pass through it to reach the Arnon, then cross this considerable river to reach enemy country in the land of "racial" Moab.

It does not say which tribes Orpah and Ruth belonged to, but, since the names *Ruth* and *Reuben* have very largely the same meaning—"friendship"—it is probable that Ruth belonged to the tribe of Reuben.

It was not permitted for Israelites to marry woman of racial Moab; such unions would have met with immediate punishment. (See Numbers 25:1–8.)

The Lord had given a divine command in Deuteronomy 23:3 (KJV): *"An Ammonite or Moabite shall not enter into the congregation of the LORD; even to their tenth generation shall they not enter into the congregation of the LORD for ever."* The prophet Samuel could not consistently enforce the divine command and, at the same time, condone so flagrant a disregard of that command on the part of a prince of Pharez-Judah, as was Ruth's first husband, Mahlon, and also her second husband, Boaz. This racial law was never canceled or annulled.

When Naomi, widowed and having suffered the loss of her sons, heard that the famine was over in Canaan, she prepared to return. Her daughters-in-law prepared to accompany her, for, as Israelites, they were aware of the Mosaic law that says, "*The wife of the dead shall not marry without unto a stranger*" (Deuteronomy 25:5 KJV). Knowing that she had no more sons to take them to wife, Naomi knew she must send them away. Her advice to these young widows—to return to their people—is evidence that they had never left the maternal roof, and also that Naomi was living in close proximity to them.

Ruth's immortal words to Naomi, "*Thy people shall be my people*" (Ruth 1:16 KJV), are not the clear Hebrew, for in the actual Hebrew, Ruth points out to Naomi that leaving her own family is not so great a sacrifice in view of the fact that they are one in race and worship. Ruth uses the holy name Jehovah, also evidence of her being an Israelite.

Another reason Naomi was anxious to return home was that it was the seventh Jubilee year, when the parcel of land belonging to Elimelech, possibly sold before they left, would revert back to her, his widow. The problem was that she had no male person to take possession of it for the family. And Boaz's marriage to Ruth overcame this difficulty.

When they arrived in Bethlehem, the city rejoiced and gave them honor, not to a couple of travel-worn women but to Naomi and Ruth, as widows of princes of the great House of Pharez-Judah, and they were given all the respect due their rank. Ruth, having come from the "Land of Moab," would naturally be called a Moabitess, as a woman from California would be called a "Californian."

In speaking to Boaz, Ruth refers to herself as a stranger, but the word used is *nokri*—"stranger in a new land"—not *zar,* which refers to an alien of another race. Boaz would not have invited a racial Moabitess to sit at meat with him. He was an orthodox Jew who would have avowed to a Gentile, "I will not eat with thee, drink with thee, or pray with thee."

Finally, Ruth was known by the townsfolk to be a woman of courage and strength of purpose, which had enabled her to set aside the agelong custom and leave her own people on the other side of the Jordan to take up residence with them. The townsfolk would not have so approved of a woman of racial Moab.

At the gate of the city, Ruth is not referred to as anything other than an Israelite. The national law of redemption was given exclusively to Israel, to be administered to Israelites alone, never to aliens.

All through the Scriptures, God stresses racial purity for the Israelites, while those who intermarried were condemned by Him and punished. The opportunity for Gentiles to be grafted into the Tree of Life, Israel, was presented when Christ died on the cross for us. For it is by His grace, not by race, that we are now saved and received into the kingdom.

About the Author

Diana Wallis Taylor was first published at the age of twelve, when she sold a poem to a church newsletter. Today, she has an extensive portfolio of published works, including a collection of poetry; an Easter cantata, written with a musical collaborator; contributions to various magazines and compilations; and six award-winning novels, including four biblical fiction stories: *Journey to the Well* (the story of the woman of Samaria); *Martha*; *Mary Magdalene*; and *Claudia, Wife of Pontius Pilate*.

Diana lives in San Diego with her husband, Frank. Among them, they have six grown children and ten grandchildren. Readers can learn more by visiting her Web site, www.dianawallistaylor.com.